*She was as naked*
*as the day she was born. . . .*

"Who are you?" she asked. "You aren't like the others. Who are you?"

The Indian dropped to his knees beside her, then leaned over and kissed her.

At first Crimson was terrified. Had she been saved from one assault only to be subjected to another? As the kiss lengthened and deepened, her terror turned to outrage, then, to her surprise —and shame—the spreading sensations of the kiss washed away the anger. The disquieting rush of feeling both thrilled and confused her. These were the same sensations she had experienced in those garden walks back East. But it couldn't be, for then she had been with well-bred gentlemen. Now she was with a savage—and being abused as well. How could she feel this way?

The kiss finally ended, and the Indian pulled away. He looked at her with a broad smile on his face.

"I . . . I thought Indians never kissed," Crimson blurted. It was a foolish statement, she knew; she said it to try to regain control over her spinning senses.

"I kiss," the Indian said, cutting the thongs that bound her wrists and ankles.

She was free to go, but he once again pressed his lips against hers, now caressing her nipples . . .

**Pinnacle Books by Paula Fairman:**

*In Savage Splendour*
*Forbidden Destiny*
*Storm of Desire*
*The Fury and the Passion*
*Ports of Passion*
*The Tender and the Savage*

# The TENDER and the SAVAGE

## Paula Fairman

PINNACLE BOOKS      LOS ANGELES

THE TENDER AND THE SAVAGE

*Copyright © 1980 by Script Representatives, Inc.*

An original Pinnacle Books edition, published for the first time anywhere.

First printing, July 1980

ISBN: 0-523-41006-9

Cover illustration by Bill Maughan

*Printed in the United States of America*

PINNACLE BOOKS, INC.
2029 Century Park East
Los Angeles, California 90067

# The Tender and the Savage

# 1

Her name was Crimson Royal, and because she was the daughter of one of America's most famous men, her name was often found in the social columns of the New York newspapers. She was twenty-two years old, of medium height, slender, with hair the color of burnished copper. Her emerald eyes were dusted with flecks of gold, which in a certain light seemed to match her hair. She had a fine, fair complexion, though she had an occasional tendency to freckle when exposed to the sun.

Crimson wasn't exposed to the sun at this moment. It was the evening of August 30th, 1875, and she was standing under the golden glow of the chandeliers and gas-jet lamps of the New York Art League's Show Gallery's foyer. The League was sponsoring a showing of her father's work, and she was acting as one of the hostesses.

Crimson's father, Artemus Royal, was one of America's best known artists. His fame and reputation did not end on this side of the Atlantic—he had shown in Paris, London and Vienna, and was nearly as highly acclaimed in Europe as he was in America.

Artemus Royal counted among his friends such men as Renoir, Monet, and Albert Sisley. He studied in Paris under Eugene Isabey, but was not unduly influenced by his teacher's academic romanticism. Artemus's unique style was best explained by a noted art critic for the *New York Tribune* in a glowing account of Artemus's work, *Train Shed:*

> It gives one a remarkable feeling of presence in the interior of a train shed. This is accomplished in part by a brilliant use of diffuse light, but also by the optically perfect perspective of his subject. Atmosphere is captured in a bold and imaginative way. Royal is a major artist with an exquisite feel for form. . . . It is most noteworthy to discover that Artemus Royal is constantly growing as an artist. A new spirit and vitality has appeared in his work. Certain elements in the canvases displayed in this show did not appear in his earlier painting. Royal has developed an eye for the variations of light and color that breathe life into his work.

When Crimson read the last comment, she and her father held a small, private celebration. Such a statement, they both knew, was a compliment to Crimson's own skill with the brush.

Artemus Royal was suffering from Rheumatoid Arthritis. Because of that, he had trained Crimson to take over much of his work. She was nearly equal to him in skill, and she now made most of the preliminary drawings as well as some of the finished work.

The "new vitality" the art critic had noticed in Royal's work was in fact the result of her own technique.

It was not simply vanity that caused Artemus

Royal to keep secret his arthritis. It was to protect a dream. For years, he had nurtured the ambition to go to the Indian Territories and paint the American Indian in his natural habitat.

Crimson had been so long a part of that dream that she felt a compulsion just as strong. So when the New York Art League commissioned Artemus to do a series of paintings that would accurately portray life among the plains Indians, she was as delighted as her father.

They both knew that the commission would be in jeopardy if the Art League knew of Artemus's affliction, so they kept it—and Crimson's involvement in his work—a closely guarded secret.

Despite their caution the project was almost jeopardized by another matter beyond their control. The Indians were beginning to make trouble in the Black Hills, and the Department of Interior refused to grant permission for Artemus and Crimson to undertake their assignment.

But Artemus had one last card to play. President Grant was a great fan of Artemus Royal's work, and had hung what was possibly Artemus's most famous painting, *Toward Higher Office,* in the White House. This work depicted President Lincoln lying on the bed after having been shot, surrounded by the anxious friends who made up the deathwatch. Above Lincoln, painted in glowing colors, was his soul being transported to heaven by a host of angels.

The President responded to Artemus's personal appeal, and overrode the Department of Interior with a presidential order allowing Artemus and Crimson free access to any and all Indian lands.

"You understand, of course," Grant cautioned, "that this just clears you with regard to the United States Government and her military forces. As far as I know, this will have absolutely no effect on the Indians."

3

"I understand, Mr. President," Artemus replied. "But I am told that the Indians have a way of measuring the intention of a man's heart. If that is the case, then I need not fear them, for they shall see the peaceful purpose to which my mission is dedicated."

"Well," President Grant responded, "we can only hope that there is some validity to your belief, though I fear that there may be dishonorable Indians as well as dishonorable white men. I give you this pass with reluctance, and ask that you be ever vigilant. But I give it to you in full appreciation of your contribution to preserving our culture for generations to come."

"Thank you, Mr. President."

"Now, when do you intend to leave?"

"I have an art show in New York on the thirtieth of August, and I have booked train tickets for the following day."

"An art showing, eh? Oh, how I wish that I could quit Washington for a brief spell and enjoy the show with the other patrons of the arts."

"Mr. President, I shall reserve one of the canvases of my Indian campaign just for you," Artemus promised.

And it was just that promise of which Paul Gideon was now voicing his disapproval. Gideon, Royal's agent, was standing quietly with Artemus and Crimson in the back of the gallery, sipping wine and watching the people file through the show.

"You have just promised him two hundred and fifty dollars of my money," Paul was saying.

"What makes you say that?" Artemus demanded.

"Because that painting would be sold for something like twenty-five hundred dollars and you know it. Ten percent of twenty-five hundred dollars, which would be my commission, would be two hundred and fifty dollars. But no, you had to *give* it away."

4

"I felt moved to do so," Artemus said, as if that simple statement explained everything. And indeed it did, for Paul Gideon understood enough of his client's artistic temperament that he dropped the subject. But he returned to another subject that had been troubling him—the Royals' upcoming journey into the Indian territories.

"Have any of my convincing arguments taken effect yet?" he asked.

Crimson laughed. "No, Paul," she said. "We are still going."

"You are both crazy," Paul said.

This time it was Artemus's turn to laugh. "Why are you so adamant against it? By your own admission, the project will earn us a lot of money from the Art League. And ten percent of that is yours."

"Yes, but suppose some Indian takes your scalp? Ten percent of nothing is nothing."

Artemus ran his hand across his nearly bald head and chuckled. "I'm afraid I have little to offer any Indian who is bent upon scalping me," he said.

"What about Crimson? She offers enough," Paul said. "I should hate to think of that beautiful head of hair hanging from some savage's belt, or from the tip of his lodgepole."

Artemus looked down at the floor, his face troubled. Crimson knew that Paul had struck a telling blow with his argument, for this was the same argument she and her father had been carrying on for some while. Therefore it was up to her to convince her father once more, she should make the trip out West with him.

"Paul, we have been through this a hundred times," Crimson said. "Nothing you nor anyone else says can change our minds now. We are going, and that is that. Am I not correct, Father?"

"Crimson, I don't know," Artemus said. "Perhaps . . ."

5

"Perhaps what?" Crimson replied. "Father, we've come too far now. Our dream is nearly realized. Don't falter at this late date."

Artemus smiled at his daughter's insistence, then looked back at Gideon. "There," he said. "Has any man ever had a daughter more deserving of admiration than I? She has spirit and determination to match my own. I tell you, Paul, nothing shall prevent our going. And no evil will befall us upon the way."

"I hope you are right," Paul said. He saw a wealthy patron admiring one of Royal's more expensive canvases and excused himself. "Oh, perhaps we are about to have a successful evening after all," he said. "If we sell that painting, it will little matter whether anything else sells, for that painting alone can make the entire season." He hurried off.

"Ah, good old Paul," Artemus chuckled. "Show him the opportunity to make a little money, and all other problems crumble before him."

"That's good," Crimson said. "I'd just as soon he find something to occupy him other than our trip West. And we will need whatever money he is able to bring in tonight if we are to be able to afford the trip."

"Yes," Artemus agreed. He sighed and ran his hand across his head, a characteristic gesture. "I hope, Crimson, my dear, that we are truly making the right decision."

"We are, Father," Crimson said. "I am convinced of it."

A man approached them. "Mr. Royal, sir, I am Stuart Philson of *Harper's Weekly*. Perhaps you would allow me a moment of your time?"

"Of course," Artemus said, smiling.

"Do you believe, as many others do, that color photography, should it ever be perfected, would render a death blow to the artist?"

6

"No, of course not," Artemus answered easily.

Crimson stepped several paces away from the conversation. The reporter would not want her opinion, and indeed, she would be little able to provide an answer with her father's articulate exactness.

Crimson studied the two men under the light of the gas jet, and composed a painting in her mind. Her father was tall, with a nearly bald head, heavy, expressive white eyebrows, and deep, piercing eyes. He was very dignified looking—even handsome, she thought, and she was proud of his appearance.

The reporter, by contrast, was short and rather plump, and he scribbled quickly on a tablet to keep up with Artemus's remarks.

Reporters were always attempting to elicit a remark from the famous artist that would shock or titilate readers and art patrons around the world. But for all their efforts, they generally received well-defined answers consistent with his philosophy of art. What most reporters did not realize was that their trick questions were old hat to Artemus Royal. He had heard them all before and had all the answers for them.

Crimson wandered through the gallery, enjoying the people fully as much as they were enjoying the paintings. The women were all dressed in butterfly bright dresses, yards of silk with bustled skirts, and sported dangling earbobs of diamond, emerald, or ruby. The jewels caught the light and sent out flashes of rainbow color.

Crimson felt a heat on the back of her neck, and she turned to see a man looking at her. He was more interesting than handsome, with an intriguing scar on his forehead, and flashing black eyes that stared at her with unabashed desire.

Crimson was caught up with a sharp feeling of feminine pleasure—that she had attracted the interest of such a man. For there was a look of cool recklessness in his face, and a cynical humor in his mouth as he smiled at her. She returned his smile boldly, as if issuing an invitation she knew he dare not accept.

Crimson knew flirting was ill-becoming a lady, that she should turn haughtily away from him to show him her disdain for such impertinence. But in truth, she derived a degree of titillation from the experience. She was, after all, perfectly safe here in the gallery; she could play with fire without getting burned. She could be reckless without courting danger. A casual flirtation under such controlled circumstances could do no harm.

And besides, she and her father would be leaving in the morning. And with that thought, she wondered what would be in her future. More importantly, she thought . . . who would be in her future?

## 2

Crimson and her father spent a magnificent five days in the spacious comfort of the train's Wagner parlor car, a commodious car equipped with deep, plush seats, decorated wood panel and velvet upholstered walls, lovely carpets, and bright kerosene lamps. The nights were passed in a comfortable sleeping car and all their meals were taken in the dining car.

"Can this be true?" Artemus asked. He was sitting in one of the great chairs of the parlor car, reading a copy of the *Lightning News,* a newspaper composed on the train for the passengers.

"What, Father?" Crimson asked.

"According to this story, a man named Alexander Graham Bell is working on a device that would send the human voice over a wire. He calls it a telephone, and says it will one day replace the telegraph."

"My," Crimson said. "Isn't it amazing what marvelous things men can do now?"

"Yes, it is," Artemus said. He folded the paper and looked through the windows at the wide open spaces flashing by outside. "This train, for instance. Now, in comfort rivaling that of a person's own living room, one can span the continent. New York to San Francisco in seven days! Why, it wasn't too many years ago it took nearly six months to make that same trip." He was quiet for a moment, and only the rhythmic clacking of the wheels over the track joints intruded. "That's why this mission is so important, Crimson. If we don't record life among the Indians as it is now . . . I mean as it really is . . . then their culture will be lost forever. And that would be a sin."

"I know," Crimson said. She put her hand on her father's and smiled at him. "And you are right when you say this record must be made by an artist, and not by a photographer."

"Photography!" Artemus said disgustedly. "Any fool can squeeze a bulb, and any mechanic can develop the plate. And then what do you have? A flat, expressionless black-and-white blob that they call a picture. There has never been a photograph taken that could compare with a painting. A photograph slices just an instant out of time, but a painting is much, much more. A painting lives."

Crimson laughed. "You don't have to convince me, Father. I'm on your side, remember?"

Artemus put his other hand on top of Crimson's and smiled at her, shedding instantly the harsh expression that had come over his face while he discussed photography.

"I'm sorry, daughter. Of course you are on my side." He held up his hands, now knotted and bent. "You are more than on my side," he added quietly. "You have become my hands . . . my talent . . . my expression. I am so proud of you."

"Everything I might be, I owe to you, Father," Crimson said. "You taught me everything I know."

10

"I cannot teach talent, my daughter. That has to come from God, and from Him you received a generous share."

"Excuse me, Mr. Royal, Miss Royal," a uniformed steward said, approaching their seats. "But your table is ready."

"Thank you," Artemus said. He stood up, then smiled at Crimson. "Well, as this shall be our last meal aboard the train, we wouldn't want to be late, would we?"

"No," Crimson agreed. She was hungry, and the meals had been excellent, but she always approached the trip to the dining car with trepidation. She drew a deep breath, as if about to plunge into an icy stream, and opened the rear door of the parlor car. As soon as she stepped out onto the platform, she felt as if she had entered another world. The noise was tremendous, and the wind whipped against her dress and hair. The car's normal rocking motion was greatly exaggerated back here, and she held onto the railing to keep from being tossed off.

There was a gap between the platforms of the two cars, narrow enough to be stepped across but wide enough that a misstep could drop an unfortunate passenger onto the tracks below. Negotiating that gap was a very frightening experience, and though Crimson had already done it many times during the trip, she approached each time with as much caution as she had the first time.

She stood there for a moment, feeling the rhythm of the car and looking down to make sure that the heights of the platforms were equal before she stepped off. She could see the ties of the railroad bed beneath them, rushing by in a blur, evidence of the fifty-mile-per-hour speed the train was traveling.

Crimson timed her move, then stepped across,

and held her breath until her father had made it across as well. Then they opened the door and stepped into the dining car.

The elegance of the dining car was in keeping with the rest of the train; Crimson saw richly paneled walls, plush drapes and upholstery, and vases with fresh flowers on the tables. She and her father were met by a waiter as soon as they stepped inside.

"Your table is ready," the waiter said. "Right this way, please."

Crimson and her father sat down and perused a menu that featured blue-winged teal, antelope steaks, roast beef, boiled ham and tongue, broiled chicken, corn on the cob, fresh fruit, hot rolls, and cornbread. Crimson ordered boiled ham, and her father took the roast beef.

Across the aisle from them, a man in uniform kept looking toward them. Finally, when the waiter left, he leaned over to speak to them.

"Excuse me," he said. "I am Colonel Olin Gray, with General Terry's staff. Are you Mr. Artemus Royal, by any chance?"

"Yes," Artemus said. He looked puzzled. "Do I know you, Colonel Gray?"

"No, sir, I'm sure you do not," he replied. "But I heard you make a speech once when I was in New York. May I tell you how much I admire your work, sir?"

"Well, thank you, Colonel," Artemus said, genuinely flattered by his remark. "And may I present my daughter, Crimson."

"It's an honor, Miss Royal," the Colonel said to Crimson. Now it was his turn to look confused. "But what are you doing out in the middle of nowhere? Or, are you traveling to San Francisco for a lecture tour?"

"No, my dear fellow, we aren't going to San

Francisco," Artemus said. "We are going now to Fort Lincoln."

"Fort Lincoln?" the Colonel asked. "What on earth are you going there for?"

"We will be going on from Fort Lincoln into the Black Hills," Artemus said. "We are going to do a series of paintings depicting the American Indian in his natural habitat."

"What?" the Colonel asked, sputtering in surprise. "Mr. Royal, you can't be serious, sir! Don't you realize that there is a war going on right now?"

"I knew there was some Indian trouble, but I didn't know . . ."

"Indian trouble, you call it? Well, Mr. Royal, it is considerably more than Indian trouble. General Custer has his hands full trying to keep them under control. I wouldn't advise you to go through with your plans."

"I'm sorry, Colonel, but we've come too far to be dissuaded now," Artemus said with the air of one who had heard all this before. "We will be going on."

"But I can't believe it," the Colonel said. "Well, in that case, I'm afraid I shall have to issue an order forbidding you to carry out your plan."

"You are going to issue us an order?" Crimson asked. "By what authority?"

"By the authority as deputy to the military commander of the area," Colonel Gray said. "I'm certain the Department of Interior knows nothing of your foolhardy plan. Once they are informed of your intention, they will sustain my order."

"I'm sorry, Colonel, I appreciate your concern for our safety," Artemus said. "But you see, I have an order which countermands yours. I have the permission of the President of the United States."

"You've got permission from General Grant to go into the Badlands?" Colonel Gray asked incredulously.

"From *President* Grant," Artemus said. "So you see, we will be going in."

Colonel Gray pulled at his beard as he looked at Artemus and Crimson. Then he sighed in surrender.

"Very well," he said. "But I insist that you allow me to summon a military escort from Fort Lincoln to meet you at the depot in Bismark. I will wire ahead from Fargo tonight."

"You may have the military escort us to Fort Lincoln," Artemus said. "But I tell you now, we have no intention of being confined to the Fort."

"Mr. Royal, I only wish there was some way I could convince you of the danger," Colonel Gray said. He stood and wiped his hands with his napkin, then gave them a half-salute and left.

"Ah, Crimson, I fear we shall encounter many more like Colonel Gray before we can begin our work," Artemus said as the waiter served their meal.

"Then we shall handle them as we handled Colonel Gray and the others," Crimson said. "Nothing can stop us now, Father. Nothing."

"I hope you are right," Artemus said. "And I hope they are wrong."

"Everything will be fine, Father," Crimson said. "I just know it will."

Crimson's brave words of assurance were spoken for her own benefit as well as her father's, and she was relieved when the conversation changed to a less troublesome topic.

Crimson slept well that night. She had grown accustomed to the motion of the train, and the sound of the wheels clacking on the tracks seemed to have the same effect as a soothing lullaby. Within a short time after her head hit the pillow, she was in a deep and dreamless sleep.

"Bismark!"

Crimson was awakened by the conductor's crisp call. The train was slowing and in a few minutes

14

came to a stop. She pulled the curtain to one side and looked out the window. She saw a low brick building from which hung a white sign, the word BISMARK painted on it.

"Bismark. This is the end of the line, folks. Everyone gets out here."

It was early in the morning and only a few of the citizens of Bismark had turned out to welcome the train. Crimson saw a couple of old men sitting on a platform near the station house, a cluster of people who were obviously meeting arriving passengers, and a young man and woman standing together sadly, obviously soon to be parted.

With an artist's eye, Crimson surveyed the scene. She saw something that first made her gasp, then thrilled her—two Indians. They were standing away from everyone else, watching the train with dark, almost brooding eyes, as if trying to comprehend this marvel of the white man's world.

"Crimson," her father called down to her from the bunk above. "Hurry and get dressed. I would hate for the train to turn around and go back with us still abed."

"I'm hurrying, father," Crimson said. Reluctantly she let the curtain fall back into place and began the rather involved task of dressing in the confines of the narrow space of the bed without sacrificing modesty.

Moments later, Crimson and her father stepped out of the car onto the station platform. They were greeted almost immediately by an army sergeant.

"Beggin' your pardon, sir, I'm Sergeant Flynn. I was told to meet a Mr. Artemus Royal and his daughter, and escort them to Fort Abraham Lincoln. That would be you, wouldn't it?"

Artemus sighed. "Yes, Sergeant, that's us," he said. "I see Colonel Gray wasted no time in carrying out his promise."

15

"No, sir," the sergeant said. The large Irishman smiled broadly. " 'Twas easy enough to find you now, bein' as how the Colonel said 'twould be a tall handsome figure of a gentleman, and a lass as lovely as any colleen I'd ever likely see."

Artemus laughed. "Sergeant, you've a bit of the blarney in you."

"Aye, perhaps so," the sergeant said. "But by the saints, I've never spoken truer words. Where would your baggage be now?"

"Well, if the Northern Pacific has done their job properly, they should be unloading it now," Artemus said.

"If you'd like to take yer breakfast now, me 'n the men'll see to your baggage," the sergeant promised.

"Thank you, Sergeant, that's most kind of you," Crimson said. She rewarded the sergeant with a smile that caused him to brighten visibly.

Breakfast was disappointing. After having been spoiled by nearly a week of omelets, pancakes, and other delicacies, tough steak and fried potatoes were unwelcome. But, realizing that future meals may be even less appetizing, they ate heartily, if not with relish.

The sun had climbed higher in the sky when they left the restaurant a short while later and already was promising the heat of a late summer's day.

"Here, ma'am," Sergeant Flynn called as Crimson looked around for their escort. "We've got General Custer's personal coach for you. You'll like it, it rides like a cloud."

The coach was a Spring coach, built along the same lines as the Concord stage coaches, though much, much smaller and lighter. The sergeant held the door open while Crimson and her father stepped in.

"Hold that coach!" someone called, and Crimson,

16

who had already taken her seat, looked back to see a man was running toward the coach.

"Oh, bless me, it's Cap'n Tom," the Sergeant muttered under his breath.

"Who?"

"Cap'n Tom Custer, the brother of Gen'rul Custer himself. Cap'n Tom's likely spent the night in Bismark, 'n likely he's a bit likkered up. It wouldn't do for the gen'rul to see him in sech a condition."

"Surely if the general is the captain's brother, the Captain need not worry about anything?" Crimson suggested.

"No'm, that ain't the case a'tall," the sergeant said. "You see, the Gen'rul . . . he's quite a stickler for military courtesy and the like. Cap'n Tom now, he don't rightly give two hoots 'n a holler for sech things. So when you got two brothers like that, 'n one of 'em bein' a commandin' officer 'n all, why it just naturally means trouble."

"Sergeant Flynn," Captain Custer said. "My brother wouldn't be in town now, would he?"

"No, sir, Cap'n Tom," Sergeant Flynn said. "He just sent the coach in to pick up guests."

"Guests? Well now, I hadn't heard that we were to be honored with guests," Custer said. He walked to the coach and looked in. When he saw Crimson, his rather laconic smile disappeared.

"Sergeant," Tom Custer whispered hoarsely and so loud that Crimson could hear every word. "Why didn't you tell me you were escorting a lady?"

"I didn't get a chance, sir," Sergeant Flynn answered.

"I've been drinking," Tom Custer said. "I'm not fit company for a lady."

"Cap'n, why don't you stick around town for a while longer?" Sergeant Flynn said. "The Gen'rul will like as not be tied up with these folks for a time, 'n he won't be lookin' for you."

Tom laughed, a small, deprecating laugh. "Meaning that I can sober up before I come in, is that it?"

"No, sir," Sergeant Flynn said. "Why, I wouldn't . . ."

"That's all right, Sergeant," Tom said. "What you are saying probably makes sense. There's no use to cause Autie to get angry if I can avoid it, eh?"

"Yes, sir, Cap'n, that's the way I see it," Sergeant Flynn said.

Tom came back to the coach and looked in. "Excuse me, ma'am," he said. "I was going to ride back to the fort with you, but in honesty, madam, I am ill fit for female companionship. I am, sorry to say, besotted. If you forgive me?"

"Of course, Captain," Crimson said, amused.

Tom saluted Crimson and Artemus, then, executing a crisp, military about-face, he turned and began walking back toward town.

"Is he often in that condition, Sergeant?" Artemus asked.

"Yes, sir, more often than the Gen'rul would like, I'm afraid," Sergeant Flynn said. "But don't let the whiskey fool you none. He's as brave a soldier as ever fought in a battle. Aye, 'n' as good a man too. There's not a manjack in the Seventh as wouldn't soak his trousers in kerosene and march through hell for the Cap'n . . . if you'll excuse the language, ma'am."

"If, as you say, the captain is a good man, then why does he drink so much?" Crimson asked.

"He has a few devils to contend with, ma'am," Sergeant Flynn said. "He picked 'em up at Washita."

A soldier rode up.

"Sergeant, the detail is formed."

"Aye," Sergeant Flynn said. "Put two men in front, two in the back, and two outriders. I'll drive the coach."

"Right, Sergeant," the soldier said. He relayed

the sergeant's instructions, and the six mounted cavalrymen took their positions.

"Hope you folks have a right comfortable ride," Sergeant Flynn said, climbing up onto the driver's seat.

Crimson wanted to ask Sergeant Flynn what happened at Washita, but that would have to come later. The coach had already started rolling, and the depot and the town of Bismark were falling behind them.

## 3

Timothy Patrick Flynn, sergeant, United States Army, Seventh Cavalry, studied the terrain around him carefully. He was driving the coach in which Crimson and her father were riding. General Custer had told him Artemus Royal was a very famous painter. A very famous painter.

Flynn had never heard of him, but that didn't mean anything. Flynn was not a very well read man, but he did have an appreciation for art. He liked one painting in particular, he would often stand in front of it and look at it in silence for a long moment. He was ashamed to admit that he had no idea who the artist was. In fact, the painting was so real to him that he sometimes forgot that it was just a picture and not a window onto real life.

The painting hung in the Sutlers' Store at Fort Abraham Lincoln. It was of a cavalry unit on parade, and the artist had captured it perfectly. When Flynn looked at it, he could almost lose himself in the picture. He could feel the sun on his back, and smell the horseflesh beneath him.

It was a fine, fine painting, and Flynn often wished that he were one of the soldiers in the picture, suspended in time and space, immortalized forever in an important moment of your life. Of course, Flynn did not think in those words, but the meaning was there.

It would be nice, Flynn thought, if Artemus Royal would paint a picture of General Custer and his soldiers, encamped perhaps, or on the march, or maybe even in battle. But not a battle like Washita Flynn thought. He had no desire to have Washita immortalized.

"Sergeant!" one of the point riders shouted, interrupting Flynn's thoughts.

"Aye, lad?"

"The bridge is burning!"

"What?" Flynn cried. "My God, lads, there must be Indians about! Call the riders in, we're going back to . . ."

Flynn was interrupted by a swishing, thumping sound as an arrow flew into his chest. He let out a bellow of surprise and pain.

"What is it?" Crimson yelled. "Sergeant Flynn, what's happening?"

"Ma'am, get down on the floor," Flynn called down in a strained voice. "We're being attacked."

Even as Sergeant Flynn spoke, two of the outriders fell, mortally wounded by the attackers, fifty strong, who were now charging toward the escort party, yelling and screaming and waving war clubs.

Sergeant Flynn managed to turn the coach around, and he whipped the horses into a gallop, but from Crimson's position in the coach, she could see that the Indians were easily gaining on them.

"They are going to catch us!" she cried, her voice shrill with panic. Never in her life had she been more frightened than she was at this moment.

22

"Is it to end here?" Artemus asked, as much in surprise as in fear.

Two more soldiers fell, then, to Crimson's amazement the remaining two soldiers broke off the running fight with the Indians and galloped off, leaving behind the coach with its wounded driver and two terrified passengers.

Sergeant Flynn, weakened from loss of blood, lost control of the frightened horses, and soon the Indians had surrounded the coach. One of them leaped from his horse to the coach and, clinging to the side, stared in through the window at Crimson and her father. His grotesquely painted face leered at them, then he let out a war whoop and climbed onto the top of the coach.

The coach gradually came to a stop. It was quickly surrounded by dozens of Indians, all shouting and yelling, and some laughing to celebrate their victory. One of them opened the door to the coach and motioned for Crimson and her father to get out.

"We'd better do as he says, Crimson," Artemus said. The calmness her father showed amazed Crimson . . . and helped calm her, too, as he had no doubt intended. As they stepped outside, Crimson saw Sergeant Flynn slumped in the seat, clutching the arrow in his chest. She started to climb up to see him.

"No!" one of the Indians said gruffly.

"But I must see to him," Crimson insisted. "Can't you see he's dying?"

"Don't worry, ma'am," Sergeant Flynn said. He coughed. "I ain't dyin'. The arrow didn't hit 'nythin' vital."

"Thank God for that," Crimson said.

"Sergeant, what's going to happen to us?" Artemus asked. "Are we going to be killed?"

"I don't think so," Flynn said. "If we was, why

like as not we'd already be dead. They'd'a kilt us the moment they stopped the coach."

One of the Indians spoke gruffly and pointed to the interior of the coach. Another Indian rode over to Flynn and roughly jerked him off the seat. Flynn fell to the ground and cried out in pain.

"You savage beasts!" Crimson said angrily. "Can't you see what you're doing?" She knelt beside Flynn.

"I'll be all right, ma'am," he grunted. "Just help me to get inside. That's what they're wantin'."

"Father, help me," Crimson said, and her father bent down to help her get Flynn back on his feet. Flynn was a fairly big man, so they depended on him to provide most of the work as they hefted him aboard.

Crimson and her father were no sooner in the coach than the Indian who had climbed on top took the reins and snapped them against the animals' backs. The coach lurched forward.

"Where do you suppose they'll take us?" Crimson asked.

"They are Hunkpapa Sioux," Flynn said. "They must be down here on a hunting party, so my guess is they have a hunting camp somewhere nearby. They'll be taking us there, I reckon."

Crimson unbuttoned Flynn's shirt. The wound was a jagged tear, still spilling a little blood, though by now the blood around the hole had begun to coagulate. The shaft of the arrow protruded from the middle of the ugly hole.

Crimson made a face and turned her head away.

"Sorry, ma'am, I should'a maybe told you. It ain't such a pretty sight," Sergeant Flynn said.

"Should I . . . try to pull it out?" Crimson asked.

Flynn managed a weak smile. "Bless you, ma'am for thinkin' about it. But it's best to just leave it in there until I can get somewhere to lay still for a

24

while. Besides that, I'm not all that sure you could yank it out, lass, even if you tried. 'Tis flared, you see, 'n the little devil goes in a mite easier than it comes out."

"Oooh," Crimson said, flinching at the very thought of pulling out the arrow.

"If the heathens ain't got it in mind to kill us right off, I reckon they'll have one o' their medicine men yank it out for me."

"Surely, Sergeant, you wouldn't allow yourself to be operated on by a savage medicine man?" Crimson asked, shocked at the thought.

"Ma'am, I figure they've had a heap more practice jerkin' out arrow heads than most white doctors. Yes'm, I reckon I would let 'im do it."

Crimson glanced over at her father and was shocked to see him holding a sketch pad on his lap. He was looking out the window, sketching a picture of one of the Indian guards.

"Father, what are you doing?" Crimson asked.

"Just what I came out here to do, daughter," Artemus said.

Crimson didn't know whether to laugh or to cry. She was terrified . . . she had no idea what was going to happen to them, and yet here was her father, sketching a picture as casually as if he were in his own studio.

"Let 'im be, lass," Sergeant Flynn said. "When the Indians see it, perhaps we can convince them that you mean no harm to 'em. At any rate, it can't hurt."

"If you say so, Sergeant," Crimson said.

The next hour was one of the strangest Crimson had ever passed in her life. She was sitting in a coach that was bouncing across the open plains, holding Sergeant Flynn's head on her shoulder. The sergeant was unconscious, grunting only when the coach hit an occasional severe bump.

Across from Crimson her father sat making sketch after sketch. By now he had done drawings of five of their Indian escorts.

Crimson was envious of both of her fellow passengers—Sergeant Flynn because he was unconscious for most of the trip, and her father because his dedication to his art left no room for fear in his heart.

The coach rolled across a small stream of water, and silver spray shot out from both sides of the coach. Then they stopped.

"Sergeant Flynn," Crimson said. "Sergeant Flynn, we're here."

The door to the coach was jerked open, and a tall, fierce Indian stood there looking in. He was handsome in a savage, frightening way.

"It's Crazy Wolf," Sergeant Flynn said.

"Who?"

"The fella at the door," Flynn said. "He's one of the war leaders. I don't think the Gen'rul knew he was in the area though. If he did, I don't think the Seventh would be in garrison right now."

The Indian said something in a harsh, guttural language, then motioned them to get out of the coach.

"Sergeant Flynn is wounded," Crimson said. "He needs help."

"Don't waste your breath, ma'am," Sergeant Flynn said. He grunted in pain as he stepped out of the coach. "They see that I'm wounded. If they are going to help, they'll do it without being asked. If they ain't gonna help, all the askin' in the world ain't gonna do no good."

Crazy Wolf looked at the three of them, then shouted something and pointed to Sergeant Flynn. Two Indians came up to him, took his arms around their necks, and led him away.

"Thank you," Crimson said.

Crimson and her father remained by the coach, surrounded by the people of the village. The people didn't seem particularly ferocious, many were women and children, and they seemed more curious than anything else.

Several times the children would edge close to Crimson and stare at her, fascinated by her long red hair. Then, when she smiled at them, they would turn and run back to cling to their mothers.

Artemus raised his sketch pad and began drawing a picture of one of the children. Finally, the one called Crazy Wolf came back to stand before them.

"Why do you come to soldier-fort?" Crazy Wolf asked Crimson. "Are you soldier-squaw?"

"You speak English," Crimson said. "Oh, am I glad to know you can speak to us."

Crazy Wolf slapped Crimson, and the sudden blow shocked more than hurt her.

"Here, what do you think you are doing?" Artemus shouted. He dropped his sketch pad and started toward Crazy Wolf, but he was grabbed by two warriors.

"Father, no!" Crimson said. She was holding her hand up to her jaw. It stung from the unexpected slap, but her face burned more in anger and embarrassment than anything else. "I'm all right. Don't cause any trouble."

"When Crazy Wolf ask woman question, woman must answer," Crazy Wolf said. "Why do you go to soldier-fort? Are you soldier-squaw?"

"No," Crimson said. "I am . . . that is, my father and I are artists."

"What is artists?"

"We paint pictures," Crimson said. She pointed to her father's sketch pad on the ground, its pages riffling in the soft breeze. "There," she said. "Look at that pad."

Crazy Wolf picked up the pad, and a strange expression came over his face. He flipped through the pages then called out. The Indian whose likeness Artemus had captured came over to look at the drawing. He laughed and showed it to several others, and soon half the camp was yelling and straining to see the drawings. In the melee that followed, several of the drawings were torn.

The two Indians who had been holding Artemus released him so that they, too, could see the pictures. Artemus and Crimson stood together, wrapped in each other's embrace, wondering what their fate would be.

"Why do you do pictures?" Crazy Wolf finally asked.

"I am doing it to preserve your culture for all time," Artemus said.

"I think you do it to show soldiers," Crazy Wolf said. "Maybe you will go to the fort and the soldiers will see the pictures and come to arrest us."

"No," Artemus said. "That's not what I had in mind at all."

"Crazy Wolf," Crimson said. "We want to stay on the Indian lands and draw many pictures of many Indians."

"No," Crazy Wolf said.

"But why not? We mean you no harm."

"No," Crazy Wolf said again. He spoke in the same short, guttural language, and then Crimson and her father were taken by several of the Indians and separated.

"What's going on?" Crimson asked. "Crazy Wolf, where are they taking us?"

Crimson struggled against the grip of the two men who held her, but she wasn't strong enough to break free. They took her into a tent and pushed her roughly to the ground. Then they spread out her arms and legs and tied them with rawhide thongs to stakes that had been driven in the ground.

"What are you doing?" she asked. "Please, let my father and me go. We mean you no harm. Can't you see that?"

Despite Crimson's entreaties, the captors left her, helpless and vulnerable to indignity that might be perpetrated against her.

Crimson lay tied to the stakes for the rest of the day. She yelled for the first several minutes, pleading with Crazy Wolf to come talk to her, trying to see if she could get a response from her father or Sergeant Flynn, but no one answered her.

In fact, no one paid any attention to her. For one maddening hour, half a dozen children played some game that required them to dart through the tipi where she was being held. Laughing they jumped over her and ran around her, but didn't seem to pay the slightest attention to her. Once, an old woman came into the tipi and she squatted between Crimson's legs, staring in silence for several moments.

"Do you speak English?" Crimson asked.

The woman made no response. Not even a flicker in the eyes, or the slightest change of expression on her face showed that she had heard Crimson speak.

"What are they going to do to us?" Crimson asked.

The woman was silent.

"My father, and Sergeant Flynn. Are they all right?"

Still no response. Finally, after the woman seemed to have satisfied whatever curiosity had driven her there in the first place, she got up and left.

No one offered Crimson anything to eat through the rest of the day, but she was so unnerved by the events of the day that she had no appetite.

Night came and the wavering orange of the campfires' glow bathed the inside of the tipi in erie light. The Indians seemed to be celebrating, for they were dancing around the fires and singing, a strange, haunting, discordant chanting. The incessant pounding of the drums seemed to coincide with the rhythm of Crimson's own pulsing heartbeat.

It all seemed so unreal to Crimson. Less than a week ago, she had been standing in the foyer of the New York Art League Gallery . . . and now, she wasn't at all confident that she would survive this night.

A conversation began just outside her tipi. Crimson twisted her head, straining to see who it was, but she could see nothing more than two shadows.

She couldn't understand the words being spoken but she could understand their discordant intent. Finally the two arguers drifted away, and Crimson was left alone again. She lay there, listening to the drums' crescendo, trying to reckon the passing of time. She had come to the somewhat irrational conclusion that if she could just survive beyond midnight, she would not be killed.

Crazy Wolf came into the tent. He stared down at her, his eyes reflecting the red glow of the fires, his face looking demonic in the flickering light.

"Crazy Wolf, what have you done to my father and Sergeant Flynn?" Crimson asked, hoping that by hearing him speak some words of English, she would not find his demeanor so terrifying.

Crazy Wolf didn't answer her.

"What . . . what are you going to do?" Crimson asked, frightened by the way Crazy Wolf was staring at her.

Again, Crazy Wolf did not answer. Instead, he knelt down beside her and held a knife to her throat.

Crimson closed her eyes tightly and twisted her head to one side. She breathed a quick prayer, then waited for the sting of the blade as it bit into her neck.

That didn't happen. Instead, she felt a slight tugging at the bodice of her dress, and heard a tearing sound. She opened her eyes and saw that Crazy

Wolf had cut her dress from the neck down to her waist. Now he was laying the dress open, exposing her nudity to his cruel eyes. Crimson realized then that he intended to rape her!

"Ahh," she heard Crazy Wolf say, then she felt his coarse hands on her body, roughly kneading a breast before trailing down to the junction of her legs and grabbing her.

What a cruel twist of fate, she thought, that the first man who would ever touch her there would be a savage Indian. For there had been many occasions when, with a handsome man in the velvet blue night of a garden stroll, she had felt a rising concupiscence. But always she had denied herself the pleasure her body sought, thus protecting her virginity, which at age twenty-two was still intact. Is this what she had saved herself for? Had she fought so hard to keep her passionate nature under control, only to suffer this gross indignity?

Crimson felt the dress being pulled from her. Now she was completely nude before the brute who would ravage her, and though she twisted and strained, she could not free herself from the rawhide thongs. In fact, her undulating body only served to further enflame the passions of Crazy Wolf—though no further fuel was needed to fire his lust.

Crimson looked up at the last moment and saw him descending over her. She readied herself for the pain and humiliation of his attack.

## 4

Just as Crimson felt him about to enter her, she heard the sound of a blow being struck and saw Crazy Wolf fall beside her. He let out a shout of pain and anger, and Crimson, who had closed her eyes against his brutality, opened them again to see a second Indian in the tipi. The second Indian began shouting at Crazy Wolf, and though Crazy Wolf answered just as angrily, he skulked away, leaving Crimson untouched.

She was saved!

Or was she? For the one who had driven Crazy Wolf away was looking down at her nudity, relish and enjoyment reflected in his face.

The Indian was strikingly handsome. Crimson was angry with herself for noticing, but it was something that couldn't be denied. He was a big man, though from her position on the ground, everyone loomed larger than life when they stood over her. Then she noticed that his eyes were blue! She had never realized that Indians could have blue eyes. His skin tone, too, was different than the other Indians.

"Who are you?" she asked. "You aren't like the others. Who are you?"

The Indian dropped to his knees beside her, then leaned over and kissed her!

At first, Crimson was terrified. Had she been saved from one assault only to be subjected to another? Then, as the kiss lengthened and deepened, she realized that the strange Indian had no intention of going any further than a kiss, and her terror turned to outrage. How dare he do this to her!

But to Crimson's utter surprise—and shame—the spreading sensations of the kiss washed away the anger. The disquieting rush of feeling both thrilled and confused her. These were the same sensations she had experienced in those walks in the garden. But it couldn't be, for then she had been with gentlemen who were well placed in society. Now she was with a savage—and being abused as well! How could she possibly feel this way?

The kiss finally ended, and the Indian pulled away. He looked at her with a broad smile on his face.

"I . . . I thought Indians never kissed," Crimson said. It was a foolish statement, she knew; she said it to try to regain control of her spinning senses.

"I kiss," the Indian said without a trace of an accent. In fact, his tone was mocking, a subtlety which Crimson knew would be very difficult for one who could speak only a rudimentary English.

"You do speak English, then," she said.

"Yes."

"Who are you? You are not an Indian."

"Yes, I am. I am Joseph Two Hearts. When I was white, my name was Joseph Baker."

"What do you mean, when you were white?"

Joseph Two Hearts pulled his knife from his belt and cut the thongs that bound Crimson. She sat up and began massaging her wrists and ankles to restore

34

the circulation, so grateful to be free that she forgot all about being naked.

Joseph walked over to the side of the tent, picked up a blanket, and tossed it casually to Crimson. Then she realized that she was nude, and she put it on quickly, blushing in embarrassment. Somehow the embarrassment seemed greater because this man was white.

"I was the only survivor of our wagon," Joseph said. "I was twelve years old, and my mother and father and I were going to Oregon. The Crow attacked us, and my mother and father were killed. I played dead, and they left me alone. The scalp of a child does not make good coup. Later, the Sioux found me and gave me a home and a new name. Two Hearts is my new name, because I am now Indian, as well as white."

"Then I beg of you, Mr. Baker . . ."

"Two Hearts," Joseph said, holding up his hand.

"Mr. Two Hearts, I beg of you, set my father and the sergeant and me free."

"I can't do it," Joseph said. "It must be decided by the tribal council."

"But surely you have some influence with them? Can't you convince them to free us?"

"I can speak for you at the council meeting," Joseph said. "Maybe they will listen to me, maybe they won't. Crazy Wolf will have angry words, I know that."

"Oh, Crazy Wolf, yes," Crimson said. "He will be very angry at you for what you have done. Will you be in any danger from him?"

Joseph smiled broadly. "Ha! Crazy Wolf doesn't frighten me. We have fought many times since we were children, and always I have beaten him."

Crimson stuck her arm out from the blanket, which fell from her shoulders, exposing her breasts.

35

But she made no attempt to cover herself. Instead, she placed her hand on Joseph's.

"Joseph, please be careful," she said. "He may be so angry that he won't attempt to fight you fairly."

"Don't worry," Joseph said. "No matter what Crazy Wolf tries, I can handle it."

Crimson readjusted the blanket, then saw that her trunk had been brought into the tipi.

"Do you want to put on clothes now?" Joseph asked.

"Yes, please," Crimson said. "Will it be all right?"

"Yes," Joseph said, "because I say it will be all right." He touched himself on his bare chest with the bravado of a boy. "Now I will go speak to the council for you."

"Thank you, Joseph," Crimson said. "From the bottom of my heart, I thank you."

Joseph left the tipi and stepped out into the soft spring night. The girl had made him feel like no other girl ever had. What was it about her that moved him so, he wondered? Was it the fact that he saw her without her clothes?

No, for the maidens of the village often bathed naked in the river, and he and the other young men would watch from the banks in open admiration. Perhaps it was because she was so beautiful.

And yet Joseph had seen beautiful girls many times. In fact, Sasha, daughter of Sitting Bear, was very beautiful, and Joseph knew that Sasha had eyes for him as well. Was it because she was white?

No! Joseph would not accept that. He was no longer white—he was Indian! He would not be turned back into a white just because he was moved by a white girl.

The council fire was burning brightly as Joseph approached, and he found a spot within the inner circle and sat down. Najinyanupi was speaking.

"When the prairie is on fire, you see animals surrounded by the fire; you see them run and try to hide themselves so that they will not burn. That is the way we are here."

"I will speak now," White Ghost said. He stood up, and the others around the council fire looked toward him, for he was older than most and considered very wise.

"The white men have driven away our game, until now we have nothing left that is valuable except the hills that they are asking us to give up. The earth is full of minerals of all kinds, and the ground is covered with forests of heavy pine, and when we give these up to the Great Father we know that we give up that last thing that is valuable either to us or to the white people."

"I want to speak," Crazy Wolf said, and he leaped up and walked across the circle to stand before Joseph. He pointed an accusing finger at Joseph. *"He* is a white man!" Crazy Wolf said angrily.

"He was born white, but now he is Indian," Sitting Bear said. "We held the sacred ceremony that made him one of us."

Crazy Wolf, who had been holding something in a clenched fist, suddenly threw two stones on the ground in front of the other council members.

"Look at the two stones," Crazy Wolf said. "If you are not blind, you can see that one is red and the other is white. Medicine men can not change the color of the stones, wishing cannot change the color of the stones, prayer to the Great Spirit cannot change the color of the stones, and no ceremony can change the color of the stones. I know, for I have tried all of these ways. And yet, as you see, they have remained the same. One is red . . ." He paused dramatically and walked back over to stand in front of Joseph. He leaned over so that his face was only inches away from Joseph's. ". . . and one is white!"

Crazy Wolf stood there in the light of the campfire, allowing the impact of his dramatic speech to sink in. Finally Sitting Bull held up his hand. It was the first time that night the great chief had spoken.

"You have demonstrated that the color of stones cannot be changed," Sitting Bull said. "It was a good speech with many wise words. But I ask you this. What has the color of stones to do with Joseph Two Hearts?"

"Just as stones cannot be changed, neither can men," Crazy Wolf said. "Tonight, Joseph Two Hearts attacked me because I am a red man and I looked upon a white woman. It is known that the white men will enjoy a red woman, but a red man is thought by the white men to be an animal. They tell their women to kill themselves rather than let a red man look at them. And so this is also true of Joseph Two Hearts."

There were several angry remarks from the other Indians at that accusation, and Joseph could feel their eyes looking at him angrily. His words, he knew, had struck at a very vulnerable point . . . their manhood.

"It is true that I attacked my brother, Crazy Wolf," Joseph said. "But he was about to rape the captive girl."

"And you could not see a red man with a white girl?" Crazy Wolf challenged.

Joseph stood up and faced the others. "I let my brother speak his angry words . . . now I ask that I be allowed to answer."

"You may answer," Sitting Bull said.

"Thank you," Joseph said. "I did not want him to rape the girl. Not because she was white, but because it would be unwise. We are very close to the white fort now, but we do not have many of our warriors with us. If the white girl or her father or the long knife sergeant are hurt by us, then I think Custer

38

will attack us before we are ready and many of our people will die."

"We are not afraid to die," Crazy Wolf shouted.

"No, we are not," Joseph said. "Nor were the warriors afraid to die at Washita. But it was not the warriors of Washita who died. It was the women and children, and the old men and the babies. Do you want such a thing to happen here as well?"

The Indians looked at each other, remembering the tragedy of Washita.

"Hear me, my brothers, for what I speak is true," Joseph continued. "We should not have attacked the wagon that took the girl and her father toward the fort. They are of no danger to us. But Crazy Wolf was foolish, and without the consent of the council, he led an attack. It is said that he killed four soldiers. But it is also said that two soldiers were not killed. They returned to the fort, and they will tell Custer what we have done. Custer has many more soldiers than we have warriors, and he will come destroy our small camp and kill the women and children."

"You speak with the fear of women and children," Crazy Wolf said.

"No," Joseph said. "I speak with the wisdom of one who is a member of the council. For I say that if we release the girl and her father unharmed and tell Custer that he may send the medicine wagon for the sergeant, we can make a truce that will allow us to fight another day."

"He speaks wisely," Fool Dog said. "I say we should listen to him."

"And I say he is a white man and will trick us with his white words!" Crazy Wolf insisted.

"No," Sitting Bull said. "He is not a white man. He is an Indian. Your story of the stones has no meaning because a stone has no heart."

"Thank you, Sitting Bull," Joseph said.

"What would you have us do, Two Hearts?"

"Let us free the girl and her father," Joseph said. "Let us send a message to Custer. Let us tell him that we do not want to make war here. Let us tell him we are sorry we attacked his wagon, and let us tell him that he can send a medicine wagon in safety."

"Go," Sitting Bull said. "Get the girl and bring her here, so that she may hear my words."

Joseph left the council fire and went back into the tipi. He worried suddenly that she might be gone. He had cut her loose but hadn't cautioned her to stay in the tipi. If she was gone, it might be bad for her because then he wouldn't be able to convince the others that she could be trusted.

He breathed a sigh of relief when he stepped back inside the tipi and saw her sitting quietly, fully dressed.

"Will I be released?" Crimson asked, looking up as Joseph entered.

"Yes."

"Oh, thank God," Crimson said. "And the others? They will be released too?"

"Yes. At least your father will be."

"And Sergeant Flynn?"

"Sergeant Flynn will stay here until Custer sends the ambulance wagon for him. Then he, too, will be released."

"How badly hurt is Sergeant Flynn? Will he live?"

"Yes," Joseph said. "Now, come to the council fire. Chief Sitting Bull wants to speak to you."

Crimson stood up and stretched a bit to restore the circulation, then followed Joseph outside. The village, which had been frightening enough in the daytime, was terrifying by dark. The flickering fires cast grotesque shadows, and faces that had expressed curiosity in the daytime now seemed like demonic masks.

"This is Sitting Bull," Joseph said, pointing to one of the Indians.

Crimson had heard of Sitting Bull. From the reading on the Indians that she and her father had come to paint, she knew that he was the chief of the Hunkpapas and that he had never lived on a reservation. He was an impressive looking man, and despite the uncertainty of her position, she looked at him with the practiced eye of the artist. The lines of strength and wisdom in his face comforted her.

"What is your name?" Sitting Bull asked.

"I am Crimson Royal."

"I am Tatanka Iyotake. In your language, that means Sitting Bull."

"I have heard of you, Sitting Bull," Crimson said. "I am proud to meet you."

"Why have you come?"

"My father and I are artists," Crimson said. "We wish to paint pictures of Indians and their way of life."

"Crazy Wolf says you will give pictures to soldiers so they will know how to hunt and kill us."

"That isn't true," Crimson said. "We want to take the pictures back to New York and let the people see what you are really like."

"Crazy Wolf says you should be killed."

Crimson looked at Crazy Wolf, and because she felt safe with the council present, she spoke frankly.

"Crazy Wolf is a coward. He would have his way with me while I am tied, and then he would kill me."

Crimson's words were translated to the others, and they laughed. Crazy Wolf glared at her with anger and hate in his eyes, and she knew that she had made an enemy for life. She wondered if that would make their mission a lost cause, if indeed, it was not already. On the other hand, she would not be cowed by him.

41

"Joseph Two Hearts said you should be set free to return to your people."

"I do want to be free," Crimson said. "And I want to return to the fort so I can send help to Sergeant Flynn. But I do not want to stay with my people. I want to stay with you."

"If you stay with us, you will have an enemy in Crazy Wolf," Sitting Bull said. "Does this not frighten you?"

"Yes," Crimson said. "But I wish to stay anyway."

"We will speak of this," Sitting Bull said.

Crimson walked to the outer edge of the circle of light and sat watching as the council discussed her fate, and that of her father and Sergeant Flynn. Joseph Two Hearts and Crazy Wolf both spoke several more times, angry and accusing. Finally, even though she couldn't understand the words, she knew that the council was turning against Crazy Wolf, because he grew angrier. Then, after a particularly sharp exchange of words, Crazy Wolf stormed out of the meeting, glaring angrily at Crimson as he walked by. The ferocity of his stare sent shivers running down her spine.

Joseph came to her and, smiling, held out his hand to help her to her feet.

"The council will let you and your father return as I have said," Joseph said.

"Then will my father and I be able to return to paint among the Siox?"

"I will let Sitting Bull tell you."

Once again Crimson found herself standing before Sitting Bull. He held his hand up, palm out, and bowed his head for a moment before he spoke.

"I have listened to your words, and I have discussed your words with the others. Now here is what we say. After you return to the fort, if the soldiers say you may come, we will not harm you. We say it

42

is good if people in the large white villages such as New York know of our ways. Perhaps then they will say to the Great Father in Washington to let Indian children go in peace. Now, you must take these words to Custer. Tell him these are the words of Sitting Bull, chief of the Hunkpapa Sioux."

Sitting Bull stood up and walked toward the fire. He gazed at it for a moment, as if composing his thoughts, then turned back to Crimson.

"Tell the whites the Black Hills belong to me! Look at me and look at the earth. Which is the older do you think? The earth, and I was born on it. . . . It does not belong to us alone; it was our fathers' and should be our children's after us. When I received it, it was all in one piece, and so I hold it. If the white men take my country, where can I go? I have nowhere to go . . . I love it very much. Let us alone. That is what they promised in their treaty . . . What is the white man doing here? To spy out the land, to build more forts and more roads and to dig out gold? The Black Hills belong to me. The white man must go back."

Sitting Bull finished his speech, then walked out of the circle of light and disappeared in the night. Crimson looked after him, staring into the dark for a long moment. His words, though simple, were eloquent, and they rung with the power of truth.

"Mr. Two Hearts," she said quietly. "Please inform Sitting Bull that I would be proud to carry his words to Custer."

# 5

The dream came to Tom again.

It had come to him so often over the last seven years that he referred to it in his thoughts as "the dream." He had never mentioned it to anyone; not to his sister-in-law, who had always taken a maternal interest in him, and certainly not to his brother. He would have told them about it if he had thought they could understand. He would have spoken about it to anyone if it would have helped him rid himself of the dream.

But no one would understand, so he tried to forestall the dream by drinking.

"Too much alcohol is inconsistent with the tenants of command," his brother said, chastising him for his intemperance. "It is unbecoming an officer, and it is unbecoming a Custer."

But Autie just didn't understand, because Autie didn't have the devils of Washita chasing him. Autie was able to set human emotions aside and deal only with the issues of military operations. To George

Armstrong Custer, Washita was just one more in a string of brilliant victories over the enemy.

How Tom wished he could approach Washita with the same sense of detachment. But he couldn't ... and it had haunted him for seven years.

The oddest thing about the dream was that, regardless of the number of times it occurred, it would be so vivid that at the moment he was dreaming, he was unable to distinguish it from reality. He was forced to relive the incident time and time again ... hundreds of times over the last seven years.

In the dream was the fog, a thick blanket pinned to the earth by the tall pine trees. The fog shielded the Indian village where Black Kettle's people were sleeping in the pre-dawn hours. There were no warriors in the village to give the alert of the cavalry's approach—only women, children, and old men.

The ground was covered with a heavy snow, as if the fog had solidified at its base, and the snow and fog deadened all sound so that the horses and men moved in absolute silence.

Tom was sitting on his horse in the front rank, and his company and the others of the Seventh Cavalry were drawn up in line with him. He had no idea how he got there or how long he had been there.

The band dismounted and began playing *Garry Owen*, the regimental song. Then the regiment swept forward. The horses hooves made no sound, as if the animals were running on the thin air. The shouts of the men, the rattle of their equipment, and even the first, tentative gunshots were also without sound.

Though the soldiers and horses were mute, the band was not, and Tom could hear the incessant sound of *Garry Owen*; the band was invisible in the fogbank behind them, a ghostly orchestra, not of heaven, but of hell.

Then the savage butchery began. Tom could see

it all as a slowly danced ballet, a grotesque, amazingly detailed choreography. Women and children were cut down by flashing sabers . . . old men were shot at point blank range, and babies were trampled by the horses.

It was a soundless dance of color—white snow, red blood, blue coats, and the golden hair of his brother as Tom stood back and watched the carnage.

A loud, incessant knocking at the door of Tom's quarters finally awakened him. He sat up quickly and looked around in terror, thinking for a moment that the massacre was still going on.

"Cap'n Custer! Cap'n Custer, sir!" Again, knocking sounded at the door.

Tom ran his hand through his dark, curly hair and let out a long, slow sigh of relief as he realized that he had only been dreaming.

"Cap'n Custer, sir? Beggin' your pardon, sir, but the general wants to see you."

Tom slowly swung his legs over the side of the bed and put his feet on the rough-hewn plank floor, returning to the world he had so reluctantly abandoned the night before.

The soldier pounded on the door again.

"I'm awake," Tom said. He walked to the door and opened it, then went over to the water basin. He poured in some water from the jug. "Come in, Sergeant Kennedy," he said.

The sergeant stepped into the room and gave a crisp salute.

"My brother would be proud," Tom said dryly, returning the sergeant's salute with his own sloppy version. "Now, what is on the 'general's' mind?"

"General" was a courtesy extended to his brother because he had been breveted a general during the Civil War. His actual rank was that of lieutenant colonel though possibly he was the best known lieutenant colonel in the United States Army.

47

"The General wants you to take the search party out today," Sergeant Kennedy said.

Tom had splashed water in his face, and now he was drying himself with a towel. "Search party? What search party?" he asked. "What am I to search for?"

"Oh, beggin' your pardon, sir, I thought you knew," Sergeant Kennedy answered.

"No, Sergeant. I, uh, was unavoidably detained in Bismark yesterday, and I didn't return to the fort until quite late last night. I spoke to no one. What's missing?"

"That artist fella," Sergeant Kennedy said. "And Sergeant Flynn, and the artist's daughter. They was comin' back to the fort in the gen'rul's coach when they was attacked by Crazy Wolf."

Suddenly Tom remembered the beautiful young lady he had seen in Autie's coach on the day before. He pulled the towel away from his face and stared at Sergeant Kennedy.

"What? You mean those people I saw in town yesterday never made it back to the fort?"

"No, sir."

"Why, that is incredible! Crazy Wolf attacked them, you say? How do you know?"

"Chance and Evans got away 'n made it back," Sergeant Kennedy said.

"You mean to tell me that Chance and Evans *abandoned* the others?"

"Well, not exactly, Cap'n. We did find the other guards. They was dead. But we haven't been able to find the village."

Tom put on a buckskin tunic. "Tell my brother I'll be right there, Sergeant. Have my horse saddled, and get the men mounted up."

"Yes, sir," Kennedy said. He started out the door, then stopped and looked back toward Tom. "Excuse me, sir, but will you be wantin' any breakfast?"

48

Tom made a face. "No," he said. "I don't even want to think about eating."

"Yes, sir," Kennedy replied.

After the sergeant left, Tom examined himself in the mirror. His brother was a stickler about his officers' appearance, and he would be no less strict with his own brother than he would be with the others. The figure who looked back from the mirror was of medium height, trim, with flashing blue eyes in which one could readily see a resemblance to his brother. But, whereas the general had long, golden hair, Tom's was cut short, and was curly and dark. And he was clean shaven.

Tom decided that he could pass his brother's critical inspection. He strapped on the belt that held his service pistol, ammunition pouch, and saber. Giving his mirror image a sarcastic salute, he was about to start for his brother's quarters when he saw a bottle of whiskey on a shelf. He took a quick drink, feeling it burn its way down his throat. He was grateful for the sense of calm and well being it gave him.

Tom's quarters were next door to his brother's house, and it was but a moment before he was knocking on the door.

"Tom, do come in," his brother's wife said, greeting him with a cordial smile.

Elizabeth Bacon Custer—Libbie, as she was called —showed no signs of early age from the rigors of military life in a remote fort. In fact, she seemed to thrive on it. She was a very pretty woman with skin that one New York reporter described as being "of the white transparency of alabaster." The writer went on to say that "her cheeks were apple red. Her hair, luxuriant and wavy, was chestnut brown. Her features were well cut, and her eyes were the light, gray-blue of Lake Erie, from whence she came."

"Where is Autie?" asked Tom.

"He's taking his breakfast. Won't you have something to eat?"

"No, thank you," Tom said.

"Don't tease him so, Libbie," George Custer said, as Tom and Libbie stepped into the dining room. "He has no time for breakfast."

Custer buttered a biscuit as he spoke. He was already elegantly dressed in a black, velvet tunic with gold ornamentation. He looked at Tom with a disapproving expression.

"Where were you yesterday?"

"I . . . uh . . . was detained," Tom said.

"You were drunk," Custer said.

"Autie, don't be too hard on him," Libbie said.

Custer pointed his knife at Tom and started to speak, then sighed and put the knife down.

"Tom, oh, Tom, do you think I enjoy reprimanding you?"

"I suppose not," Tom said.

"No, of course I don't," Custer replied. "In fact, when Libbie and I go to New York this Christmas, I intend to leave you in command. You, Tom. Not Reno or Benteen. That will surely mean promotion for you. And when I fulfill my manifest destiny . . . who better to leave in command of the Seventh than another Custer? The Custers have an obligation, Tom, a pivotal role to play in the history of our nation. You must never forget who you are."

"That hardly seems likely," Tom replied. "Autie, what happened yesterday?"

"Yesterday," Custer said. "Yes, a terrible business. I sent Sergeant Flynn and an escort detail in to meet the train. Mr. Artemus Royal and his daughter were on the train, you know. He is probably America's best known painter. . . . I visited a gallery showing of his work last January when I was in New York. He is a brilliant, brilliant artist."

"But what happened yesterday?" Tom asked. Tom was used to his brother's digressions.

"Yes, well, as Sergeant Flynn and the escort detail were bringing them to the fort, they were attacked by Crazy Wolf. Four of the men were killed, two escaped to bring word of what happened, and we don't know about the fate of the other three."

"Did you not find them yesterday?"

"No," Custer said. "We sent out two patrols yesterday, one north and one west. Today we'll go east and south."

"There's no need to go east," Tom said. "I know where they are."

"You do? How do you know that?"

"When I was in town yesterday, I heard some buffalo hunters talking about a large stand. The herd was south of here, that's where we'll find Crazy Wolf."

"If Crazy Wolf is with them, then that means that some of the other chiefs are there as well," Custer said. "White Ghost, Sitting Bear, Fool Dog . . . maybe even Sitting Bull."

"And Joseph Two Hearts?" Tom asked.

The smile left Custer's face, which set in an expression of determination and hate.

"Yes," he said. "Maybe even Joseph Two Hearts."

"Autie, why do you have such a personal vendetta against him? He isn't the only Indian ever to beat you in a skirmish."

"Because he is a traitor to the white race," Custer said. "And when I capture him, I shall take great delight in hanging him for treason."

"It's only natural that he would fight for the Indians. After all, he was raised by them. He knows no other life."

"I cannot countenance treason," Custer said. "Don't attempt to defend it."

51

There was a knock on the front door.

"That'll be Sergeant Kennedy," Tom said. "My troop is formed. I must be off."

"Tom," Custer said as Tom started to leave.

"Yes?"

"It would not look well for me if something has happened to them. The newspapers back East would tear me to pieces . . . you know how badly they want to discredit General Custer."

Tom suppressed the smile at hearing Custer refer to himself in the third person.

"Find them for me."

"Is your only concern how this would look to the Eastern papers?" Tom asked.

"No, of course not," Custer replied.

"Good," Tom said. "I would hate to think that was the sole reason for the search."

Libbie stepped over to her brother-in-law.

"Tom," she said, kissing him lightly on the cheek. "You mustn't be too hard on your brother. After all, he looks out for all of you. Custer is one of the best known names in America. We are family, Tom . . . and we will always stand united as family."

Tom smiled. "You're right, Libbie. You don't have to worry about me. And Autie doesn't have to worry about the Royals. If they are out there, I'll find them."

"I have no doubt of that," Libby said.

Tom's horse had been brought to his brother's front doorstep. Tom put his foot into the stirrup and swung on, then, standing in the stirrups, he surveyed the assembled troop of sixty mounted cavalrymen, sitting tall and strong in their saddles, stretched out in a long, single line.

"Sergeant, prepare to move out," Tom said.

"Troop, form column of twos!" the sergeant yelled, his voice echoing across the fort.

The men executed the command.

"Guidon, post!" the sergeant yelled, and a soldier carrying a red and white flag galloped to the head of the column.

The few wives and children of the soldiers and the men who were not going on this patrol were standing by to witness their departure. Tom, for all his laconic military spirit, couldn't help but be moved by the scene.

"Move 'em out, Sergeant," Tom ordered.

"Forward, ho!"

The troop started through the gates as beneath the flagpole, the regimental band played *Garry Owen*.

# 6

The column was one hour out of the fort, moving slowly but steadily. The plains stretched out before them in folds of hills, one after another; as each ridge was crested, another was exposed, and beyond that, another still. The dusty grass gave off a pungent smell when crushed by the horses' hooves.

The golden light of morning had long since given way to the white brightness of day, and though it was already September, the heat of a long, hot summer lingered on. Tom had sweated away all the alcohol in his system, and the merciless sun gave him a headache. He held his hand up to bring the column to a halt.

"D'ya see anythin', sir?" Sergeant Kennedy asked.

"Have the men dismount, Sergeant," Tom said. "Give the animals a five minute blow."

"Yes, sir," Kennedy replied, and he passed the order on to the men.

The soldiers dismounted and walked their horses to cool them down. Some of the soldiers stretched out on the ground for a moment; several others used the opportunity to relieve themselves.

Tom handed the reins of his horse to Sergeant Kennedy, then took his binoculars and climbed the hill to scan the horizon. But he saw only dusty rocks, shimmering grass, and more ranges of hills under the beating sun. He started to drop the glasses, when he saw one outcropping of rock that looked different from the others. He stared at it more closely.

"Sergeant Kennedy!" he called. "On the double!"

Sergeant Kennedy ran up the hill, puffing loudly by the time he reached Tom. "What do you see, sir?"

"The coach, Sergeant," Tom said. He handed his binoculars to Kennedy, who looked in the direction Tom pointed.

"Aye, it's the coach all right," Kennedy said. "But where are the horses?"

"The Indians took them, of course," Tom said. "The question is, where are the people?"

"My bet is they are inside the coach, sir."

"Or lying dead alongside it," Tom answered grimly. "Let's get the men mounted."

Sergeant Kennedy ran back down the hill. "Mount up, men!" he called. "We've spotted the coach."

"D'ya see Sergeant Flynn?" one of the men called.

"Just the coach," Kennedy said. "We don't know what else we'll find."

Tom reached his own horse and swung into the saddle. He wondered what they would find when they reached the coach. He had seen dead and naked bodies hacked to pieces and left to turn purple and bloated under the relentless plains sun. He knew what they looked like, and what they could do to you inside.

He also remembered how beautiful the girl was he had met yesterday, and his stomach twisted as he thought of what she would look like without her long, radiant hair.

"Forward at a trot, Sergeant."

The column broke into a trot at Sergeant Kennedy's command, sabers, canteens, and rifles jangling and dust boiling up behind them. The coach loomed larger until they were within a few hundred yards of it.

"At a gallop!" Tom called, and he stood in his stirrups and drew his saber, pointing it forward. It wasn't just showmanship; it was a signal to the soldiers to be on the alert for a possible Indian ambush. Every soldier drew his rifle from the saddle scabbard and held it at the ready.

At first, Crimson thought the Indians were returning. It didn't seem like they had been gone more than half an hour, and when she heard the hoofbeats, she was frightened that perhaps Crazy Wolf had changed the council's mind. But when she looked out, she saw that the approaching riders were cavalrymen.

"Father, it's the cavalry," Crimson said. Happily, she opened the door of the coach and stepped outside to greet them.

"Troop, halt!" Tom called, and the soldiers reined in their mounts.

"Are there Indians about, miss?" Tom called.

"No," Crimson said. "They've gone."

"Sergeant Kennedy, send out two squads. Clear the area for three hundred yards in every direction."

"Yes, sir," Kennedy replied.

Tom swung down from his horse and walked over to Crimson. It was only then that Crimson recognized him as the officer she had met the day before.

"Are you all right, Miss Royal? And you, sir? Have you been harmed?"

"We are fine," Crimson said, smiling in apparent amusement. "And you, Captain Custer. How are you, today?"

"I'm fine," Tom said, then looked at her with a curious expression. "I must say, Miss Royal, you seem in remarkably fine spirits for one who has just gone through such an ordeal."

"We were not harmed," Crimson said.

"What about Sergeant Flynn?"

"He was wounded in the battle," Crimson said. "The Indians removed the arrow. He is weak, but not in serious condition. Sitting Bull said you may send an ambulance for him."

"Sitting Bull? Did you say Sitting Bull?" Tom asked.

"Yes."

"Are you positive?"

"Would you recognize a likeness of him?" Artemus asked.

"Yes, of course," Tom said.

Artemus reached back into the coach and pulled out a pad. He thumbed through the pages until he found the sketch of Sitting Bull and showed it to Tom.

"Yes," Tom said. "Yes, that's him, all right. Well, my brother will be happy to hear this. He's been looking for Sitting Bull for this entire year . . . and you found him on your first day out here."

"I think it would be more accurate to say that he found us," Artemus said.

"Cap'n Custer, the men report the area is clear," Sergeant Kennedy said, riding up to the coach.

"Good," Tom said. "Have a couple of the men hitch their horses to the coach. We'll form a screening detail and lead them back to the fort."

"Yes, sir," Kennedy said.

It was early afternoon by the time the coach and escort reached Fort Abraham Lincoln. But Tom had sent a fast rider out ahead, and by the time the coach rolled in through the front gates, the entire garrison had turned out in full parade dress uniform. The band struck up a crisp march as the detail came through the gates.

"Look sharp now, men," Tom said to his tired troopers. "Sit tall in the saddle."

"Oh, Father, look," Crimson said. "There, over there by the flagpole. That's General Custer, isn't it?"

Artemus nodded. "That's Custer, all right."

The escort detail passed in front of the flagpole.

"Eyes—right!" Tom called, and as the cavalrymen, two by two, snapped their heads toward General Custer, Tom held his saber out in a salute. General Custer returned the salute.

"Troop, halt!"

The coach creaked to a halt in front of Custer.

"Dismount!"

Crimson could hear the jangle of equipment as the men swung off their horses.

"Sir, Captain Custer and A troop returning from the mission," Tom said. "Pleased to report, sir, both civilians are safe and well."

"Thank you, Captain," Custer said. "Well done. You may dismiss your men."

"Dismissed!" Tom called, and at that instant pure bedlam broke out. There were cheers and shouts of hurrah, and the men who but moments before had been blue statues in the sun now came running toward the coach.

General Custer was the first one to the coach. He opened the doors and helped Crimson and her father out.

"Are we glad to see you!" Custer said, smiling broadly. "I must say, you certainly gave us a scare."

"Well, thank you," Crimson said, somewhat flustered by all the attention. "I must confess to a moment or two of fright myself. Oh, and General Custer, Sergeant Flynn is alive, though wounded. Sitting Bull said you may send an ambulance for him."

"Yes, I will lead the party myself," Custer said. "We will get underway right after lunch. Have you eaten?"

Suddenly Crimson realized that she was hungry. Her appetite, suppressed by fear and uncertainty, had returned with a vengeance.

"I am starved," she said. "We haven't eaten since yesterday morning."

Custer laughed. "Well, Libbie will be happy to hear that you are hungry. She has been cooking ever since she heard you were safe and returning to us."

Crimson touched her hair, which was hanging in unkempt strands. "General, would it be possible to take a bath before we eat?"

Custer laughed appreciatively. "Don't tell me that women do not know women, for my own Libbie said you would make just such a request. You'll find a tub of hot water waiting for you in Tom's quarters. Tom, I hope you don't mind—you'll be moving in with Will Benteen."

"No, of course I don't mind," Tom said. "Sergeant Kennedy, detail someone to carry Miss Royal's trunk to my quarters."

Half a dozen men volunteered, and Kennedy smiled as he chose one. "Lads, why is it you aren't so quick to volunteer for any of the other nice details?"

"If there is a pretty lady involved, Sarge, you can count me in any time," one of the troopers yelled, and the others laughingly agreed.

Crimson followed the sergeant and the trooper across the quadrangle to Tom Custer's small house. The room was cozily furnished, and, sitting right in the middle of the floor, was a large tub, filled with hot, soapy water.

"Ohh," Crimson said happily. "How wonderful!"

"Enjoy, ma'am," Sergeant Kennedy said, touching his brow in a salute as he left.

And enjoy Crimson did. She luxuriated in the hot water, feeling the prairie grime wash away. Finally, only because she knew that the others would be waiting lunch for her, she got out of the tub and dressed.

Tom was waiting on the front porch for her. He had cleaned up and was wearing a parade dress uniform. He offered Crimson his arm.

"I'm sorry if I kept you waiting," Crimson said.

"You were worth waiting for," Tom said. "Libbie is a beautiful woman and brightens up this post, but your beauty is a match for hers any day."

"Well, how nice of you to say so," Crimson said.

When Crimson walked into the Custer home, she was introduced to a half-dozen officers and their wives, but there were so many at one time she had trouble keeping the names and faces straight.

She had no trouble with Elizabeth Custer, though. The woman dominated the meal. She was beautiful, true enough, but it was more than her beauty that held sway over everyone, for even the women deferred to her. As wife of the commanding officer, her rank was as indelibly stamped upon her person as the silver leaves on her husband's shoulders.

"To provide you with the privacy I know a young woman needs, I've prevailed upon Dr. Sprague to share his quarters with your father," Libbie explained.

"Thank you," Crimson said. "You've all been so nice to us, I don't know how to thank you."

"How far away is the Indian camp, Miss Royal?" Captain Benteen asked.

"Now, Will, we'll discuss none of that until after we have eaten," Libbie said sharply. "After all, Miss Royal has been through quite an ordeal. We must give her a chance to relax."

"I don't mind," Crimson said.

"Well, I *do* mind," Libbie said with authority.

61

"So," Custer said. "I suppose the two of you will be returning to New York on the next train."

"Of course not," Artemus said. "What makes you think such a thing?"

"But surely you don't intend to go on with your plans now?" Custer asked.

"Yes," Crimson said. "Yes, we do. The Indians have given us permission to return."

Custer laughed. "My dear lady, it is not the Indian's permission you must seek. It is mine."

"But we already have President Grant's permission," Artemus said.

"President Grant isn't commanding the fort," Custer said easily. "I am."

"But General, surely you can see the importance of what I am trying to do?"

"Mr. Royal, please look at this from my point of view," Custer said. "I am charged with protecting the lives and property of the white settlers and travellers in this territory. I am responsible for six thousand square miles. Now you are one of the most famous artists in the world. If something happens to you out there, the responsibility will fall right on my shoulders."

"But surely I can assume the responsibility for my own actions?"

"No, sir, you cannot," Custer said. "Alas, my dear Mr. Royal, I'm afraid it is neither in your hands nor mine. Back there," he pointed east, "you have only loyal fans. They will not fix responsibility upon your shoulders should something happen to you. They will fix it upon mine."

"But surely, General, you have fans too?"

"That is true," Custer said. "In fact, I have supporters who have suggested that I might seek political office." Custer coughed. "The highest political office," he went on. "But it is precisely because of this that I also have detractors, political enemies who would stop at nothing to prevent me from achieving my destiny. It is they who would hold me to blame. No, Mr. Royal, I cannot let you venture back into the Black Hills."

"General, you don't understand . . ." Crimson started, but she was interrupted by Libbie.

"More tea, my dear?" Libbie asked, smiling sweetly.

Crimson knew that it was useless to pursue the matter any further now, so she let it drop for the time being.

"Mr. Royal, perhaps I could engage you to do a portrait of me," Custer said. "It certainly could not harm my cause to have a portrait done by America's greatest painter."

"Perhaps," Artemus said noncommittally.

The meal was finished shortly afterward, and then Custer asked Crimson and Artemus to tell them the location of the village.

"Before I tell you, I must relay a message from Sitting Bull," Crimson said.

"You don't have to tell me anything he said, Miss Royal," Custer said. "You are safe here, now."

"But I want to tell you," Crimson said. "I promised that I would."

"Very well."

Crimson relayed the message about the Black Hills, and when she was finished, Custer chuckled quietly.

"They're still trying to claim the hills for themselves," he said.

"But . . . aren't the Black Hills the sacred grounds of the Indians?" Crimson asked.

"Miss Royal, I'll tell you what is sacred about the Black Hills," Custer replied. "Gold."

"Surely, Miss Royal, you've read my brother's famous comment that the Black Hills are full of gold from the grass roots down?" Tom asked.

"No," Crimson said. "No, I don't believe I have."

"Then you are one of the few who haven't," Tom said. "There are ten thousand prospectors out here, and every one of them came because of that statement."

"And each one of them is a potential target," Major Reno said.

"Gentlemen, we have a mission to perform," Custer said, standing. "Ladies, if you will excuse us?"

Libbie held her cheek out for a kiss, and Custer dutifully gave her a peck. The other wives and husbands followed suit, and the officers left.

"Well, ladies, shall we quilt, then? Crimson, we would be pleased if you would join us," Libbie said.

# 7

"They're comin' back! The regiment's comin' back!"

This announcement, shouted just outside her window, awakened Crimson. She had tried to maintain her end of the conversation during the ladies' quilting the night before, but Libbie had noticed her drooping eyelids and bobbing head and finally sent her off to bed. Crimson dropped off to sleep the moment her head hit the pillow and was just now waking up. At that, sleep still pulled at her, and she lay in bed for a few moments more until she heard the band begin to play. Only then did she get out of bed and start to get dressed.

The patrol must have had to travel very slowly with Sergeant Flynn to just now be returning, she thought, leaving the post yesterday afternoon. She wondered why they hadn't left immediately upon her return or else waited until morning. As it was they would have reached the village after nightfall, which seemed to her a strange time to call upon the Indians for the return of Sergeant Flynn. She had wondered about it, but she hadn't questioned it. She didn't know about such things, and besides, she was just too tired.

"How's Sergeant Flynn?" Crimson heard someone ask just outside her window.

"He's all right," came the answer. "But they was two troopers kilt last night. The General brought their bodies back, though. They're sayin' we'll have a military funeral for 'em tomorra' afternoon."

What were they talking about? Crimson wondered. How could anyone have been killed?

"How many Indians was kilt?"

"I hear tell near on to twenty."

Crimson finished dressing and stepped quickly outside. She looked around to see who was talking, but they had left.

Then she saw the regiment returning, and she gasped. She had not watched them leave yesterday, and had no idea how many had gone out. This was no simple rescue mission! This had been a full-scale raid!

"Isn't it wonderful, Crimson?" one of the women she had met last night asked. "What a glorious victory!"

"What is this?" Crimson asked. "They weren't supposed to attack the Indians! They were just supposed to rescue Sergeant Flynn!"

"Dear, you didn't really expect them to keep a bargain with savages, did you?" the woman asked.

"Yes," Crimson said. "I gave Sitting Bull my word."

The regiment was dismissed then, and Tom came over to Crimson.

"Miss Royal, Crimson, can I talk to you?" Tom asked.

Crimson turned her back on him. "I've nothing to say to you, *Captain* Custer," she said.

66

"Please," Tom said. "I must talk to you for a moment."

Crimson had started to walk away from him, but now she let him catch up to her.

"I want you to know that I didn't approve of this," Tom said.

"You went, didn't you?"

"Yes."

"Then you must have approved."

"That's not true. I went because I am an officer and I was ordered to go. I had no choice. But believe me, Crimson, I didn't want to go."

"Tom, what happened?" Crimson asked. "I thought you were just going to go get Sergeant Flynn. Now I hear men were killed on both sides."

"Yes," Tom said. He sighed and stared at the floor as he spoke, as if ashamed to look her in the eyes. "We arrived just before dusk." The main party stayed away from the village, out of sight. We sent in the ambulance with a two-man escort under the white flag. The men picked up Sergeant Flynn, but all the time they were looking around, gauging the strength of the Indians, looking at the lay of the land. When they came back they gave all the information to Autie. We waited until about one o'clock this morning, then, when we knew they would be asleep, we hit them."

"Oh, no," Crimson said.

"Most of the chiefs got away," Tom went on. "Sitting Bear was killed. Joseph Two Hearts—"

"Was he killed?" she asked anxiously, her heart in her throat. Oh, Lord, please let it not be so!

"No," he said, obviously surprised at her reaction.

"Oh, good," Crimson replied, unable to disguise her relief.

"He fought a rear-guard action so that the others could get away," Tom said. "Most of the ones who stayed with him were killed. Miraculously, Joseph Two Hearts wasn't even wounded . . . but he was captured."

"Captured?"

"Yes," Tom said. "He's in the guardhouse now."

Crimson looked toward the guardhouse, where a mob had already gathered around, looking in through the barred window.

"He is going to be hanged tomorrow," Tom said simply.

"What?" Crimson gasped. "You can't mean it!"

"I'm afraid I do," Tom said.

"But . . . doesn't he get a trial or anything?"

"Autie is the military commander of the district," Tom said. "He is his own judge and jury."

"I see," Crimson replied. "How convenient for him."

"Crimson, don't think too harshly of him," Tom said. "He has a big responsibility. Big? It's awesome. I don't know how many men could handle it. I know I couldn't."

"Perhaps you are selling yourself short," Crimson said. "You have compassion and humility, qualities that seem to me the general is sadly lacking."

"You just don't understand," Tom said sadly. He turned and started to leave, then he stopped and looked back toward her. "Oh, there is a dance in the Sutlers' store tonight to celebrate."

"To celebrate? What—the General's treachery? *My* treachery?"

"No, of course not," Tom said. "It's to celebrate your safe return, and your father's and Sergeant Flynn's. Sergeant Flynn will be as good as new in no time, you'll see."

"Thank God for that, at least," Crimson said. "I rather like Sergeant Flynn. And I gather he thinks highly of you."

"Sergeant Flynn has been with me since I was a

68

shavetail," Tom said with a laugh. "He figures I belong to him."

"A shavetail?"

"A second lieutenant," Tom said. "When the army buys a new mule, they shave its tail. New mules are notoriously stupid."

"And new lieutenants?" Crimson asked.

"You've made the connection," Tom said. "Now, about the dance tonight. I would be honored if you would allow me to escort you."

"I don't suppose there is any way to get out of going altogether," she said.

Tom smiled. "Not if you want to remain a guest on my brother's post."

"And the alternative to staying here as a guest?"

"Returning to New York, I suppose," Tom said. "At the very least, going back to Fargo."

"Then I have no alternative," Crimson said. "I will go to the dance, and you may escort me."

"Oh, that's wonderful," Tom said. "You'll have a fine time tonight, Crimson. You'll see."

"Yes, I'm certain I shall," Crimson said without enthusiasm.

Tom saluted and left. Crimson, unsure of where she was to take her meals or what was expected of her, went next door to speak with Libbie.

"Well, so you are up, I see?" Libbie said, greeting her sweetly but without warmth.

"Yes, Mrs. Custer," Crimson said.

"Please, call me Libbie, dear," Libbie interrupted.

"Thank you," Crimson said. "Libbie, where shall I take my meals? There is no kitchen in Tom's . . ." Crimson flushed at saying Tom's first name, and she cleared her throat and stammered before continuing. "In Captain Custer's quarters."

"Captain Custer takes his meals with us," Libbie said, and Crimson suddenly got the distinct notion that Elizabeth Custer was discouraging any relationship that might develop between Crimson and Tom.

"Oh, but I can't do that," Crimson said. "That would be such an imposition."

"Nonsense," Libbie said. "As the wife of the commanding officer of this fort, I am expected to provide for our honored guests. You and your father shall always be welcome at my table."

"How very kind of you," Crimson said.

"As Autie was in the field this morning, I didn't serve breakfast," Libbie went on. "I trust you can wait until lunch?"

"Yes, that will be fine," Crimson said.

Crimson heard some hammering from the quadrangle, and Libbie walked over to look through the window. "Oh, dear, they are building a scaffold. I suppose there is no way to avoid this unpleasantness."

"Unpleasantness?"

"The hanging," Libbie said. "Autie captured a traitor last night, and he will hang tomorrow. Imagine, a white man living like a savage, fighting against his own kind."

"Libbie, I can't believe this," Crimson said. "A man is going to die tomorrow, and you call it an unpleasantness?"

"I don't enjoy these things," Libbie said defensively. "But as an army wife, I have learned to accept them. I must say, it is easier to accept when the person to be hanged is guilty of treason."

"He is not guilty of treason," Crimson said. "And that man who is in the jail now, waiting for tomorrow's 'unpleasantness', saved the lives of Sergeant Flynn, my father, and me. Is this how we are to repay him?"

"Crimson, my dear, you are getting yourself needlessly overwrought. I told you, it is our duty to accept such things without question. Autie knows what he is doing. I am sure he weighed the fact that this

... person ... played some small part in securing your freedom. But it may just have been to further his own cause, you know. However, I can see that this upsets you, so we must change the subject and talk about something else. Was it a lovely summer in New York?"

"What?" Crimson replied. Her mind was on the guardhouse, and on the prisoner inside.

"The summer in New York. Was it lovely?"

"Oh ... uh ... yes," Crimson said.

"Autie has promised that we can spend Christmas in New York. Of course, that is four months away, but I am already looking forward to it."

"Will Captain Custer be going with you?" Crimson asked, trying to sustain the conversation, to keep her mind off the terrible sound of the hammering outside.

"It would not do for you to get too interested in Tom, dear," Libbie said.

And with that, at least, Libbie managed to recapture Crimson's attention. Here it was, in the open. Libbie did not want Crimson to associate with her brother-in-law. Crimson hadn't given it too much thought, but now that Libbie had forbidden it, she was curious to know the reason.

"The interest thus far has been expressed by Captain Custer, and not by myself," Crimson said coolly.

Libbie smiled sweetly. "Please, don't be offended, my dear. I know Tom has been the aggressive one. And heavens, who could blame the poor boy? You are a beautiful young woman, and Tom has been in the field, denied the company of an attractive woman. But my request to you, dear, is that you do all in your power to discourage it."

"Why should I?" Crimson asked.

"You are not right for him," Libbie said.

"You mean I don't measure up to your standards?" Crimson asked angrily.

"That's not it at all," Libbie said. "You are a lovely girl with many fine qualities, and I would dearly love to have you as my own, sweet, sister-in-law. But Crimson, think about it for a moment. Tom is a Custer . . . a United States Army officer, as is his brother. You would have to be aware, all the time, of what that means. Here, in the confines of my own house, I will tell you that Autie will be president one day, and after Autie, perhaps Tom, and after Tom, maybe Boston. To marry a Custer, one must become a Custer, and that means one must be prepared to meet demands."

"You became a Custer," Crimson said.

Libbie laughed. "My dear, I *created* the Custers. I took an obscure little Ohio family and made it into one of the best known families in America. Heavens, do you think Autie was the *only* hero of the war? There were dozens of others, but my lectures and my writing has generated a whole nation of Custer followers. That must be protected, and I must ensure that Tom's future bride, whomever she may be, will add to the brilliance of the Custer name, and not detract. Can you understand that?"

"Don't worry, Mrs. Custer," Crimson said. "I have no designs on Tom Custer. And it's a good thing, because I could not become what you want. I could not dedicate myself entirely to the preservation of the Custer luster you have created."

"Custer luster, that's very good," Libbie said. "Perhaps I can use that some time, if you don't mind?"

"Be my guest," Crimson said. "Now, if you would like to, you may inform Captain Custer that I will be unable to attend the dance as his guest tonight."

"Oh, heavens no, don't do that," Libbie said. "I think you should go to the dance with him . . . and see him socially, too. Now that we have had our little conversation, I feel much better about things."

General Custer came in then. He looked over at Crimson and smiled.

"Well, girl, we rescued Sergeant Flynn for you, and got a bonus besides. Oh, and Libbie, news of the battle is going back by wire today. I talked with Toby from the *New York Tribune*. He's calling it the Battle of Two Creeks because there were two creeks near the village. Another victory can't hurt our cause back East now, can it?"

"No, Autie," Libbie said. "That's wonderful news."

"General, is it true you are going to hang Joseph Two Hearts?" Crimson asked.

"Yes," Custer said. He walked over to Crimson and took one of her hands in his, gazing at her with sympathy. "I know the thought of hanging another human being must seem distasteful to you, but such is the harsh reality of war."

"Joseph Two Hearts saved my life!" Crimson said.

"I know. And if it weren't for the fact that he committed murder on so many other occasions, I would have taken that into consideration before passing judgment on him."

"Autie, Crimson is going to the dance with Tom tonight," Libbie said, artfully changing the subject.

Custer smiled. "Well, now isn't my brother Tom the lucky one, though? And isn't it nice that we have an occasion to celebrate tonight? But, Libbie, I was in the saddle all night and if I am to be fresh for this evening, I must rest now. Crimson, if you will excuse me?"

"Yes, of course," Crimson said.

"I shall have lunch ready promptly at noon," Libbie said, and Crimson knew that she was being dismissed.

"Thank you," Crimson said. "I shall see you then."

# 8

That night the rigors of the campaign were put behind as the men, handsome in their dress uniforms, and the women, resplendent in shimmering gowns, gathered in the Sutlers' Store for the dance.

It wasn't until that moment that Crimson realized how greatly outnumbered the women were at Ft. Lincoln. Only six of the twenty officers and nine of the thirty Sergeants had wives. There were five laundresses, the only women officially authorized to be on the fort. There were, counting Crimson, twenty-one women and over three hundred men.

Though Tom had brought Crimson to the dance, he generously allowed her to fill her dance card with the other soldiers' names. Like every other lady at the dance, she soon found that every moment of her evening was to be taken.

The band played a fanfare, and Custer stepped in front of them and held out his arms, calling for quiet. He was smiling broadly, and when a couple of his men called him Yellow Hair, he laughed good-naturedly.

"Ladies, officers, men," Custer said.

"Speech!" someone called. "Speech!"

"Well, that's just what I'm going to give you," Custer said. "If you'll be quiet and let me."

Again, there was laughter from the men.

"Gentlemen, I want you to know that 'Custer's Own,' as they are calling the Seventh Cavalry now, is the finest fighting outfit ever to wear the uniform of the United States Army."

"Hurrah!" the men shouted, and stamped noisily on the floor until Custer quieted them again.

"Last night, we had a great victory, and we rescued Sergeant Flynn, so we have much to be grateful for. We also have two distinguished guests who themselves were held captive by the savages for a short time. We are grateful for their safe return as well."

"And don't forget that traitor we're gonna hang tomorrow, General!" someone shouted to a chorus of cheers.

"Yes," Custer said. "Though I find little to celebrate there. Tomorrow will be a somber day, for we will have one execution and two burials. Gentlemen, I propose a toast to Baker and McKean, two of the finest troopers who ever made the trip to Fiddler's Green."

"Hear, hear," someone yelled, and the toast was drunk.

"What is Fiddler's Green?" Crimson asked Tom.

"It's a cavalryman's legend," Tom said. "When a cavalryman dies, he doesn't go to heaven or hell. He goes to a grassy glade under the cool shade of trees, and there he sits and drinks with all the other cavalrymen who have gone there before him, to await Judgment Day." Tom laughed. "It's just a legend, but it seems to comfort a trooper who knows that the next day, or the day after that, may be his last."

76

"Do you ever think about dying, Tom?"

"Of course I do." Tom smiled. "But if I know Autie, he will have some grand and glorious scheme in mind for us when we die, to create the maximum amount of publicity. My brother has lived by that code, I've no doubt that he will die by it."

"And you will just go right along with it?" Crimson asked a bit sharply. "Tom, don't you ever question *anything* he does?"

"No."

"Why not?"

Tom sighed. "Crimson, I don't expect you to understand," he said. "But I am bound by honor."

"Honor? And you would let a man die tomorrow, because you are bound by honor? Where was the honor in capturing him?"

"Sometimes one must weigh honor in one's soul," Tom said. "It is not difficult to do the right thing, Crimson. It is only difficult to *know* what is right."

The music started then, and the first dance began. Tom looked at Crimson with a pleading expression on his face, begging her to torment him no further with questions of honor or right and wrong. And Crimson, because the whole thing was painful to her, held out her hands to him and allowed him to sweep her out onto the floor amidst the laughter and the music.

Finally the dancing ended, and the men began drinking and exchanging campaign stories. The women settled into another corner of the room to carry on their own conversations. Crimson slipped, unnoticed, through the door, leaving the party behind her.

Outside the stars shimmered like crystals of ice. As she walked through the coolness of the September night, she wondered what she would say to the guard to get him away from the guardhouse. Incredibly there was no guard there. Whether they thought there was no need for one, or the guard had deserted his post, Crimson didn't know.

The front of the guardhouse faced the quadrangle, and Crimson knew that if she stood under the front window, she undoubtedly would be seen. So she dipped into the shadows alongside the guardhouse and stepped up to the barred window. It was so dark inside that she could see nothing.

"Joseph!" she whispered. There was no answer. She called again, more loudly this time.

"I heard you," Joseph finally said, his voice as dry as a broken twig.

"Joseph, are you all right?"

Joseph suddenly appeared out of the dark. "Why do you ask?" he wanted to know. "Do your white friends want to make sure they have a healthy Indian to hang tomorrow?"

"Joseph, I'm sorry," Crimson said. "I didn't want this to happen."

"It is not your fault," Joseph said. "I should have known Custer could not be trusted. He has always lied before, I knew he would lie again. I was the fool."

"I'm going to set you free," Crimson said.

"Can you do this?"

"Yes. The door is held by a bar and I can remove it from out here."

"Open the door. I will leave now," Joseph said.

Crimson stepped to the edge of the shadows and looked across the moonlit quadrangle. At the opposite end were the enlisted quarters, to her right the officers' quarters, the house where she was living, and the Sutlers' Store. Only the store showed light through the windows, and from inside, she heard a loud guffaw of laughter. On the left side of the quadrangle was the stables, the stockade wall, and front gate. The two guards at the front gate were facing out, looking for signs of trouble from without.

The way was clear, so Crimson pulled the heavy bar through and swung the door open.

"Go, quickly," she said.

Joseph moved through the door in a flash and slipped across the open space to the back wall. Without a sound, he was up and over the wall.

Now Crimson realized that she, herself, was in danger. If anyone saw her near the guardhouse and discovered the open door, she could be arrested for letting Joseph escape. She started to walk back across the quadrangle, but, frightened that someone would see her, she stayed in the shadows of the stockade wall and walked all the way around the fort, back to the store. Then, quietly, she let herself back inside and rejoined the women. A moment later, Tom came over to her.

"Where have you been?" Tom asked.

Crimson was so frightened by the question that she was unable to answer. Had he seen her? Had someone else seen her and reported her? Then she was rescued by an unexpected source.

"Tom, for heaven's sake, you don't always ask where a lady has been," Libbie said. "There are certain delicate things . . ."

"Oh," Tom sputtered. "Oh, of course . . . excuse me, I should have realized . . . I mean, I'm sorry."

"It's quite all right," Crimson said.

Libbie started asking Crimson questions about New York. Crimson, grateful for the opportunity to speak about a subject of which she had some knowledge held forth while the others listened.

"He's gone! The Indian has escaped!" someone yelled, sticking his head in through the front door.

"What?" Custer yelled, standing up so quickly that his chair tumbled over.

"General, I was just taking my regular tour around the post, and when I got back to the guardhouse, the bar was slipped and the door was open."

"Damn!" Custer swore. "An Indian must have sneaked over the walls somehow. Major Reno!"

"Yes, sir."

"Turn out the regiment, Major. We are going to bring him back."

"Beggin' the General's pardon, sir," Reno questioned. "Do you intend to take out the entire regiment for *one* Indian?"

"If I had a division, I would turn it out," Custer said. "Now hurry it up. In intend to be on the move in no more than fifteen minutes."

"Yes, sir," Reno said. "Bugler, sound *Boots and Saddles!*"

The trumpeteer in the band picked up his instrument and began sounding the call that every cavalryman lived by—*Boots and Saddles,* the order for the mounted march.

Only a few men were left in Sutlers' Store after the bugler sounded his call—the store operator, a man named Frank Blue, a handful of soldiers who would serve as the rear guard detachment, and, of course, Artemus Royal.

"I have some sketches I would like you to work on tomorrow," Artemus said to Crimson.

"The Indian sketches?"

"No," Artemus said. "Not yet. The sketches I have in mind now are of General Custer and some of his officers. I would like for you to make some preliminary drawings for me."

"Father, you can't be serious!" Crimson said. "You are going to trade in our dream to feed Custer's ego?"

"No," Artemus said. He smiled wryly. "I am going to play on his ego to preserve our dream."

"How?"

"If we do some drawings of Custer, I think I can convince him that the showing wouldn't be complete without drawings of the Indians. If he is as vain as I think he is, he'll see our point of view."

"Perhaps so," Crimson said. Her eyes sparkled as a thought came to her. "Libbie is the one to work on, Father. She is the driving force behind the General."

"Really, now?" Artemus said. "Well, I wouldn't be surprised. She does seem to be a dynamic woman, and they say that behind every successful man, is a woman."

"That's what they say," Crimson said. "Father, I'm ready to go to bed. Would you walk me to my quarters?"

"Of course," Artemus said. "Just let me take my leave." He walked over to the few remaining men to wish them goodnight. Crimson did the same with the women, and a moment later she and her father were walking across the quadrangle toward her quarters.

"You took a great chance tonight, you know," Artemus said when they reached the middle of the quadrangle, well beyond anyone's hearing range.

"What are you talking about?"

"I saw you leave the dance," Artemus said. "At first I thought you might be ill, so I walked over to look through the door to see if you were all right. I saw you walk to the guardhouse. I waited, and a moment later, I saw Joseph Two Hearts escape."

"Oh," Crimson said. She was silent for a moment. "Do you think anyone else saw?"

"I don't think so," Artemus said. "I looked very carefully." He chuckled. "I even thought of a way to create a diversion, should anyone come toward the door."

"How?" Crimson asked, joining her father in laughter. "What were you going to do?"

"I pulled the punchbowl to the edge of the table, and I was going to knock it off."

81

"Heavens, Father, Libbie's Waterford punchbowl?" Crimson gasped laughing. "If you had done that, they might have hanged *you* tomorrow. You don't know how proud she is of that. It was given to her by Julia, you know."

"Julia?"

"Mrs. Grant. You aren't the only one with fans in the White House."

"Oh, my," Artemus said. He chuckled. "Then I suppose I am doubly pleased that you weren't seen."

They reached the house.

"I hope he gets away," Artemus said and he kissed his daughter goodnight.

"He will," Crimson said. "I know he will."

# 9

She didn't know how long she had been asleep when she was awakened. Laying awake in her bed, she was aware only of the silence of the night. Then a cold chill passed over her. She had been awakened, not by a sound, but by a touch! Someone was in the room with her!

"Who is here?" she asked in a frightened voice.

And then she saw him. He had been standing in the shadows, but he moved into a shimmering pool of moonlight so that she could see his features. He stared down at her with deep, penetrating eyes and lips pursed in thought. Around his neck was a strand of bear's teeth. His shoulders and chest were bare.

Crimson sat up, letting the cover fall away, so that the moon splashed on her silk nightgown. The silk clung to her like a second skin and the nipples of her breasts stood out in bold relief, but she was so surprised by Joseph's presence that she was oblivious to the enticing picture she made.

"Joseph, what are you doing here?"

"I came to see you," Joseph answered, his voice as dry and flat as it had been earlier in the guardhouse.

"But you shouldn't be here. They are looking for you. Don't you know that?"

"Are they looking for me in your house?"

"What? Why, no, of course not."

"Then I am safe here."

"But you can't stay," Crimson said. She ran her hand through her hair, her breast rising with the movement. "Surely you realize that you can't stay."

"I will not stay long," Joseph said. "I have come for something."

"What is that?"

Joseph's eyes started at her neck, then traveled down the smooth skin and the silk gown until they rested, unabashed, on her breasts.

Crimson knew then what he had come for, and the realization both frightened and thrilled her.

"You have paid for your life with my life," Joseph said. "Now, you will pay for my honor with your honor."

"I . . . I don't know what you are talking about," Crimson stammered.

"When you tricked me, you dishonored me before the council. I can never get that honor back. Now, I will take something from you that you can never get back."

Joseph reached for her.

"No," Crimson said, leaning away from him. "Don't do anything, Joseph, please. You are frightening me."

"I will do this," Joseph said thickly.

"Joseph, no, please, no."

He put his hand on her shoulder. "I should have done this when you were in the tipi in the village. I wanted to then, but I respected your honor."

"Joseph, please, you don't know what you are

84

doing," Crimson said. Her fear was rising, not because of Joseph, but from her own strange, tumultuous feelings.

Joseph leaned down and touched her mouth with his, and Crimson marveled that the kiss could be so tender, yet so urgent.

"Joseph . . . no . . . please . . ."

"I will do this thing," Joseph said. His voice was insistent yet strangely unhappy, as if he was unwilling to hurt her but was unable to stop. He had no choice now. His desire had taken charge, sweeping away all barriers, forcing him to go on.

Crimson made a strange animal sound in her throat, but whether of passion or fright, she couldn't be sure. She closed her eyes and waited for Joseph to make the next move, longing desperately for it, yet still afraid. She could no longer trust her own body to put up a fight. She realized that she should resist him, but she knew she would not, because she was no longer in control.

Joseph stretched out on the bed beside her and put his arm around her. He kissed her again, this time pressing against her, pulling her body against him. She could feel the hardness of his muscles, and a rapidly spreading warmth growing from within. Her mind told her it was wrong. Her body told her it was needed. Her heart told her it was wonderful.

Joseph grew bolder at her lack of resistance. His kisses became more demanding, and Crimson felt the tip of his tongue darting across her lips. She opened her mouth instinctively and Joseph's tongue stabbed inside, changing the warmth to fire. Through her thin sleeping dress she easily felt the sudden growth of his maleness. It aroused her as she had never been aroused before. Eager hands pulled at the hem of her nightgown and clutched at the rawhide laces of buckskin trousers. With a passionate sense of freedom, Crimson felt for the first time in her life the warmth of a man's naked body against her own. The white heat rising in her created a pent-up feeling, and she felt an urgent craving in her loins for more than a mere touch. And when, finally, Joseph moved his hard and demanding body over her soft yielding thighs, she was ready to receive him.

Crimson let out a low whimper of pain as he found her and then a sharper exclamation as she felt him thrust into her. The pain was soon mixed with the most intense pleasure she had ever known. Gone was all pretense of caution and fear. She felt only a hunger to be satisfied, a need which was being completely fulfilled. He thrust her with his manhood up to the crystal stars, and Crimson cried when at last it was over—but only because it was over.

Crimson lay beneath him for a while, feeling his weight on her, enjoying the warm and pleasant dampness that filled her. She stroked his shoulders with her hands for a moment, then he rolled over and lay beside her. They were both silent; their breathing was just returning to normal.

"That wasn't just to punish me, was it, Joseph?" Crimson asked.

Joseph folded his arms behind his head and stared at the darkness that was gathered under the peaked roof of the cabin. He said nothing.

Crimson raised herself up on one elbow and looked down at him. Her breasts swung like pendulums, and a nipple trailed across the muscle on Joseph's forearm, sending tiny tingles of pleasure coursing through her.

"You didn't answer me," she said.

Joseph sighed. "The answer will do no good for either of us," he finally said.

"Why?"

Joseph looked at Crimson, and for the first time, Crimson saw pain in his eyes.

"Must you hear the answer?"

"Yes."

"I did it because I wanted you," Joseph said. "I was not thinking of honor when I came to your house. I was not thinking of honor when I came to your bed. I was thinking of you."

"And what were you thinking of me?" Crimson asked. She was playing the coquette now, letting her hair hang down to touch him, leaning against him, feeling the hard muscle of his legs against her, pressing against him to intensify the feeling.

"I was thinking that I wanted you more than I have ever wanted any woman," Joseph said. "And I was thinking that it would be good if you would want me, too."

"And do you now know that I did want you?" Crimson asked. "That I do want you?" She leaned over and kissed him.

The fires that had been banked were rekindled, and she lay back to let him come to her. He returned her kiss slowly, as if he didn't care if the entire regiment was watching. He was here at peril to his life, and yet there was nothing hurried or anxious about his movements.

Crimson no longer had misgivings or disquieting thoughts to contend with. She surrendered to her desires, and to Joseph's virile strength. She bent to his will, eager to do his every bidding.

Joseph didn't wait this time, but moved over her and began, once again, to make love. She felt his weight on her, and she thrust against him, giving him the unbridled limits of her passion. This time their union was as it should be, a man and woman making love on every plane of communication—emotional, spiritual, and physical. And for Crimson, Joseph was all men and she was all women, sensual beyond measure.

Then it started, a tiny tingling that began deep

in her, pin-wheeling out, spinning faster and faster until every cell in her body was caught up in a whirlpool of pleasure. Her body was wound like the mainspring of a clock, tighter and tighter, until finally, in a burst of agony that turned into ecstasy, her body achieved the release and satisfaction it had long yearned for. A million tiny pins pricked her skin, and cries of pleasure rose from her throat. She felt as if she lost consciousness for just an instant, and lights passed before her eyes as her body gave its final, convulsive shudders.

They lay side by side in the dark, without speaking, feeling for the moment that they were the only two people in the world, and Crimson knew then that she loved him. She knew that she would face her father's displeasure and society's ostracism, but she loved him.

Joseph had not spoken of love to her, not in words, at least. But she knew he loved her, of that there could be no doubt.

Finally, Joseph spoke.

"The Indians have a saying," he said. "A bird and a fish may fall in love and marry. But where will they live?"

"Joseph, you don't have to go back to the Indians," Crimson said. "You are a white man. You could live as a white man."

"The white man wants to hang me," Joseph said.

"You don't have to live out here," Crimson said. "You can cut your hair, grow a beard, and put on the clothes of a white man, and no one would know who you are."

"And this would be good?" Joseph asked.

"Yes," Crimson said. "Don't you see? You could start all over . . . make a new life. And I would go with you."

"Crimson, I have a life. I do not wish to start over."

"But you aren't an Indian," Crimson said.

"Yes, I am."

"No, you aren't, and I can prove it," Crimson said. "A moment ago, you said 'the Indians have a saying.' You didn't say 'we', or 'my people'. Don't you see?"

Joseph swung his legs over and hopped up quickly. He pulled his trousers on as he looked back at the bed.

"No," he said. "No, I will not let you trick me into dishonor."

"There you go, talking about honor again," Crimson said. "Can't you talk about something else? Can't you talk about love?"

"Does love mean I must leave my people?"

"They *aren't* your people," Crimson insisted.

"Would you come with me, tonight, as my squaw?"

Joseph made the statement as a challenge, knowing full well what her answer would be. . . . And yet, for a fleeting instant, something deep down inside Crimson almost made her say yes.

"You know I cannot," Crimson finally said.

Joseph stepped over to the window and opened it, then looked outside. With the grace of a cat, he jumped up onto the window ledge, then looked back toward Crimson and gave her a wry smile.

"A bird and a fish may fall in love and marry. But where will they live?"

# 10

Joseph slipped through the shadows of the fort, staying close to the wall, working his way around to the stables. He smelled burning tobacco and pressed himself against the wall and waited. A moment later a soldier appeared, walking guard and smoking a pipe.

"Bill, you got 'ny idea what time it is?" a soldier yelled down from the parapet.

The soldier with the pipe answered. "I make it nigh on to two in the mornin'. We'll be gettin' relieved 'afore too much longer."

"I'll be proud to see that," the soldier on the parapet said. He walked over to the edge and sat down so that his legs were dangling over the walkway. If Joseph wanted to, he could reach out from the shadows and grab the soldier's legs and pull him down. But of course, he would have the pipe-smoking soldier to worry about then. Joseph stayed quiet.

"Hey, Pete, do you think the General will catch the half-breed?" Bill asked.

"Pass me up some tobaccy," Pete said. He took

the tobacco and stuffed it into his pipe. "The feller's not a breed."

"Why do you say that? He's half-white, ain't he?"

There was the flare of a match, and Joseph was afraid that the light would give him away, but Bill was looking up at that moment as the soldier lit his pipe.

"He's all white," Pete said between long, audible puffs. "Fact is, I know'd his pappy—fella by the name of Jason Baker. We was both at Shiloh during the war."

"Shiloh?"

Pete laughed. "You Yanks called it Pittsburgh Landing. Whatever it was called, it was one bloody hell of a battle. Baker, he was a cap'n then, rose up to colonel 'afore the war was over. Afterward, he didn't have nothin' to go back to, 'n no army left to be a colonel in, so he come out to these parts. Me, I'd done paroled myself over to the Yankees, and was posted out here, 'n I run across him in Omaha. Him 'n his wife, 'n a strappin' youngster name of Joseph."

As Joseph listened to the soldier talk, he felt a strange sadness for a time that was, and a future that was never to be.

"Dad, I've been reading these broadsides about Nebraska," Joseph said. "They sound pretty good. I'll bet we could have a farm in Nebraska as good as Trailback in no time."

"There will never be another Trailback," Joseph's mother said.

"Martha, I know you have happy memories of Trailback," Joseph's father said. "I do, too. But Joseph is right to think of the future. We can build us a farm as good as Trailback. At least it will be as large and as productive, and in time, why I'll even build you a house as nice as The Glades." He tousled Joseph's hair. "But it's going to be in Oregon, and not in Nebraska."

"But, dad, these broadsides," Joseph said, holding one up to his father.

"Son, that's just snake oil, put out by the Union Pacific Railroad. Of course they want people to settle in Nebraska. They've got a vested interest in it. If there are no people in Nebraska, the railroads can't make money. You can understand that, can't you?"

"I guess so," Joseph said.

"Don't worry. You are going to love Oregon."

The conversation between the two guards went on, and Joseph, trapped as he was, could do nothing but listen. Their words brought him out of his recollections.

"Him bein' white, how come him to be livin' with the Injuns?"

"Well sir, ole Jason signed up to go West with a wagon train, but he didn't hit it off none too well with the wagonmaster. It seems the wagonmaster was a private in the Ohio Volunteers durin' the war, 'n he learned that Jason was a Confederate officer at Shiloh. The wagonmaster was in the hornets' nest at Shiloh, and got whupped pretty good. So he commenced to take it out on Jason. Jason figured if he didn't cut hisself loose from that wagon train, either he or the wagonmaster was goin' to wind up dead. Jason didn't figure to gain nothin' no matter which way it wound up."

"What happened then?"

"They was attacked by Crow Injuns. For some reason the Injuns didn' take the boy's scalp. I guess they figured it would be even meaner to leave 'im there with his scalped mama and papa, 'n' just let 'im starve to death."

"But he got away," Bill said.

"Sort of. Some Sioux, travelin' with Sittin' Bear,

93

come by, 'n' they picked the boy up. Sittin' Bear raised the boy like as iffen he was his own."

"Sittin' Bear? Ain't he the chief was kilt the other night?"

"Yep," Pete said. "I guess you might say ole Joseph's done lost two papas in one lifetime. That can't be none too easy."

"You say that like as iffen you feel a mite sorry for him."

"Oh, I don't know as I do," Pete said. "Joseph's a man full growed now, 'n' he could pretty well make up his own mind about what he's a'doin'. 'Course, bein' raised partly by the Injuns I can see where it might be hard for him. But he was white longer'n he was Injun."

"Oh, oh," Bill said. "I just seen Sergeant Caine. We best get to walkin', or he'll be havin' our tails for breakfast."

"Right," Pete said, and Joseph saw the legs drawn up as the man above him stood up. "I don't think they will find Joseph. He might of been white longer'n he's been Injun, but he's been Injun long enough to learn their ways. I figure he'll get away clean this time."

The guards continued on their rounds. Joseph waited a few moments longer, then slipped through the shadows toward the stable, where he intended to steal a horse.


"But stealing is wrong," Joseph had told Sitting Bear.

"When you are white, you do honor to the things which are white," Sitting Bear said. "When you are Indian, you do honor to the things which are Indian. There is great honor for the Indian to steal from his enemy. If you wish to become accepted as a warrior, you must steal a horse from the Crow camp."

"I stole a horse from the Crow last spring," Crazy

Wolf said. Though Joseph had made friends with most of the other young men his age, an immediate animosity developed between him and Crazy Wolf. "I made a present of the horse to Sasha."

Sasha was also Joseph's age, fourteen, and just coming into nubile womanhood. She was graceful and beautiful, and though as Sitting Bear's daughter she was Joseph's step-sister, she had already let it be known that she regarded him much more as a potential suitor than as her brother. She was an outrageous flirt, and no one was safe from her deep brown eyes and infectuous smile.

"Then I shall steal *two* horses and give them both to Sasha," Joseph said.

"Ha! Brave talk from a white boy who has never proven himself."

"I've proven myself in fights with you," Joseph said. "And I am ready to do it again, anytime you want."

Joseph wasn't just boasting. He and Crazy Wolf had fought several times already, with Joseph usually coming out on top.

"Joseph, will you *really* get two horses for me?" Sasha asked, her eyes glowing. She had no real use for two horses, but the thought of someone risking his life for her was thrilling to her.

"Sure," Joseph said. "I'll get them for you."

It was much easier said than done. The nearest Crow village was three hours' ride away. If Joseph left just after sundown and rode hard, he would reach the Crow Village in the middle of the night. He could take the horses and be back just before sunup—provided he wasn't caught.

Joseph reached the village at about midnight. It was pitched on the banks of a small stream; Joseph could see by the light of the moon dancing on the water, two dozen tipis and a remuda of horses. The remuda was right in the center of the village, so that he would have to pass by the tipis in order to reach it.

Joseph tied his horse to a bush, then got down on his hands and knees and began crawling toward the village. He had practiced crawling great distances for the last several nights. Two nights ago, he had crawled from a long distance outside his village into Crazy Wolf's tipi. There he had stolen one of Crazy Wolf's most prized feathers, and had worn it proudly the next morning for all to see.

"I took it from your tipi as you slept last night," Joseph said, returning the feather to an angry Crazy Wolf.

Now that stealth would be put to the maximum test, for if one of the sleeping villagers woke up to see him, he would be killed.

A dog barked. The Crow were noted for their dogs, which they kept, not as pets, but as domesticated livestock to be eaten. Joseph had a sack full of buffalo bones around his neck. He opened it and scattered the bones. The dogs converged on them, and in a moment's time, they were completely absorbed in their eating.

Joseph was right outside one of the tipis when a warrior came out. Joseph felt a quick stab of fear shoot through him, and he dropped to his stomach and lay very quietly, looking up at the warrior. He held a knife in his hand, watching warily as the warrior relieved himself, then walked over toward the remuda and looked at the horses.

Finally, after what seemed like an eternity, the warrior returned to his tipi. Joseph lay quiet for a few moments longer, then cautiously slipped over to the remuda.

As he tried to grab a couple of the horses, they became skitterish. They whinnyed and stamped and snorted, and Joseph was afraid that someone would come out to see what was going on.

"Easy, horses," he said in English. He could speak Sioux, but in this moment of stress and tension, he slipped naturally into English, which was less difficult for him. "Easy, horses. We are just going to take a little trip together. Now, who would like to belong to a beautiful girl?"

Finally Joseph's soothing talk calmed the horses, and quickly he threw halters around two beautifully spotted ponies and started leading them out of the village.

Joseph had nearly made it back to his own horse when he was jumped by a Crow sentry! The attack caught Joseph completely by surprise, and he was knocked flat. He looked up in terror to see the Crow, grinning from ear to ear, coming toward him with raised tomahawk. The Crow was going to scalp him alive!

The Crow, who was much older than Joseph, grew overconfident, intent only upon claiming coup on the would-be horse thief. He was not aware of Joseph's amazing agility or terrified strength.

Joseph rolled to one side just as the Crow swung at him, and he lunged with his knife hand feeling his blade go deep into the Crow's stomach. Joseph twisted the blade and turned the Crow over; the knife made a fatal tear across his abdomen. The Crow fell to the ground with a death rattle in his throat.

Joseph pulled the knife out, cleaned it, and slipped it back into his scabbard. He looked at the man he had just killed and fought the urge to be sick. He told himself that this was the enemy of his people, and that as a Sioux, he should be proud of his victory. And he reminded himself that it was Crow who had attacked the wagon and killed his mother and father.

And when he thought of his mother and father's scalps now decorating a Crow lodgepole, he was able to steel himself to do what he must do. He dropped down on one knee beside the Crow, grabbed the dead man's hair in one hand, put his knife to the Crow's scalp with the other, then turned his face away as he completed the scalping.

Joseph was made a warrior immediately upon his return to his village. Stealing two horses on one raid was, Sitting Bear said, symbolized by his name, Two Hearts. One of the horses the white heart stole, and one the red heart stole. And claiming coup on the Crow warrior entitled Joseph to sit on the war councils from that time on.

His action raised him in the eyes of Sasha and the other villagers. But it created so much jealousy in Crazy Wolf that it just drove the wedge between them deeper.

From that day on, Crazy Wolf had been his enemy. Now, Joseph knew, Crazy Wolf would have ammunition to use against him. He would claim that Joseph allowed his white heart to dominate his judgment and had helped the whites to trick them. Sitting Bear, Sasha's father and his own step-father, was killed by the treachery.

And Joseph knew that it was true—he had betrayed his people because he had been moved by the white girl.

Joseph reached the stable and saddled a horse, and wrapped another saddle blanket around his shoulders to keep his naked skin from shining in the moonlight, then climbed on the animal's back and rode it boldly up to the front gate.

"I'm goin' out for Sergeant Caine," he called to the two guards on the wall. He stayed in the shadows against the wall so the soldiers couldn't see him clearly.

"Close the damn gate good, will you? I don't want to have to come down."

98

"I'll get it," Joseph said.

Joseph went through the gate, closed it behind him, then stayed tight against the wall and worked his way around the outside of the stockade until he could ride away without being seen.

Finally, he reached the corner that provided a blind spot and whipped the horse into a full gallop. It was a feeling of great exhilaration.

And yet, as he thought of Crimson, and what he was leaving behind him, he felt a sadness he couldn't deny. A fish and a bird may fall in love and marry ... but where would they live?

# 11

While in search of Joseph, the regiment encountered a rather substantial war party led by Rain In The Face. Tom led a small unit of men on a daring strike at the rear of Rain In The Face's war party, causing the Sioux chief to break off the fight and retreat. Fourteen of Tom's men were killed, and all but three sustained some sort of wound, including Tom himself. They returned without having found Joseph.

Crimson heard of Tom's wound shortly after the regiment returned, and she hurried over to the infirmary to visit him. "Well," Tom said, smiling brightly when he saw Crimson. Tom was sitting on a chair and Dr. Sprague was bandaging his shoulder. "For a visit from you I would gladly take a bullet in my other shoulder."

"Are you badly hurt, Tom?" Crimson asked, showing genuine concern.

Tom laughed. "Only a scratch."

"And lucky at that," Dr. Sprague said. "Miss Royal, I don't know if you are able to exercise any influence over this young hellion, but I wish you would advise him that he is not invincible."

"Oh, but I am, doc," Tom said sardonically. "I'm a Custer. Don't you know what that means? My brother would never let anything happen to me." He took a long drink from a bottle of whiskey he was holding.

"Here," Dr. Sprague said, reaching for the bottle. "You were supposed to take some whiskey to kill the pain, and that's all."

"Doc, I got pains you can't begin to understand," Tom said with disarming candor. Then, realizing he had shown more of himself than he intended, he smiled and put the bottle down. "I don't need it anyway," he said. "One look at this beautiful young lady, and I can take anything."

"How you do carry on, Captain Custer," Crimson said.

"There is truth in what I say," Tom said. "As you shall see by my improved appetite at the dinner table. Because I am wounded, I was able to persuade Libbie to change the seating arrangement. I am now sitting by you."

"Miss Royal, I don't wish to be inhospitable," Dr. Sprague said. "But if you don't leave so he will settle down, I shall never finish this."

Crimson smiled. "Very well," she said. "I have some work to do for my father, anyway, and I certainly have no wish to hinder Captain Custer's convalescence."

Crimson returned to her quarters where she was, indeed, working on sketches for her father.

And one of her own.

In the three days since Joseph left her bed, she had been working on a drawing of him. Normally she required a model to present an accurate likeness, but this time it wasn't necessary—she could see

Joseph's features every time she closed her eyes just as clearly as if he were standing before her.

She had captured him perfectly in her drawing. The black and white shading of his face and the melancholy tilt of his head, summed up all the emotions that coursed through him—his sense of honor and loyalty to his adopted people, his desire for Crimson and the love they could share, and his despair over the hopelessness of the situation.

Crimson's portrayal of Joseph clearly showed her understanding of his dilemma. But it didn't relieve her of the hurt she felt, and the sense of betrayal by this man who had taken her virginity, scorned her honor, and spurned her offer of love.

The hurt festered in her soul with each passing day, and now, with the sketch completed, the discontent and anger boiled up in her. She put her hands together on the drawing and tried to summon the will to rip it apart.

But she couldn't.

With a small cry of rage and frustration, she tossed it under her bed. She was determined that she would forget Joseph Two Hearts.

"I thought you would want me to be brave in battle," Tom was saying. He, the other Custers, and Crimson and her father were all gathered around the Custer table for dinner. Crimson, as Tom had promised, was sitting next to him for the meal, and was witnessing the rather spirited conversation between Tom and his brother.

"Of course I want you to be brave in battle," Custer said, replying to his brother. "But, Tom, sometimes you go beyond bravery. You act as if you want—" he stopped.

"What are you saying, Autie?" Libbie asked.

"Nothing," Custer said. He wiped his mouth with

his napkin. "It just distresses me to see Tom throw himself into battle with such reckless abandon."

Tom laughed, not with mirth, but with a ring of mockery. "Can this be George Armstrong Custer talking? The same man who once said, 'I shall always go to the sound of battle'?"

"It's not the same thing, Tom, and you know it," Custer said. "There is a difference between bravery . . . and some insane wish to commit suicide."

"Autie!" Libby scolded. "I'll not have you talking about your brother in such a way! And before guests!"

Custer looked down at his plate as if he were a small boy chastised. "I'm sorry," he finally said. "Tom, forgive me. It was a brave thing you did, and I have no right to question it."

"That's all right," Tom said. He slid back from the table. "If you will excuse me, I think I'll go to my quarters."

The meal continued in silence for a few moments after Tom left, then Libbie spoke.

"Autie, what did you mean . . . a wish to commit suicide?"

"Sergeant Kennedy told me," Custer said. "There were three warriors holed up in some rocks and Tom went right in after them, standing as bold upright as if he had been on parade. I think he was successful only because he so shocked the Indians."

"But perhaps that was his plan," Libbie suggested. "You have often stated that bold action against Indians is the most effective key to success."

"Bold, yes. Not suicidal. It's just that Tom's actions—not just in this campaign, Libbie, but all his actions lately, including his drinking—remind me of Colonel Cooper."

"Oh, Autie, no," Libbie said, putting her hand on his arm.

Custer patted his wife's hand, then excused himself from the table.

"Who is Colonel Cooper?" Crimson asked after Custer left.

"He was an unfortunate man who was once Tom's very close friend," Libbie said. "He drank to excess, much as Tom does now. After the Battle of Washita Colonel Cooper began drinking more and more until . . . well . . . perhaps this will explain better than I. It is from Autie's field notes."

Libbie walked over to a roll-top desk and looked through it for a moment until she found a ledger book marked *Campaigns of 1868*.

"Autie is going to write his memoirs someday, and he keeps copious notes of his expeditions. Read this part," she said, opening the book and handing it to her.

Custer's writing was bold and clear, as easy to read as if were set in type:

> The officers of the 7th—the entire camp, in fact—is wrapped in deep gloom by the suicide of Col. Cooper while in a fit of delirium tremens.

"Suicide?" Crimson asked.
"Yes," Libbie said. "Read on."

> "We reached present camp after a march of 17 miles over broken country. I had just risen from the dinner table where I had been discussing with Tom, Col. Cooper's actions, when Col. Meyers came rushing in. Calling Dr. Sprague we hastened to Col. Cooper's tent, and found him lying on knees and face, right hand grasping revolver, ground near him covered with blood, body still warm and pulse

beating, the act having been committed but 3 or 4 minutes before. Placing him on his back we saw how well the shot had been aimed. Only the eyes wore the ghastly look of death. Conversation with other officers revealed he had contemplated the act under the influence of rum and suffering some misguided guilt from his part in the recent battle of Washita. One by one all came to gaze on one who but a few minutes before had been companion of our march.

Actuated by what I deemed my duty to the living, I warned the officers of the reg't of the fate of their comrade. I hope the example will not be lost on them.

But for intemperance, Col. Cooper would have been a useful and accomplished officer, a brilliant and most companionable gentleman.

Crimson returned the melancholy diary to Libbie, and sat for a moment in quiet contemplation.

"You can see how Autie might be disturbed by Tom's actions, when he compares them to those of the late Colonel Cooper's."

"Yes, of course I can," Crimson said. "Libbie . . . what happened at Washita?"

Libbie smiled. "Washita was one of Autie's greatest victories."

"Then what did the General mean when he said that Colonel Cooper was suffering from misguided guilt over Washita? And what did Sergeant Flynn mean when he said that Tom lived with the devils of Washita?"

"I'm sure I don't know," Libbie said. "The General's notes on the battle are in this same ledger. Here, read for yourself."

Libbie returned the ledger to Crimson. Crimson

couldn't help but notice that Libbie had referred to Custer as "the General" rather than his Christian name. Even Libbie seemed defensive about Washita. She read in the ledger:

November 1868, the Washita valley, Indian Territory:
Recorded by G.A. Custer, Commanding.

I rode with the scouts so as to be as near as possible in the advance. The cavalry followed from a quarter to a half mile back, lest the crunching of the crusted snow signal our whereabouts.

Orders prohibited a word above a whisper, a match struck, or a pipe lighted—great deprivation to a soldier. Thus, silently, mile after mile we went until the guides rode back and reported that we were within two or three miles of the Indian village.

The command resumed the march with guides, who were afoot, in the lead. At the crest of the hill, the Osage guide shielded his eyes with his hand and peered into the valley below.

"Heap Injuns down there."

It was after midnight. Complete silence was to be observed. I ordered the officers to remove their sabers so the clank of metal not be heard. Then I divided the command into four detachments of equal strength. One was to move to the woods bordering the village, another downriver to the timber below, a third to occupy the crest north of the village, and the fourth, my own, to remain at the point of the discovery. The attacks would be simultaneous and the enemy, being surrounded, would have little chance to escape. Everything depended on accurate timing and the element of surprise.

We waited until two hours before dawn. The moon had gone down and the night was perfectly black. A brilliant light, the morning star, appeared, but even that soon disappeared with the morning fog, which limited visibility to only twenty yards.

Then came the moment to advance. I gave the signal and the band broke into *Garry Owen*. Cheers resounded from the other detachments. The entire command rushed into action, four units as one. The battle of the Washita was enjoined and carried on by my brave men to a successful conclusion—103 Indians killed, 53 captured.

The sad side of the story is our killed and wounded. Captain Hamilton and Major Elliott led their men after a small band of Indians and pursued them too far . . . nineteen enlisted men, with these gallant officers, were killed. Three officers and eleven enlisted men were wounded.

Crimson looked up from her reading.

"Those who regard Washita as anything less than a glorious victory simply wish Autie ill will," Libbie said.

"Then what devils do Tom face?" Crimson asked.

"Tom is a sensitive young man," Libbie explained. "He was very close to Colonel Cooper, and when Colonel Cooper committed suicide—no doubt because Washita was his first experience with the horrors of battle—Tom assumed the Colonel's burden of guilt. That burden has plagued Tom all this time."

"Oh, how terrible for him," Crimson said.

"But Tom is also an honorable man," Libbie went

on. "And he would do nothing to bring dishonor to the Custer name. I have no doubt but that the excitement of command will bring him out of his despair. Autie intends to leave him in command of the Seventh while we are in New York, you know."

"No," Crimson said. "I hadn't heard."

Libbie's face grew serious. "Crimson, you do recall the talk we had about Tom's destiny?"

"I do."

"Good. I hope you will bear that in mind while we are gone. I should not like to see Tom suffer because of some ill-considered act."

"I assure you, madam, I am not the person you need fear on that score," Crimson said shortly.

"I find that comforting," Libbie said sweetly. "Now, if you will excuse me, I shall see to Autie."

Crimson stared after Libbie, barely concealing her annoyance with the woman. In fact, even her father, who normally retreated into introspection during "woman talk," commented on his daughter's vexation.

"Crimson, why are you angry with Mrs. Custer?"

"No reason, Father," Crimson replied.

Artemus chuckled. "Am I to believe that you are angry just because it is in your nature?"

Crimson smiled, relaxed by her father's easy banter. "Mrs. Custer is afraid that I will show undo affection for Tom."

"I see."

"Of course, I explained that such a thing is unlikely, but, nevertheless she persists in her fear. Perhaps I shall go to her again and try to put her mind to ease."

"Why?"

"Why?" Crimson repeated, surprised by her father's question. "Don't you think I should?"

"Do you like the young man?"

"Well I . . . I must admit that he has all of his brother's charm with none of his conceit," Crimson said. "And there is a kind of sweetness about him, too."

"Then pay no attention to Mrs. Custer," Artemus said.

"Father . . . are you *encouraging* a relationship with Tom?"

"Yes," Artemus said. "Didn't she just say that he will be in command while they are gone?"

"Yes," Crimson said.

"Perhaps he could be made to see the validity of our request to go into the Indian lands and paint," Artemus said.

"Oh," Crimson replied. "I see. In other words . . . you want me to use him."

"Yes," Artemus said. "But only if you can use him without hurting him."

"I don't think that can be done," Crimson said.

"Oh, I don't agree with you at all. In fact, your attention may be just what he needs to rid himself of these devils that plague him."

## 12

If Joseph was worried that he might not be accepted back into the village, it was because even now he did not understand the depth of the Hunkpapa commitment to him. He had become one of them through sacred ceremony, and as far as they were concerned, he was as truly Indian as any who had been born a Sioux.

The joyful acceptance of his return and the celebration of his escape made him realize more than ever that he had done the right thing by returning. He would deny what he felt for Crimson Royal, and in so doing, deny the white race. He was an Indian, now and forever.

Shortly after he returned, Joseph announced his intention to go into the sweat lodge, a tightly sealed tent under which rocks were fired to a very high temperature. When one entered a sweat lodge one faced a physical ordeal, for often the temperature would be so high that the skin would burn; sometimes one would pass out from the heat. Yet it was considered the single most spiritual act a Sioux could perform. It was in the sweat lodge that those individuals blessed with great spirituality received messages from the Great Spirit. And though Joseph had never seen a vision, he never left a sweat lodge without an uplifted feeling and a sense of purpose.

"Perhaps you would not mind sharing your sweat lodge with me?" Sitting Bull asked.

Joseph and those around him gasped. Sitting Bull was the most respected of all the chiefs, greater even than Rain In The Face, Gall, or Crazy Horse. Sitting Bull had never shared a sweat lodge with anyone, for he often received visions during such meditations. To request to share the lodge with Joseph was the greatest honor he could bestow upon the young man.

Joseph took great pains in building the lodge, and when it was ready he walked proudly through the village to Sitting Bull's wickiup to inform him. Without a word, Sitting Bull rose from his seat on a mat of soft furs and followed Joseph into the lodge.

They sat in silence for a long time which Joseph was certain would be the pattern for their entire stay. But Sitting Bull surprised him again.

"Do you know how I got my name?" Sitting Bull asked.

"No," Joseph replied.

"It was my father's name and he gave it to me for an act of bravery when I was the same age as you when you counted coup against the Crow warrior. The name was a great gift from my father, for he was given the name by the Great Spirit, and that is the story I will tell you, if you wish to hear."

"I would very much like to hear," Joseph replied.

"One night when my father was on a hunting party, a great bull buffalo came slowly toward the hunting camp. The bull made many strange noises from its throat, and the hunters were afraid, but my father was not. My father's name then was Returns Again, and he thought the bull was sent by the Great Spirit to speak to him, so he didn't run from the bull. He went out to listen to what the bull had to say.

"What do you wish, messenger of the Great Spirit?" my father asked the buffalo bull.

"The bull slowly moved his head from side to side and continued to speak in buffalo language. Finally, the Great Spirit gave my father the power to understand the language of the buffalo. The bull was saying four names over and over. Four, as you know, is a magic number for the Sioux. Each of the four names had the word Bull as a part, and one of them was Sitting Bull. My father took that to be his name, and now it is mine. Tatanka Iyotake, which the white men call Sitting Bull."

"That is a good story, Tatanka Iyotake," Joseph said. "I am pleased that you told it to me."

"And now, shall I tell you of a vision I have seen?" Sitting Bull asked.

"I would be honored."

"There will be a great battle between the Indian and the soldiers. All the Indian nations will fight under me, and all the soldiers will fight under Yellow Hair. The Indians will win the battle with a great victory. There will be much crying and wailing in the homes of the soldiers, for all will be killed."

"That is a great vision," Joseph said.

"You are a man of two hearts," Sitting Bull went on. "After that battle, one of your hearts will die and one will live. But I do not know which one."

"My Indian heart will live," Joseph said.

"This may be so," Sitting Bull said. "But for now I cannot say."

"Sitting Bull, do you fear that I will betray you?" Joseph wanted to know.

"No, this I do not fear," Sitting Bull said. "For

if it is to be your Indian heart which dies, it will die a brave death and will not betray its people. But neither will your white heart allow you to betray the whites. There will be a battle between your two hearts as great as that I will fight with Yellow Hair."

"The Indian will win the battle you fight with Yellow Hair," Joseph said. "And the Indian will win the battle between my two hearts. I will not bring dishonor to myself."

"You would bring dishonor only if you disobeyed the heart that wins the battle," Sitting Bull said. "If your Indian heart is victorious, it would be dishonorable for you to deny what it tells you to do. But if your white heart is victorious, it would be dishonorable for you to deny what it tells you to do."

"How will I know which is right?"

"You will know."

Sitting Bull fell silent, and Joseph, out of respect for Sitting Bull's meditations, was silent, also. But he did think about Sitting Bull's words, and he vowed that he would not betray his Indian heart. He wasn't sure how long they sat in silence, but presently his jumbled thoughts stilled and a tranquillity descended on him.

"I have a song for you," Sitting Bull said then. "It has come to me as I sit here. I will sing it for you now."

Sitting Bull started to sing his song, a two-note chant repeated over and over. The words of the song, though delivered in Teton Sioux, rang clear in Joseph's ears:

> *Like the empty sky it has no boundaries,*
> *Yet it is right in this place.*
> *When you seek to know it you cannot see it.*
> *You cannot take hold of it,*
> *But you cannot lose it.*

*If you do not understand,*
*Then you can understand.*
*When you are silent it speaks,*
*When you speak it is silent.*

Joseph did not consciously try to decipher the meaning of the words but instead, let the phrases soothe his mind. Joseph did not see Sitting Bull leave. Songs were chanted outside his tent, but he did not hear. Joseph had glimpsed the truth.

Sasha tried not to think about the soldiers who had come in the night to kill her family, but she couldn't help it. Sometimes the memories came back to chill her like a cold wind blowing from the winter mountains. Often the memories came while Sasha was asleep and she would cry out in terror and wake up shaking with fear.

It wasn't always like that, though. There were times when Sasha would wake up and it would still be night and she could see the moon, hanging cold and quiet in the early morning darkness. At that moment, just between sleep and wake, she would think of the man she loved.

As the stepson of her father, Joseph had become the head of her family, and he provided for her and made the decisions for her, and treated her as a father would his daughter, or a brother would his sister. This was as it should be for a woman with no husband.

But Sasha did not want to be a woman without a husband. There was nothing in tribal law that forebade her from marrying the stepson of her father, which was just what she wanted to do. She wanted to be Joseph's wife.

One night in late fall as Sasha lay thinking of Joseph, she heard the shamans leaving to go to the mountains to pray and meditate. Sasha stayed in

115

bed for a few minutes until she could no longer hear the sound of the shamans climbing. Then she removed her buckskin gown and walked to the door of the wickiup to let the night breeze cool her skin. The wind was cold and bracing, and she felt that such a thing would be healthy for her.

As Sasha stood in the soft, silver light of the full moon, she could hear Joseph moving in his sleep. She was naked and knew that she should cover herself in case he woke up, but there was such a wonderful sense of freedom to her nudity that she just couldn't give it up.

Then the sounds changed and Sasha realized that Joseph was awake. She also knew that she was going to give herself to him. She walked over to him, and crawled into his bed.

Joseph put his arms up to receive her, then rolled onto her, pressing her down into the furs of his sleeping pad. Sasha felt him upon her, and soon, she was caught up in a quickly rising tide of passion. She welcomed him into her with a small groan of pleasure.

Joseph took her with an amazing tenderness, and a pleasantness began in her loins and flowed through her body, awakening her senses and heating her blood. The chill of the fall night was melted away now by the heat of their lovemaking.

Now Sasha was no longer a young Indian maiden; she was a creature of the Great Spirit in whom lightning and thunder had ignited a passionate fire and an unquenchable erotic thirst. Then the peak of sensation hit her, a fire-burst of rapture that licked her with tongues of flame.

Afterward they both slept.

Joseph awoke in the early morning darkness. The moon, high in the velvet sky, was still shining brightly. It spilled a pool of iridescence through the tipi

116

opening and onto the bed, bathing Sasha in a soft, shimmering light.

Sasha was asleep and breathing softly. Joseph reached over gently and put his hand on her naked hip. He could feel the sharpness of her hip bone and the soft yielding of her flesh. The contrasting textures were delightful to his sense of touch. He let his hand rest there, enjoying a feeling of possession until finally sleep claimed him once again.

Sasha was Joseph's woman after that. At first, they took their pleasure only in the middle of the night and spoke nothing of it during the day. But within a few weeks, their beds were no longer separated in the wickiup, and they would make love when they wanted, even during the long, cold, rainy afternoons. Finally, by the time of the first snow, Joseph took Sasha to the tribal council and announced that he was taking her as his wife.

Crazy Wolf spoke angry words, and stormed away from the council, but the council thought it was good, and one of the shamans performed the ceremony.

And now, Joseph thought, as he held his wife in his arms, warm and snug in their own wickiup as snow blanketed the valley of their winter encampment, my Indian heart has made its choice.

Joseph had never known greater happiness.

## 13

Dear Tom,

It is New Year's Eve as I write, thus you will receive this letter in the New Year. I trust all is well with you and with our military family at Fort Lincoln. Please give my kindest regards to Artemus Royal and his daughter. Autie and I have met with Paul Gideon, their agent here, and he reports that some of the earlier work from Fort Lincoln has enjoyed a tremendous popularity, particularly the portraits of Autie. He agrees with us, incidentally, that Artemus Royal is much too fine an artist to be allowed to venture into the Indian Territories.

The holidays have been rainy and gloomy. I did not have the fun I had anticipated looking at the shop windows. On Christmas morning I went to church, Episcopal, of course, but came back, weary and disgruntled from the ritual prayers and processions. Autie always finds the day somewhat of a bore and is glad when it is over. I missed the home atmosphere and all of you. Autie gave me a black silk dress which I am making, as I have no one to help me. I gave him a solid silver tablespoon and teaspoon, Maggie gave him a fork and dessert spoon to match.

Autie has so many invitations, I have to drive him to accept them, as it is a privilege to meet interesting people. One night he dined at three places. One night a dinner at the Lotos Club, another at the Stoughtons to meet Sir Rose Price, a noted sportsman—and, greatest treat—a lunch in Mr. Bierstadt's studio, where we met the Earl Sunracen. Then we dined twice with the Barretts.

Mr. Barrett is making an enormous success in *Julius Caesar* at Booth's Theatre. The scenery is perfect and the stage is full of people . . . three hundred sometimes. And at the close there is a grand tableau. Brutus is burned on a funeral pyre. Why, Tom, it makes you want to scream to see the funeral pyre blazing and Brutus rising above it.

We have seen Oakey Hall in his own play, sensational and lawyer-like, but imagine an old man of fifty starting as an actor.

Autie and I have a room opposite the Hotel Brunswick (where we have our meals and get our mail.) We live cheaper than at Fort Lincoln.

We are waiting to hear about the journey back. I enjoy New York, but I miss you and our military family.

Don't spend more money than you can help at the Sutlers', drinking and card-playing. Don't be influenced by the badness around you. Oh, if only I could find a companionable wife for you . . . one who would understand her role as a Custer, one who would foresake all her own ambitions and desires for the fulfillment of yours. That's the kind of wife you need, Tom. Don't be fooled by loneliness

. . . or kindness . . . or a pretty face from someone who may seem right, but isn't, if you know what I mean!

Libbie

"What do you suppose she means?" Tom asked. He had been reading the letter aloud to Crimson, who, with Tom, was sitting on the floor of the commandant's house, eating popcorn and drinking apple cider.

"Well, Captain Custer, I'm sure I don't know," Crimson replied innocently. "She couldn't mean me, could she? Surely she doesn't think I would fool you by loneliness, or kindness."

"No," Tom said sternly. "It couldn't be you . . . Libbie said this person had a pretty face."

"Tom Custer!" Crimson said in mock anger, throwing a handful of popcorn at him.

"Here!" Tom retorted. "We'll have none of that, now. I'm the commanding officer of the Seventh Cavalry. How would it look if some of my officers came in and saw popcorn all over the floor?"

"Better some of your officers than Libbie," Crimson said.

"You've a point there, girl," Tom said. He looked toward the window. "But there's little chance that she'll show up unexpectedly tonight. The snow is already knee deep and still coming down strong. I've known people to get lost twenty-five yards from their house in this kind of a blizzard."

"I know, it's awful," Crimson said. Crimson picked up the popcorn and put it in a bowl, then brushed her hands together. "But, let her come now, if she wishes. There's not a sign of our unmilitary frivolity."

"There was a letter from Autie too. You want to hear it?"

"Of course," Crimson replied. "I'm always interested in what a future president has to say."

"All right, here goes," Tom said, and began to read:

"We have been here over a month now. We have delightful rooms at the back, quiet, opposite the Brunswick. We are having the most delightful and interesting time possible. I have entry to all the theaters in the city. At a reception at the Historical Society, its president and a group of other men over eighty flocked around Libbie. At a reception of the Palatte Club, the president took her in to supper with dancing afterwards. The ladies danced in hats. Artemus Royal's paintings of Army life at Fort Lincoln were exhibited, and much was made over them. I was told that one young lady fell in love with me, through the portrait by Mr. Royal; Libbie showed admirable restraint at the news.

"The latest in regard to Army reduction is that the House will not interfere with the cavalry, but will cut off five regiments of infantry, and one of artillery.

"I have no idea of obtaining my promotion this spring or summer. On the contrary, I expect to be in the field in the summer with the 7th, and think there will be lively work before us. I think the 7th Cavalry may have its greatest campaign ahead. Congressmen and senators have told me privately that my best method of advancing into the political arena would be by producing a sterling victory over the hostiles this summer, possibly even over Sitting Bull himself. I will seek that scoundrel out and ride him down to the tune of *Garry Owen*, you may count on that.

"Get plenty of rest this winter, brother, for in the summer I shall cover us all with glory.

Autie"

"Well," Crimson said as Tom finished the letter. "You certainly have your life all planned for you, don't you, Tom?"

"Yes," Tom said. "It would seem that way, wouldn't it?"

"Is it what you want?"

Tom didn't answer Crimson. Instead, he walked over to the fire and stirred it with a poker, moving the logs around until they were blazing brightly.

"Excuse me," Crimson said. "I should have known better. It's a question of honor, right?"

Tom looked at Crimson with a pained expression on his face.

"Oh, don't bother to explain," she said. She lay down on the bearskin rug in front of the fireplace and stared into the fire.

"I have learned much of honor since I have been out here. You aren't alone in your slavish devotion to it."

"Meaning Joseph Two Hearts?"

Tom's offhand comment caught Crimson totally unawares. She felt as if she had been hit in the stomach with a club, and she stared at Tom in absolute shock. "What?" she asked in a very small voice. "What did you say?"

"I found the drawing you did of Joseph Two Hearts," Tom said. "And I know that you are the one who set him free. I know how you felt about him. Or, maybe, you still feel."

"How . . . do . . . you . . . know?"

"Crimson, a drawing isn't like a photograph. A drawing shows the artist's emotions. The drawing you made of Joseph? I would give anything if you would make such a drawing of me."

"I see," Crimson said.

"And when you found out that Joseph had married Sitting Bear's daughter . . . I saw the look in your eyes. You are in love with him, aren't you?"

"No," Crimson said.

"Oh?"

"At least . . . I don't think I am," Crimson said. She ran her hand through her hair and looked away from Tom. "I may have been at one time. But not anymore."

Tom put his hand on Crimson's arm. "Then could that mean there is a chance for me?"

"For you?" Crimson asked, looking back at him. "Tom, do you know what you are saying?"

"Yes," Tom said. "I am telling you that I love you. I love you, Crimson, and I want to marry you."

"But what of Libbie?"

"Libbie is already married," Tom said.

"You know what I mean," Crimson replied. "Libbie doesn't approve of me."

"Libbie just doesn't think you would make a good Custer wife, that's all."

"She's right, Tom," Crimson said. "I could never do for you what a wife is expected to do. At least, not the kind of wife Libbie has in mind."

"Dammit, Crimson, I don't care what Libbie has in mind! I love *you*!"

"And honor be damned?" Crimson asked.

"And honor be damned," Tom replied. Tom moved to her and put his arm around her. He kissed her once, on the temple, then whispered softly in her ear, his lips caressing her ear as lightly as the flutter of a butterfly's wing. "I'll fit my life to yours," he said. "I love you, Crimson."

Crimson stared at him for just a moment, then, in the length of a breath, they were kissing.

The kiss wasn't a tentative, exploratory one, like most first kisses. It was full born as a lover's kiss, open-mouthed and hungry.

Crimson wasn't quite sure how things had reached this point, but she felt her insides growing white with the heat of her passion for Tom. She knew now that she had been attracted to him all along, though theirs had been a strange, and somewhat melancholy relationship. Never before had Tom made a move or spoken a word that could be considered improper. And yet he had borne a hidden, smoldering desire for her all this time.

The kiss deepened, and Tom's hands began moving gently yet skillfully across the bodice of her dress, releasing fastenings, and soon Crimson lay nude upon the bearskin rug. The wavering orange fire painted her nude body with a golden glow, and she looked up at him through half-closed eyes as he undressed. Then he lay beside her, touching her skin with fingers that seemed to scorch her with their intense heat.

Outside, the soft snow continued to drift down, isolating the two lovers in the small house, while inside the burning wood played an ancient melody to their embrace. Crimson felt the nap of the bear's fur against her bare legs and back, then Tom's hard, muscled legs against hers as he moved over her.

Tom's weight came down on her, and she took him willingly, eagerly, thrusting up against him, helping him as he made slow and wonderous love to her.

"Oh, Tom," she breathed, but her words were smothered by a kiss and a darting tongue that moved in and out of her mouth in perfect rhythm with the rest of his body. Then a jolt of pleasure struck her; once, twice, three times, and her body was lifted to the stars, a blazing comet exploding in a golden ecstasy that went on and on and on.

All at once Tom's body went rigid. A groan escaped from his lips and convulsions of pleasure racked his body. Crimson could feel the convulsions transferred from his body to her own. His manhood strained inside her and then slowly slackened.

When finally he rolled off her, she could feel the pleasure of him within her.

"Will you marry me, Crimson?" Tom asked.

"Tom, I . . ."

"Marry me."

"Tom, you don't know what you are asking. You . . ."

"I'm asking you to marry me," Tom persisted.

"Yes, Tom," Crimson finally said. "Yes, I'll marry you."

## 14

General Custer's leave was officially over by the first week of February. But he was ordered to Washington to testify before Congress regarding the building of new posts and forts in the Western territories.

General Terry petitioned to have Custer relieved of this duty so that he could take charge of the spring campaigns, but his entreaty went unheeded. The result was that while the Custers were attending gala balls and glittering parties in Washington, sandwiched in between Custer's appearances before committees, Tom was left in command of the Seventh.

Though Crimson continued to work in her quarters, she spent many of her nights with Tom in the commandant's quarters.

Artemus asked her about her relationship with Tom one morning while the two of them were working.

"Are you sleeping with him, daughter?"

"What?" Crimson gasped. They had been talking

about light and color, and his abrupt question had surprised her.

Artemus dabbed a bit of color onto his canvas and worked it in, as if it were much more important than a discussion of Crimson's nocturnal habits.

"I asked you if you are sleeping with Tom Custer."

Crimson was cleaning a brush with turpentine, and she studied it closely.

"Well?" Artemus asked. He looked over at her, his expression neutral.

"Yes," Crimson said quietly, almost inaudibly.

"Do you love him?"

"I . . . I don't know," Crimson said. "I think I do."

"Well, I should hope you love him, if you intend to marry him."

"That's funny," Crimson said. "I would have thought you would have said, 'I hope you marry him, since you are sleeping with him.' That's what most fathers would tell their daughters."

"I'm not most fathers," Artemus said. "And you aren't most daughters. I spent a good many years in Paris, as you well know. The French are much more understanding about such things, and perhaps, some of that understanding has reached me. Besides, we are artists, you and I. Artists feel things much more deeply, and it is only natural that our emotional sensitivity would carry over into our physical feelings. I'll not condemn you for sleeping with him, for I think you wouldn't do it if you didn't love him very much. But I would condemn you for marrying him if you don't love him enough to sleep with him. And I certainly don't want you to feel that you must marry him because you are sleeping with him."

"Father, I'm sorry," Crimson said. She walked over to stand behind her father and put her arms

128

around him. "I don't want to do anything that would hurt you."

"Then don't do anything that would hurt yourself," Artemus said.

"I can't promise that," Crimson said. She walked away from her father and looked through the window. Outside in the quadrangle, a troop of mounted soldiers were preparing to leave on a detail.

"What's wrong?"

"It's Tom's dreams," Crimson said. "Or rather, I should say his nightmares." She turned around to look back at her father. "Father, have you ever heard what really happened at Washita? I mean, really?"

"I read General Custer's report, the same as you."

"Which said that one hundred and three Indians were killed, right?" Crimson said. "But did you know that only eleven of those were warriors. The rest were women and children . . . even babies."

"No," Artemus said. "No, I didn't know that."

"And the fifty-three captured—they were all women and children," Crimson went on. "In addition to that, more than six hundred horses were slaughtered."

"Did Tom tell you all that?"

"No," Crimson said. "No, that would be disloyal to his brother. Tom could never tell me all that. He just has nightmares, and drinks too much, and keeps it all bottled up inside him. And it's driving him insane."

"I can see how something like that would," Artemus said. "So that was what drove Colonel Cooper to suicide."

"Yes," Crimson said. "I learned of it through Sergeant Flynn."

"You don't think . . . I mean, there's no chance that . . ."

"That Tom will do the same thing?" Crimson asked.

"It's a possibility isn't it?"

"No, I don't think so," Crimson said. "At least, not in the same way. Tom would find a way to accomplish the same thing, but with honor. That's why I worry about this upcoming campaign so. The General isn't back, and the Seventh has to go out and round up a group of warriors who have strayed beyond their bounds."

"And Tom is going to lead the expedition?"

"Yes."

"But surely the prospect of marrying you will deter him from any foolhardy action?"

"I hope so," Crimson said. "But I can't be sure, Father. I can't be sure."

As Crimson and her father were discussing him Tom was at that moment sitting behind his desk reading Libbie's latest letter. He had not shown it to Crimson, nor even told her of its existence. It would only upset her, and he didn't want to do that. The last part was particularly venomous, and Tom had read it many times over:

I do not blame you, Tom, for supposing you have "fallen in love" with Crimson Royal. She is a most beautiful woman, and you, so long denied the joys a wife would bring, have suffered what any man in your circumstances would suffer, a loss of good judgment.

Crimson is not for you, Tom. She will do nothing to further your career, nor will she even have your best interests at heart. She is an artist, ambitious only in her own chosen endeavor. I will not allow this proposed marriage to take place, and neither will Autie. When at long last this Washington business has ended, and we are allowed to return, Autie will invoke his right as military commander of the district to require Miss Royal and her father to leave. I know this may sound unnecessarily harsh to you, Tom, but believe me, we are doing this for your own good.

Tom walked over to the fireplace and tossed the letter in. He watched it turn gold, then brown, then finally blacken and crumble as it burned. Then he spread the ashes around with a poker.

"Tom, the detail is ready to go," said Captain Benteen, who had been seeing to the preparations for the expedition to return the hostiles to the reservation.

"Thanks, Will," Tom said. "I guess I'd better get started."

"Tom, are you sure you want to take this detail out?"

"Why do you ask?" Tom asked, slipping into his coat.

"It's just that . . . well . . . as acting commander you have every right to stay back at the post and let Reno or me handle this. After all, the majority of the troops will be here at the fort."

"I'll take it," Tom said. "Look, I've got enough trouble with Major Reno now. He outranks me, and by all rights he should have command while Autie's gone. But Autie gave it to me. I didn't ask for it, mind you . . . I didn't even want it."

"The General made the right choice," Will Benteen said.

"The General chose his brother," Tom replied. "Anyway, what's done is done. But if I send Reno out with this detail, I'm afraid it would be rubbing salt into the wound. No, I'll take the detail out . . . Reno will stay here, in command of the fort."

"You're the boss," Benteen said.

"Let's go."

They stepped out onto the front porch, and Tom buttoned the coat around him. Most of the snow had given way to the cold, gooey mud of early spring. It was the brown time, between the white of winter and the green of spring, a dismal, ugly day.

"Will, have someone bring my horse over, will you? I want to tell Crimson goodbye."

"All right," Benteen agreed. He smiled at Tom, a friendly, sharing smile. "If I had someone as pretty as Crimson around, I wouldn't be telling her goodbye. I'd be telling the troop goodbye."

Tom walked down the wooden walkway to the front door of the small house and knocked lightly.

"Well, hello, Tom," Artemus said, opening the door.

"Hello, Artemus. I've come to tell Crimson goodbye."

"Sure, come on in. But if you'll excuse me, I have to get a couple of brushes," Artemus said diplomatically, wanting to let the two young people be alone.

"I'm going to be gone for a few days, Crimson," Tom said after Artemus left.

"I know," Crimson said. "Tom, please, for my sake if not your own, be careful. Don't do anything foolish."

"I promise you I won't," Tom said. He smiled. "Besides, I've reason to be careful." He put his arms around Crimson. "I don't want to wait to be married. I want to be married as soon as I return."

"Tom, are you sure that's a good—"

"As soon as I get back," Tom said.

"Tom, I thought we were going to wait."

"I want us to already be married by the time Autie gets back. I want to surprise him."

"I see," Crimson said. She turned and walked out of his arms. "It isn't really Autie, is it? It's Libbie.

132

And you don't want to surprise her, you want to defy her. Only you can't do it in front of her."

"Libbie has nothing to do with it," Tom said. "She isn't leading my life. I am."

"Then have the courage to wait until she returns," Crimson said.

Tom sighed, then smiled sadly. "Very well, if that is the way it must be . . . then that is the way it shall be. But the thought of our being married would have sustained me during the next two weeks in the field."

Crimson returned to Tom and kissed him, slow and deep. After several seconds, she broke it off and looked at him with a half-smile on her face and a twinkle in her eyes.

"Think of that," she said. "Let that sustain you, if you must have something."

"Crimson, with that kiss in my heart I could be sustained for a forty-mile march on foot through ten-foot-deep snowbanks." Tom gave her one final squeeze, then turned and walked back through the door.

Crimson wrapped herself in a blanket and stepped out onto the front porch to watch Tom form the column, then ride through the front gate. The entire post had turned out to see them off. The band was playing and flags were flying, and as the detail passed by the other troops, they came to attention and saluted.

Even Crimson was affected by the scene, and for a few moments she contemplated a life of being the kind of wife Libbie wanted for Tom. But even as she was thinking about it, she knew she could never do it. And if she couldn't be the right kind of wife for Tom . . . she shouldn't marry him at all. Oh, why did she agree to do it? And why didn't she have the courage to refuse him?

As the gates closed behind the detail, Crimson

went back inside to return to her work. Reaching for a brush, she knocked the whole tray on the floor, and as she got on her hands and knees to retrieve them, she saw in a stack of old drawings and sketches the drawing she had done of Joseph Two Hearts last summer. She saw again his smoldering eyes, his powerful shoulders and arms, and his bare chest. A pulse of heat flashed through her as she recalled the rapturous moments with him, then angrily she shoved the picture to one side, out of sight and out of mind.

And even as she did so, she wondered . . . with whom was she angry? With Joseph for getting married? Or with herself for not being able to forget him?

The blankets were stained with blood from Sasha's lungs, and her fever was so high that her hand burned in Joseph's. Several totems had been placed on the ground beside her, and outside a shaman danced and chanted a holy song, but the sickness was winning the battle.

The tentflap opened and Sitting Bull stepped inside. He sat beside Joseph and looked at Sasha without speaking. The two men sat in silence for a long time, with only the labored breathing of Sasha to interrupt the quiet. Finally Sitting Bull spoke.

"When you were white, did the white doctors have medicine for such an illness?"

"I don't know," Joseph said. "I think not. I remember a cousin who had this illness and the doctors could do nothing."

"She is going to die," Sitting Bull said.

"Yes," Joseph replied. "I know."

Sitting Bull reached over and patted Joseph's hand a few times, then, without another word, he left.

Joseph looked at his wife, and tried to choke

back the lump in his throat. Why had she gotten sick? Was it God's punishment against him for becoming a heathen?

"Why do they call Indians heathens, Ma?" he had asked his mother.

"Because they are Godless, son," his mother had answered. "Indians are lost children in the Kingdom of God."

"Why? Doesn't God love everybody?"

"Yes, but you must love God, and you must love his son, Jesus Christ. If you don't, you are a heathen."

"Don't the Indians love God?"

"Some Indians do. Those who have been civilized. But most Indians have some pagan god, and they are lost."

"What does it mean if you are lost?"

"Why, Joseph, you know what it means. You've been to church enough to understand that."

"I've heard the preachers talking about saving souls," Joseph said. "I know what that means."

"What does it mean?"

"It means going to heaven."

"All right. If somebody is lost, then that means they aren't saved."

"And they are going to hell?" Joseph asked.

"Yes," his mother said. "Unless someone can save them. Some heathens can be saved if they listen to the word and change their ways. But there are some who are even more lost than the heathens."

"Who?"

"A person who knows about God and Jesus, and yet turns his back on the Lord. That's the worst kind of sin."

Joseph remembered the conversation with his mother as clearly as if it had happened yesterday.

And from the dim past he tried to remember how to pray, to ask God for forgiveness, and to beg Him to spare the life of Sasha.

But he couldn't.

## 15

They had been on patrol for fifteen days, but so far their search had been fruitless. Twice they had seen small, mounted bands of warriors, but the warriors were travelling light on fast ponies and they easily outdistanced the soldiers, then returned to laugh and mock them. It was, thus far, a most frustrating expedition.

That afternoon the Rhee scouts had found signs that they may be close to a large party. Tom halted his troop and made camp while the scouts went out looking.

Tom, his second-in-command, Captain Benteen, and Lieutenant Godfrey were sitting by a campfire that night with sergeants Flynn and Kennedy. The fire provided some warmth in the chilly spring night and kept the coffee hot.

"If the scouts have found nothing, we'll go back tomorrow," Tom finally said.

"Oh, Tom, we're so close," Benteen said. "If we just press on a little further, I know we'll find them."

"But my brother will be back shortly," Tom said. "By rights he should be doing this."

"Wouldn't you like to surprise him with a successful mission?" Benteen asked.

Tom smiled. "I'm not all that sure he would want to be surprised like that."

"Tom, you stand in his shadow too much," Benteen said. "It isn't fair."

"You don't understand, Will. You are like Crimson. I don't mind standing in my brother's shadow. There is no jealousy between us. And I have no ambition, beyond serving my brother."

"Even if you don't always agree with your brother?" Benteen asked.

"And when have I disagreed?"

"Washita, perhaps?"

Benteen and the others knew of Tom's trouble with Washita. And yet none of them had ever heard him speak one word about it.

Tom sucked the coffee noisily from his cup before he spoke.

"It was my place to neither agree or disagree," he finally said. "It was only my place to follow orders. And it is not your place to question me now."

"I'm sorry," Benteen said.

"The scouts are returning," Sergeant Flynn said, the interruption easing the awkward moment. The men stood up as they rode into camp. Sergeant Flynn filled two tin cups with coffee, which he handed to the two men.

"Good, good," Bloody Hand said, wrapping his hands around the cup, enjoying the warmth as much as the coffee's bracing effect.

The officers were silent while the scouts drank their coffee and warmed themselves by the fire. Finally Bloody Hand spoke.

"I have found the village," he said.

"Where?"

"There," he said, pointing westward through the darkness.

"How far?"

"Three hour march," Bloody Hand said.

"What is the village like?"

"Good village for us," Bloody Hand said. "This many tipis." He flashed both hands twice, indicating twenty.

"Warriors?"

"Same," Bloody Hand said, flashing his hands again.

"Well," Benteen said, looking at Tom with excitement in his eyes. "What do you think? Shall we hit it?"

Tom rubbed his chin with his hand and stared off into space. "I know what my brother would do, and without the slightest hesitation," he said. "And as I am serving in my brother's place, I know what I should do. But . . ." he looked back at Bloody Hand. "Bloody Hand, are you sure there are warriors in the village? I don't want to attack if no one is there but women and children."

"Warriors," Bloody Hand said. "I am sure."

Tom folded his arms across his chest, then turned and walked out of the circle of light. He stood there in the darkness for several moments while the others waited by the fire for his decision. Finally he spoke.

"Will, get the men mounted," he said. "We'll move now and get in position to hit them at dawn."

"Yes, sir!" Benteen said with obvious approval.

Flynn and Kennedy returned to their companies and began hurrying the men, instructing them to check their equipment and lash everything down to prevent the clanking of metal from announcing their arrival and ruining the element of surprise.

139

Finally the troops were mounted, the fires extinguished, and, with the scouts in the lead, Tom's Seventh Cavalry detachment was underway.

As the column rode through the night, Tom prayed that this would not be a repeat of Washita. Better he would be killed in battle than lead his men into another Washita.

"What are you shooting at that kid for?" one of the troopers asked another. "He's just barely walkin'."

"Hell, his mama's dead, I'm doin' the kid a favor," the trooper answered. But his shot went wide. "Missed the little son-of-a-bitch." He fired and again his bullet kicked up snow close to the child.

"Well if you're gonna shoot the little bastard shoot 'im!" the other trooper said. He took his own rifle and fired, and blood squirted from the hole in the child's head, painting a fan of red on the white snow. "Got 'im," the marksman said proudly. "And he never even flopped once."

"Troop, halt," Tom suddenly said, holding up his arm. The memory of the incident at Washita was with him so strongly at this moment that he couldn't go on.

"What is it, Tom?" Benteen asked. "Have you seen something?"

"What?" Tom answered. "Oh . . . uh, no," he said. He looked around at the soldiers as if surprised that they were stopped. "Why did you ask me that?"

"You halted the column," Benteen said easily.

"Oh," Tom said. He turned in his saddle and looked back along the dark forms stretching out behind him. "I thought I heard someone's gear clanking," he lied. "Have Godfrey ride along the line to double-check."

"All right," Benteen said.

"Move out," Tom called, and the column began again. Far in the back, some of the privates who had come since Washita and didn't know of the devils riding with them, wondered at the reason for being stopped and then ordered on again with no explanation. But, they thought, such things were to be expected in the army. And one of the first things they learned was the old maxim, "theirs was not to reason why, their's was but to do or die."

Down in the village, Crazy Wolf went from rock to rock, checking the warriors, making certain they were ready. The warriors, armed with rifles, were waiting behind rocks on the sides of the two hills that overlooked the approach to the village. They all had buffalo blankets to keep them warm as they waited for the soldiers.

"Crazy Wolf, I think it is not good that we use the village as a decoy," one of the warriors said. "Suppose the soldiers attack the village before we attack them? Then squaws and children will be killed."

"That will not be," Crazy Wolf said. "I will give the signal when to fire, and then we will kill all the soldiers. Also their horses, so they cannot escape from us."

"But shouldn't we tell the ones in the village of your plan?" the first warrior asked. "If they do not know what is happening, they will grow frightened and try to run and then some will surely be killed."

"If we tell them of the plan they may give it away by some act or signal," Crazy Wolf said.

"But they are Sioux. They won't give away the plan."

"I will not take the chance," Crazy Wolf said. He looked back down the trail in the direction from which the soldiers would come. His eyes were glow-

ing proudly in the soft glow of early morning moonlight. "I will have a great victory when the sun
comes again. For many days the people will sing
of this victory in the lodges and tipis. Now, say no
more, for the soldiers may have scouts riding ahead."

Crazy Wolf returned to his position behind one
of the rocks and settled down, wrapped in his robes,
to wait for the soldiers and contemplate the glorious victory that was before him. He had defied orders, but when he won the battle no one would dare
challenge him at the councils.

Sitting Bull had led the main party of Sioux many
miles away, back toward the territory of Montana.
But there were many, including Sasha, who were
much too ill to travel with the main party, and they
were coming more slowly, with Joseph in charge.

Fearing that the soldiers would happen upon the
group of sick Indians, Sitting Bull ordered Crazy
Wolf to take a war party and create a diversion to
draw the soldiers away from the camp.

Crazy Wolf had other ideas though. He lured the
soldiers toward the camp, and now his scouts had
brought him word that his plan was working. He
looked up at the sky. It would be light soon. The
soldiers must be near.


At daybreak, Tom and his men nearly in position, a small boy from the camp came down to the
stream to get some water. The boy saw the soldiers,
and, knowing nothing of Crazy Wolf's plan, cried
out a warning to the village, then threw the water
bucket and started running back.

One of the troopers drew a bead on the boy but
Tom saw him.

"Don't shoot the boy!"

"But he's gonna give us away," the trooper protested.

"He already has," Tom said. "Dismount, but hold your fire. Horses to the rear."

With the soldiers now alerted, Crazy Wolf knew that if he didn't open fire now, the situation would only worsen. His signal shot was followed by a volley of rifle fire from the hills.

"It's an ambush!" Tom shouted. "Spread out into skirmishers and return fire!"

Within moments the well trained and disciplined soldiers were sending a murderous return fire into the hills on both sides, picking the Indians off one by one.

Seeing that his plan was going awry, Crazy Wolf gave the signal to retreat and himself was the first one to the ponies. The others, not wanting to risk capture or death at the hands of the soldiers, joined their leader in flight.

"Lieutenant Godfrey!" Tom called when he saw the Indians fleeing. "Follow them!"

"Yes, sir," Godfrey called. "B Troop, mount up!"

"Be careful, Godfrey," Tom warned, remembering the plight of Hamilton and Elliot, who had followed fleeing Indians from Washita only to run into a large ambush. "Go no more than a mile after them."

"Yes, sir," Godfrey yelled, the thunder of the hooves of his troop's horses nearly drowning out his reply.

Tom watched the men as they pursued the Indians, and saw the mud being thrown from the hooves, and heard the roar of the men who were caught up now in the lust for battle. He wished that he, and not Godfrey, was leading the pursuit, but as commander his duty was to remain with the column.

"Captain Custer, some white flags are flying from a couple of the tipis down there," Benteen said. "Shall we go down?"

"No," Tom said.

Benteen looked at Tom in confusion. "What do you have in mind then?"

"I'll go down there," Tom answered. "Alone."

"What if it's a trick? It could be another trap like the one we just rode into," Benteen said.

"If it is, I don't think they will be willing to close it on just one person," Tom said. "You stay back here. If you don't hear from me in fifteen minutes, attack the village."

"Right," Benteen said.

Tom mounted his horse, then rode slowly down toward the village. As he approached it, people began to come out of the tipis, mainly women, children, and old men. And a good many of them appeared to be sick. He was surprised that the warriors had set up their ambush this close to the village.

When Tom reached the village, his horse was surrounded by more than a score of Indians. Tom looked at them with sympathy. Some were so obviously ill that he didn't even know how they were still on their feet.

"Does anyone here speak English?" Tom asked.

"I speak English, Captain Custer."

Tom looked toward the sound of the voice, and saw Joseph Two Hearts standing by the opening of one of the tipis. He was tall and strong, not at all like the others. He was wrapped in a blanket, but he appeared to be unarmed.

"What is this village?" Tom asked, taking it in with a sweep of his arm.

"It is a village of the dying," Joseph said. "All you see here are ill. Most will die."

"Are you ill?"

"No," Joseph said. "My wife is. She is one who will die."

Tom turned in his saddle and looked around. The leather creaked as he moved.

"I'm sorry, Joseph," Tom said. "I'm real sorry to hear that."

"Why did you attack us?" Joseph asked.

"I didn't," Tom answered easily. "I was attacked by your warriors from the hills."

The Indian boy who had given the first warning said something to Joseph in Sioux, and Joseph spit angrily at the ground.

"It was Crazy Wolf," he said. "The fool let you follow him here, and he used the village for bait."

"Your friend Crazy Wolf sounds like a real smart fella," Tom said.

"He is not my friend," Joseph replied.

"Joseph, what are you doing here in this area?" Tom asked. "Don't you know it is beyond the limitations set by my brother?"

"Yes," Joseph said. "We came to follow the buffalo, and the women and children came to follow the men. Now Sitting Bull and the others have returned, but these people are ill and can't travel as quickly, so I am leading them back."

"And Crazy Wolf?"

"Crazy Wolf was supposed to lead you away from the village," Joseph said.

"Instead, he led us right to it," Tom replied. He pulled his watch out and looked at it. "Joseph, I have to fire three rounds to signal my men that I am all right," he said. "If I don't, they will assume I've been trapped, and they will attack."

"Go ahead," Joseph said. "I will explain to the others what you are doing."

Tom pulled out his service revolver and gave the signal.

"So, I have been recaptured," Joseph said. "I suppose now I will be returned to the fort to hang."

Tom crossed his arms and looked at Joseph and the others. He knew how pleased his brother would be if Joseph was recaptured. But he also knew that he couldn't do it, he dare not do it, because of Crimson.

"No," he finally said. "I'm not going to take you back. I'm going to let you lead these people back to the reservation."

"Send a soldier escort with us," Joseph said. Typically, he didn't thank Tom for sparing his life.

"Why?" Tom asked.

"General Crook also has soldiers out," Joseph said. "If we have an escort, Crook won't bother us."

"You may have a point," Tom said.

When the other soldiers arrived, they were just as surprised by what they saw as Tom had been. Tom asked the doctor to do anything he could for the sick, and many of the men volunteered to assist.

Godfrey returned a short while later to report that Crazy Wolf and the others had gotten away, but that there weren't enough of them left to pose a serious threat to the patrol.

"Good, good," Tom said. "I'm sorry they got away, especially Crazy Wolf. But I'm glad we inflicted enough damage on them to teach them a lesson."

"What are you going to do with all these people?" Benteen asked.

"I'm sending them back to the reservation."

"You should take them to the fort," Benteen said.

"Why?" Tom asked. "Look at them, Will. What harm can they do?"

"Well, perhaps none," Benteen said. "But there are over thirty of them."

"What difference does that make?"

"If you took them back to the fort, you'd have thirty prisoners to go with the twelve warriors we killed this morning," Benteen said. "That would look

146

pretty good in a report to General Terry's head-quarters."

"I'm not interested in looking good in a report," Tom said. "Besides, as soon as we got them to the fort, we would just let them go anyway. Only by then, many would be dead. I don't intend to subject these dying people to that ordeal."

"All right, Tom, whatever you want to do," Benteen said. "I guess we'll just take Joseph back with us."

"No," Tom said.

"What? Tom, you can't be serious! Your brother has sentenced Joseph to die, you know that! He is an escaped criminal!"

"He is a husband worried about a dying wife," Tom said. "And right now, he's the best chance the rest of these people have of getting back alive. I'll not trade his one life for twenty-nine others."

"I hope you know what you are doing," Benteen cautioned.

"I am the military commander right now," Tom said. "It's my decision. Now, I'll need an escort detail to accompany the Indians. That's to prevent General Crook's columns from hitting them."

"With the Cap'n's permission," Flynn spoke up. "That's a job I'd be up to takin'."

"Are you sure you want to?" Tom asked. "It'll mean another two weeks in the field."

"Aye, 'tis somethin' I need to do," Flynn said.

"All right, Sergeant. Pick two men and the detail is yours," Tom said.

Sergeant Flynn nodded, then started back through the column to pick his men.

Well, old friend, Tom thought as he watched Flynn. Perhaps this'll help you pay back the debt you feel you owe to these people. I hope it helps with mine.

# 16

Joseph walked alongside the travois, bending over frequently to adjust the blankets and furs that he had put over Sasha. As he did so, he could feel the burning heat of her fever and see the flecks of blood she had coughed up.

"Joseph," she said weakly.

Joseph stopped the horse and leaned down.

"Yes, Sasha, I am here."

"Joseph, I do not want to die in a travois," she said.

"You aren't going to die," Joseph said, and he knew that it was his white heart speaking, for, like a white, he was unable to accept the death of someone he loved.

Sasha smiled in understanding. "I am dying and you know this," she said. "But I don't want to die in a travois. I want to die in a wickiup. I want to be in our bed in our wickiup. Joseph, please, do this for me. Build a wickiup here."

"All right," Joseph said. "I will."

Joseph cut the travois loose, then leaving Sasha

lying by the trail, he rode quickly to the head of the column to find Sergeant Flynn.

"Flynn," he called. "My wife wants to die in a wickiup."

"A wickiup?" Sergeant Flynn said. "Damn, boy, it takes a little effort to build one of those things, doesn't it?"

"Yes," Joseph said. "They are only built at a village where you intend to stay."

"Maybe a tipi would be all right for her," Sergeant Flynn suggested.

"She wants a wickiup, and she shall have one," Joseph said resolutely.

"All right, lad," Flynn said easily. "I'll not try 'n' stop you, if you've your mind set on doin' it. But I'll not be able to halt the column, you understand?"

"Yes."

"Would there be anythin' I could be gettin' for you, Joseph? Another blanket, mebbe, or a mite more food?"

"No," Joseph said.

Flynn stuck out his hand in a white man's handshake. Joseph took it without a moment's hesitation; how easily the action had come to him.

" 'Tis awfully sorry I am about your wife," Flynn said. "I wish there was somethin' I could do."

"Thank you," Joseph said. He turned to leave and had gone but a short distance when he stopped and called back to Flynn.

"Yes?" Flynn answered.

"Flynn, do you know how to pray to God and Jesus?"

Flynn smiled. "Sure'n you'd be askin' a Catholic the likes? 'Tis not a good Catholic I am, mind you, but I've never forgot the teachin's o' the Church."

"Would you say a prayer for Sasha?"

150

"Bless you, lad, 'n' I'd be more'n honored to," Flynn said. "Though not knowin' how good a standin' I am in with the Lord, I'm not promisin' 'nythin', you understand."

"I already know she will die," Joseph said. "Just ask God and Jesus to make her dying easy."

"I'll do that, lad," Flynn said earnestly. "I'll do that."

Joseph worked with near Herculean effort and finally, just before nightfall, he had finished the wickiup. He stepped back and looked at it with satisfaction. It was the best one he had ever built.

"It is beautiful, my husband," Sasha said, her voice strangely clear and alert. Shocked, Joseph looked back toward her.

But Sasha's appearance put a lie to the sound of her voice, for she was pale and drawn.

"It's ready for us to move in," Joseph said. "I can even start a fire, see? I've built a fire hole for the smoke to escape."

"Oh, yes, build a nice fire," Sasha said. "It will be good to be in a wickiup with a fire."

Joseph carried Sasha into the wickiup and lay her on soft furs, then he built a fire, and they watched the wood burn. From his position on the bed, he could see the edges of color that the sand in the wood made in the flame as it burned.

He looked over at Sasha and saw a look of contentment on her face—that look was worth all the work and more. Silently he thanked Sergeant Flynn for saying the prayer that helped Sasha, and he wished he could say a prayer to God to thank Him as well.

Sasha was composing her own prayer. It was a song, and the rhythm and melody in her mind were as real as at a tribal ceremony:

151

*This happy site of fields and hills in*
*A land of grassy plains and colored flowers,*
*With stands of trees dancing in the wind . . .*
*I know joy in the light of the Spirit*
*At the ways it appears*
*In many varieties.*

Sasha was most happy now, with her husband and her favorite furs and rugs in her very own wickiup. She would be dying soon, this she knew. But all the rest of the life left to her would be spent in happiness.

She thought of a wise old Indian saying: The flower which blooms but a single night differs not at heart from the mighty tree which lives a thousand years. She was like that flower. She had but a single night . . . but her heart was crowded with a lifetime of joy.

Joseph crawled into bed with Sasha, and he put his arms around her and pulled her to him, cradling her head on his shoulder. He felt the burning fever of her body, and he wished he could pull it out of her, absorb it with his own body.

He remembered the day he met Sasha. She had ridden by with her father and a few others shortly after the Crow who had killed his parents had left. Then, Joseph didn't know the difference between Sioux and Crow, and he thought the Indians were coming back to finish the job. He hid from them, but they poked through the wagon until they found him. He was terrified but determined not to grovel before them, so he stood up and walked out boldly, defying them to do their worst.

Sasha, who was only fourteen at the time, jumped off her horse and ran to stand in front of him, showing him that they meant no harm. He remembered her eyes, even then, large, brown and innocent, like the eyes of a fawn.

He had watched Sasha bathe that summer, sitting on the banks with the other young bucks, feeling the heat of youth in their bodies as they watched the naked young girls. The girls, enjoying the episodes fully as much as the boys, laughed and frolicked in the water.

Joseph watched the transformation of Sasha from girl to woman. Her lithe and nubile body developed into the full rounded peaks and inviting crevices of a mature young woman. But more and more, he came to regard Sasha as his sister, and though she made little secret of her wish to be his wife, it wasn't until after Sitting Bear died that Joseph was able to look upon Sasha in any other way.

Now she had been his wife but seven months. It had been a happy seven months, and she had come with him as he followed the buffalo, and she had cooked for him and warmed him at night, and he felt that it would never end.

But then Sasha contracted pneumonia. Though Joseph didn't know the name of the disease, he did know its symptoms, for it had been quite common among the Indians the last few years, and it was almost always fatal.

Sasha felt the deep breathing of Joseph in her arms, and knew that he was asleep. She wanted to stay awake, to be aware for all the time she had remaining. And now, with the moon shining brightly in the darkness of predawn, she waited to die.

Soon the line between reality and hallucination began to disintegrate. She could hear music, and she could see people . . . her father, her brother who had died in the time before Joseph, and many others. She knew that they were all people from the world beyond life, and they were all beautiful and glowing with some inner light.

The wickiup was filled with color—reds, blues, yellows, greens—and the colors seemed to be alive. Then Sasha became part of the color, and at one with everything in the wickiup. She drifted about the wickiup like smoke, and she could look down upon the bed and see herself and Joseph, sleeping in close embrace. She didn't know how she could do this, but, strangely, she didn't wonder about it. It seemed, somehow, quite natural to her.

She drifted a bit longer, seeing a living montage of herself and Joseph on the bed, and the two of them as healthy children, bathing in the streams, riding horses, dancing to the music of the drums and the songs. Then, she began collecting the pieces of herself and returning to her body. She felt herself falling into the fur of the buffalo robes. She tried to stop herself, but she couldn't. Soon all the colors, the music, and the people were gone. She was in a forest of great trees. She looked up to see the sky, but there was none. There was only the shaded roof provided by the trees.

Sasha closed her eyes and lay on a dust mote. She drifted without mind, without body, slowly and unseeing for a time that had no beginning and no end.

Sergeant Flynn was finding it more difficult to escort the Indians than he thought. Without Joseph, he had only the two other soldiers who were able-bodied enough to work. The Indians who were less ill than the others helped, but Flynn's abilities were being taxed to the utmost.

The rivers and streams were flooded with the melting snows, and routes that were easily passable in the summer were now fraught with swirling freshets. They reached one particularly swollen river, and the little band of Indians, with their pitifully small herd of ponies and horses, wondered how they would manage.

Miraculously, Sergeant Flynn managed to get the women and children across on buffalo-hide rafts without any serious accidents. But many of the horses and ponies were lost to the swiftly flowing current, and when they regrouped on the other side, some of the Indians who had been riding were forced to walk.

"Build more travois," Flynn ordered.

"Sarge, you ain't plannin' on puttin' a travois behind our horses, are you?" one of the other soldiers asked.

"Yes," Flynn said.

"Sarge, you ain't serious?"

"Aye, lad, I've never been more serious. 'N' you tell me why I shouldn't be."

"These here is cavalry horses, Sarge," the soldier protested.

"Howe, these animals don't even know they are horses, let alone cavalry horses," Flynn said. "Sure'n it'd make no difference to a horse whether he be pullin' a travois across the plains, or the grandest Drag down Park Avenue in New York."

"It just don't seem fittin', somehow, that we gotta turn cavalry horses into Injun ponies," the soldier complained, but he and the other soldier began constructing the travois.

As Sergeant Flynn and the others worked on the travois, White Ghost, who was not as ill as many, but who was too ill to travel with the other chiefs, sneaked away from the band. He had been seeing Crazy Wolf trailing them for most of the day, and he wanted to talk to him.

White Ghost followed the bank of the stream upstream until it curved behind the ridge where he had seen Crazy Wolf. He climbed the ridge to the top and looked down on the banks of the stream, where he saw the Indians, Sergeant Flynn, and the other two soldiers busily constructing travois.

"Crazy Wolf," he called quietly.

"I am here," Crazy Wolf answered.

White Ghost looked around and saw Crazy Wolf and five warriors coming out from behind rocks. They were on the other side of the hill and could not be seen by anyone down on the bank of the stream.

"I have watched you following us," White Ghost said.

"Have the others seen?"

"Some have seen," White Ghost said.

"The soldiers?"

"I think not," White Ghost said.

"What are the soldiers doing?"

"They are helping us," White Ghost said.

Crazy Wolf laughed. "Do you expect me to believe that the soldiers are helping you back to the others?"

"Yes," White Ghost said. "They come with us so that General Crook's soldiers do not attack us."

"General Crook is a long distance from here," Crazy Wolf said.

"Perhaps. But Joseph Two Hearts feared that he was close."

"Joseph is a squaw," Crazy Wolf said. "Where is he?"

"He remained behind," White Ghost said. "Sasha is dying, and Joseph is with her."

"Sasha is dying because the Great Spirit is angry with her for marrying a white."

"Joseph is Indian," White Ghost said.

"And the white stone turned to red," Crazy Wolf said sarcastically.

Crazy Wolf creeped up to a rock and peered down at the work party. "How many soldiers?" he asked.

"Only what you see," White Ghost said. He looked at the five warriors with Crazy Wolf; there had been nearly twenty when Crazy Wolf started out. "Where are the other warriors?"

"Dead," Crazy Wolf said flatly. "White Ghost, you go back now so the soldiers do not miss you."

"You must ride to Sitting Bull," White Ghost said. "Tell him the soldiers with us must travel in peace. I would not want them to be killed for helping us."

"I am chief of the war party," Crazy Wolf said. "I will do as I decide."

"If I do not like what you do, I will take it to the council," White Ghost said.

Crazy Wolf laughed. "You are an old man, White Ghost. The council listens to your age, not to your bravery. Go now. Return to the others as I have said."

White Ghost looked at the young chief, and his heart was sad for the hate and cruelty he saw. He knew it was useless to speak more, so he turned and worked his way back to the others, arriving just as the last travois was finished.

"All right, let's move 'em out," Sergeant Flynn called, smiling at his resolution to the problem of transportation.

Ahead, in the rocks on the ridge, Crazy Wolf and his warriors waited. There were only three soldiers, and they were not suspecting anything. It would be an easy victory.

## 17

Joseph Two Hearts rode into the village with his head bowed sadly. He was greeted by White Ghost and the five other survivors of the march of the sick, and they expressed their sorrow to him over Sasha's death.

"How many survived the march?" Joseph asked.

"Only those of us you see," White Ghost said.

"You mean the others died on the trail?" Joseph asked. "But many were not that sick."

"They did not die of the sickness," White Ghost said. "We were attacked by a soldier patrol of General Crook. There were few in the patrol, or all would have been killed."

"But I don't understand," Joseph said. "How could that be? Didn't Sergeant Flynn explain to General Crook's soldiers that Custer had given us free passage?"

White Ghost looked down at the ground.

"What is it?" Joseph said. "White Ghost, what is wrong?"

"Perhaps you should see the lodge pole of Crazy Wolf," White Ghost said.

Joseph looked at White Ghost a moment longer, then swung down from his horse and walked quickly through the camp toward the tipi of Crazy Wolf.

Crazy Wolf's tipi was painted red, and red streamers were flying from the top of the tipi around the smoke hole. Joseph looked at the lodgepole and saw among the old, dried scalps, a new one. It was fresh . . . and sandy colored. The color of Sergeant Flynn's hair.

"Crazy Wolf!" Joseph called angrily.

Crazy Wolf stepped out of his tipi and, seeing Joseph, grinned broadly.

"Ah. So you have come to admire my trophies, have you?" Crazy Wolf asked. He was eating a piece of meat, and he stood there, chewing insolently, while he talked.

"Why did you attack Flynn?" Joseph asked.

"Because he was my enemy," Crazy Wolf said. "He is white . . . I am Indian."

"But he was helping us," Joseph said. "I promised him safe passage."

"One white man does not speak to another for me," Crazy Wolf said. "All white men are my enemies, and I will attack them wherever I see them."

"Where were you when General Crook's soldiers came?" Joseph asked. "Why were you not there to fight them and protect the others?"

"After I defeated Flynn, I returned to the village to tell the council of my victory," Crazy Wolf said. "I did not know that General Crook's soldiers attacked the sick march, or I would have fought them, too, and had an even greater victory."

"You didn't stay to protect them?" Joseph asked. "After you killed their escort, you abandoned them?"

"I told you. I wanted to tell the council of my victory."

"No," Joseph said. "You left because you were afraid. You are a coward, Crazy Wolf."

Joseph spoke slowly and distinctly so there could be no chance that Crazy Wolf would misunderstand. Crazy Wolf did understand, but he wasn't alone. Others heard the words too, and they spread through the village like wildfire. This would mean a fight . . . and death for one of them.

Crazy Wolf's eyes narrowed, and he tossed the meat aside and wiped his hands in his hair. Then he walked into his tipi and reappeared a moment later with his war lance in his hand. He hurled the spear into the ground by Joseph's feet.

Joseph smiled. "I accept your challenge to a duel, Crazy Wolf," he said.

Young boys who were standing nearby left quickly to tell the others in the village. "Come," they called in great excitement. "Joseph has called Crazy Wolf a coward, and they will fight."

"It will be a grand and exciting fight," one of the others said. "They will fight to the death!"

Despite the inherent horror of such a spectacle, it was just that—a spectacle—and in the village the prospect of the thrill and excitement was so much greater than the anticipation of horror that the news was welcomed.

The news was welcomed, for other reasons as well. Both Crazy Wolf and Joseph Two Hearts were natural leaders, and both had their own following. Each group saw this as the opportunity to eliminate their enemy, and around each warrior assembled his followers to wish him luck.

One hour after the challenge was issued, the entire population of the village was assembled in a grassy field alongside the adjacent stream. A large circle had been laid out on the grass, marked with small, white stones taken from the stream bed.

Neither combatant would be allowed to leave the circle, and only they would be allowed to enter it.

Joseph was on one side of the circle, and across from him, stood Crazy Wolf. Crazy Wolf's friends were gathered around him, giving him last-minute instructions, while, around Joseph, his own friends were equally encouraging.

Two braves were massaging Joseph's arms and shoulders. Joseph, who had stripped to the waist, stared across the circle at his adversary as White Ghost spoke to him.

"Crazy Wolf has chosen the war club," White Ghost said. "It is his best weapon, and he feels it is your worst."

"I know," Joseph said.

"I can appeal to the council to choose a different weapon," White Ghost said. "One in which each of you have an equal skill. It is your right."

"No," Joseph said. "The war club will be fine."

"He is very clever with it," White Ghost cautioned. "Be careful of a trick."

"I will be careful," Joseph promised.

Sitting Bull stood with the council, and he gave the signal for the two combatants to begin.

"Aiiyeeee!!" Crazy Wolf yelled, and he jumped into the circle and danced around in a crouch, holding the club loosely and confidently in his right hand. "Now, white man," he called. "Feel terror in your heart, for I am going to kill you."

"Save your threats for the children of the village," Joseph said. "I do not tremble before the boasting of a coward."

Crazy Wolf yelled again and leaped toward Joseph. His sudden move surprised Joseph. Crazy Wolf swung at him, and he managed to parry the swing slightly so that the club caught him, not on the head, as Crazy Wolf intended, but on the shoulder. A numbing pain shot through the left side of his body, and suddenly his left arm seemed to weigh so much that he couldn't lift it.

Crazy Wolf knew that he had scored, and he leaped back into position and swung again. He had correctly reasoned that his best chance lay in advancing quickly to eliminate Joseph. But Joseph was ready for him this time, and Crazy Wolf's club whistled past without touching him.

Joseph wasn't in position to counterthrust with his club, but he was able to swing his left hand, landing a resounding slap on Crazy Wolf's face. Crazy Wolf's face turned red from the stinging blow, and the villagers laughed uproariously. Their ridicule only added to Crazy Wolf's fury. He swung again, this time more wildly than before, and Joseph slapped him again.

Now the onlookers roared with laughter, and Crazy Wolf became so furious that he lost control. The grace and agility with which he had launched his first, telling blow had given way to blind rage, and Joseph realized the advantage in keeping him off balance; at the first opportunity, he slapped him again.

Finally, like a charging bull, Crazy Wolf lunged toward Joseph, holding his club out before him, thinking only of scoring one crushing, killing blow. But Joseph sidestepped him neatly, then brought his own club crashing down on Crazy Wolf's arms.

Crazy Wolf dropped his club and went down. Quickly Joseph was on him. He pinned Crazy Wolf's arms, then raised his club for the kill. One quick blow, and Crazy Wolf would be dead. The crowd held its breath in expectation of the gruesome, morbidly fascinating scene.

Joseph held his club poised for a moment, looking into the face, and terror-filled eyes of the helpless victim pinned below him. Finally, Joseph lowered his club.

"No," he said. "There is no honor in killing a coward."

"Kill me!" Crazy Wolf shouted, realizing then that Joseph was condemning him to ridicule—a fate, in his eyes, even worse than death.

"No," Joseph said. He stood up and gazed down at the defeated and disgraced warrior. "Only the brave die in combat. You do not deserve an honorable death."

Joseph tossed his war club to one side and turned his back on Crazy Wolf, leaving him lying in the dirt.

"No!" Crazy Wolf leaped to his feet and shouted at the council. "This was a duel to the death! He cannot do this! He must kill me!"

"Your life belongs to him," Sitting Bull said. "He may take it or let you live as he wishes."

"Aiyeee!" Crazy Wolf shouted, and there, before all the villagers, he began pulling his hair out in large chunks, screaming in rage as he plucked himself bald.


"It's them, Cap'n," Sergeant Kennedy said. "Flynn, Howe, 'n' Peters. They've all three been scalped."

Tom Custer looked toward the three bloated forms, but he could get no closer. He couldn't bear to look at the men he had killed. And he felt he had killed them, as surely as if he had wielded the war clubs that struck them down, because he had trusted Joseph Two Hearts.

"Wrap them in canvas and take them back," Tom said. "We'll see that they get a decent burial at the fort."

"Are we going after Joseph Two Hearts now?" Benteen asked.

"No," Tom said. "Not until Autie gets back. Then we'll take the entire Seventh out and we'll clean out all the renegades. This time I shall go along as a willing and eager participant. I want to be there when we fiinally catch up with Mr. Two Hearts. And I especially want to be there when we hang him."

One of the privates from the detail rode up to Tom and Sergeant Kennedy.

"Sir, the bodies is all sewed up good 'n' proper," he reported.

"Load them on the ammunition wagon," Tom said. "Sergeant Kennedy, we'll return to the fort now."

"Yes, sir," Kennedy said. "Troop, prepare to mount!" he commanded.

As Tom watched the soldiers moving in well disciplined drill, he thought of Sergeant Flynn. The Army had been Flynn's life. It had provided him with a home, a family, a purpose—it was his religion. Once, during an engagement, when Tom Custer's horse had been shot from under him, Sergeant Flynn had ridden back into the fray and handed his reins to Tom.

"By your leave, sir. Take my mount." Tom shouted at Flynn to remount and leave him, when a riderless horse happened by. Flynn caught it, and, with a big grin, jumped on its back. "Now, sir, we're both mounted," he shouted.

Sergeant Flynn, who had saved his life more than once, had been killed . . . betrayed by the one man who owed him the most.

Tom thought of the court-martial that would come. He would offer nothing in his own defense.

"I, Thomas Custer, captain, U.S. Cavalry, did willfully disobey the standing orders of my commanding officer, in that I failed to return Joseph Two Hearts to Fort Lincoln to stand execution."

Tom said the words quietly, weighing their impact. Yes, he thought, they alone should be sufficient in themselves to convict him and force him out of the Army. He would draw up the charges against himself as soon as he returned to the fort.

Mercifully Sergeant Kennedy didn't speak much as they rode back to the fort. That left Tom alone with his thoughts, his own guilt, his own hates. He had only one wish remaining. He would request— beg, if need be—that he be permitted to remain on active duty long enough to capture Joseph Two Hearts. In fact, if he had to, he would remain as a private, if that was the only way he could be in on the capture of Joseph Two Hearts.

It was early evening as the troop returned to the fort. The sun was dying in a brilliant display of golds and reds, and the detail was one long silhouette as Tom led it through the gate. Tired and dispirited, the troop proceeded to the flagpole in the center of the parade ground. There Tom called for them to halt, then released them to Sergeant Kennedy. He dismounted and gave his reins over to an orderly, then walked slowly across the quadrangle toward Crimson, who, with others of the fort, had turned out to greet the returning patrol.

"We found them," Tom said quietly.

"I know," Crimson replied. "The messenger told us. Tom, I'm so sorry."

Tom took off his hat and ran his hand through his hair, then pulled at the small goatee he had grown during his brother's absence. "I was such a fool," he said. "I should have known better than to trust Joseph Two Hearts. I should have brought him back to hang."

"No," Crimson said. "Tom, I don't believe Joseph did this. He couldn't have done it."

"He did it, Crimson," Tom said. "He was in charge of the Indian sick march."

"But he couldn't have. I just know he couldn't have."

Tom uttered a small, bitter laugh. "Crimson, my dear, we were both taken in by him. Only Autie saw him for the scoundrel he is. It's too bad he wasn't here when I let Two Hearts go. He would have prevented me from making such a mistake." Tom put his hat back on. "I shall have to face up to him as soon as he returns."

Crimson sighed broadly. "That will not be too long, I'm afraid," she said.

"What? Why, what do you mean?"

"They are back. At least, they are as far as Bismark. Captain Benteen went into town to fetch them. They should be here by supper."

## 18

"Unacceptable. Totally unacceptable!"

George Custer was sitting behind his desk, holding the warrant in which Tom had charged himself with disobeying a standing order by not arresting Joseph Two Hearts and with permitting a band of hostiles to trespass unmolested on restricted territory, a dereliction of duty that resulted in the deaths of Sergeant Flynn and privates Howe and Peters.

Custer tossed the papers into the wastebasket by his desk.

"What are you doing, General?" Tom asked.

"What does it look like I'm doing?" Custer asked. "I'm throwing this nonsense away."

Tom started to reach for the wastebasket to recover the papers, but Custer kicked the basket, sending its contents scattering across the room.

"Leave it alone!" Custer roared.

"I don't want preferential treatment," Tom said angrily.

"Dammit, Tom," Custer said. "Everything you did, you did as the commanding officer. All right, maybe your judgment was wrong—but it was a judgment, not dereliction of duty. If every commander who had ever made a mistake in judgment was court-martialed, there would be very few commanders left."

"But my judgment was colored by personal considerations," Tom protested.

"All judgment is colored by personal consideration," Custer said. "You remember the stink when I returned to Fort Riley during the epidemic to check on my family? It was my judgment as commander that I could go. That judgment was colored by personal considerations."

"It also resulted in a court-martial and a year's suspension from active duty," Tom said. "I deserve no less punishment."

"No," Custer said. "It isn't the same thing at all. I merely used that as an example. Tom . . . I'll not approve this list of charges, and I'll not prefer charges myself. As far as I am concerned, this incident is over."

"All right, Autie," Tom said, contritely. "But it isn't quite over."

"What do you mean?"

"Joseph Two Hearts," Tom said. "He's coming back to Fort Lincoln, and he's going to hang."

Custer smiled. "On that point, I agree with you," he said. "And that brings me to the news."

"What news?"

"Glorious news, Tom. The War Department has authorized one all-out campaign. We are going to sweep through the Indian territories and clean them up once and for all. Any Indians who oppose us will be crushed. Those who won't go back to their reservations here will be shipped to Florida. And Tom, the vanguard of the entire operation is to be the Seventh Cavalry."

"What does General Terry say to all that?" Tom asked.

"General Terry has already given it his blessing," Custer said. He hopped up and rubbed his hands together excitedly, then walked over to the window and looked out at the troopers drilling on the quadrangle. He turned to look back at Tom, a big smile on his face.

"The truth is, Tom," he went on, "Terry doesn't know a damned thing about fighting Indians, and he's admitted as much to the War Department. That leaves me in charge out here."

"Autie, after this campaign you'll get your generalcy back," Tom suggested.

"Generalcy, hell," Custer said. He tugged at his yellow beard. "After this summer campaign, Tom, I will be nominated for president of the United States."

"Autie, are you certain?" Tom asked.

"I was told that by no less a figure than the Honorable James G. Blaine," Custer said. "For he himself will make the nominating speech."

Tom smiled broadly and reached out to take his brother's hand.

"Autie," he said. "You, president of the United States. What a staggering thought."

"You can see then, can't you, how unwise it would be to have the suggestion of a scandal now among any of the Custers. We must all unite, Tom. You, Boston, Libbie, Maggie, and me. All of us. And, this is no time to be bringing in outsiders . . . if you know what I mean."

"No," Tom said. "No, I'm not sure I do know what you mean."

"Tom, Tom." Custer smiled, putting his hand on his brother's shoulder. "I know you got lonesome here while Libbie and I were back East. And I know that there was someone here who was interesting

171

and pretty to help keep the lonesomeness from over-taking you."

"You are talking about Crimson, aren't you?"

"Crimson is a pretty girl, Tom. She's more than that . . . she's a beautiful girl. Under other circumstances, I might be giving you a run for your money in vying for her attention. But, Tom, we must close now. Crimson Royal doesn't fit into the Custer plans."

"I see," Tom said.

"I hope you do."

"Autie . . . I've asked her to marry me."

"Have you now? Well, then, you shall just have to get out of it."

"I don't want to get out of it. I love her."

"Tom, do you love her more than honor, duty, and country?"

"Well, I—"

"Think about it, Tom. Think about the great destiny that waits for me . . . for all of us. Could you throw that away for this girl?"

"Autie, you don't know what you are asking of me," Tom cried.

"Yes, I do know," Autie said. "I'm asking the supreme sacrifice, and I know that isn't fair. But I am asking it, Tom."

"What . . . what do you want me to do?"

"I want you to sever all relations with Crimson Royal. If you'd like, I can send you out on a mission tonight, and by the time you return, she will be gone."

"No," Tom said. "No, that wouldn't be right. I'll take care of it myself."

"Good man, Tom," Custer said. He smiled broadly. "Some day, an historian will write a book about the Custer legacy, and there will be a special place in it for the sacrifice you are making today."

* * *

"Do you like it?" Libbie asked, twisting and turning before the mirror, admiring her new dress. "I made it from material Autie bought me for Christmas."

"It's beautiful," Crimson said. "It's as lovely a reception toilette as I have ever seen."

"I saw it in *Harper's Bazaar*," Libbie said. "Oh, I brought the magazine back with me in case you wanted to look through it." Libbie handed the magazine to Crimson.

"Why, thank you, Libbie," Crimson said, surprised by Libbie's generosity.

"My dress is on page three-seventeen," Libbie said. "Read the description aloud as I look in the mirror, would you, please?"

"Of course," Crimson said. She found the place in the magazine and cleared her throat. "Are you ready?"

"Of course," Libbie said, laughing. "I'm told that in Paris they do this very thing. Models parade around in dresses before prospective buyers while the dresses are described aloud."

"Yes," Crimson said. "It is called a fashion show. I have seen such things, even in New York."

"Well, now we shall have one in Fort Lincoln. Please go on."

Crimson began to read the description of Libbie's dress.

"This stylish dress is of black faille. The trained skirt is trimmed high up with alternate wide and narrow gathered flounces, surmounted by a ruche. The polonaise is in the princesse design, that is, one piece in front; the back separates about five inches below the waist and falls square on the sides. The intervening space is filled with large loops of faille ribbon, which form a cascade of trimming. The bottom of the polonaise, the sleeves, and large double pockets are trimmed with several rows of jet gal-

173

loon, which also form a square bertha on the waist. The front of the polonaise is edged with fringe."

Crimson finished reading and looked up at Libbie, who had been turning and flouncing with the description, and was now smiling broadly.

For the moment, Crimson forgot the circumstances that had made Libbie her antagonist. She saw Libbie only as a rather remarkable woman who lived a life of hardship and deprivation on the wild frontier, yet by the sheer force of her personality, brought some semblance of civilization to a remote military post. There was much about Libbie Custer to admire, Crimson had to admit.

"I am so looking forward to the dinner tonight," Libbie said. "It has been a long time since Autie and I entertained our little Fort Lincoln family. All the senior officers and their wives will be here tonight."

"It has been dull here without you," Crimson said. "And speaking for myself as well as the others, I can say this is an event we have been looking forward to for a long, long time."

The table was set for sixteen. The combined treasures of the Custer family and the other officers' families yielded enough silver, crystal, and china to do credit to any formal dinner, anywhere. Adorning the menu were delicacies recently brought back by the Custers: champagne, German chocolates, and tinned brandied peaches. For dinner they were served French onion soup and curried lamb. The meal and the conversations were undertaken with great relish. Then Tom stood up and cleared his throat, holding his glass high in a toast.

Crimson reached over and squeezed her father's hand. She knew that Tom was about to make the announcement of their engagement. But she wished that they had spoken of it again beforehand, for the truth was . . . she wasn't certain she wanted to go through with it.

Tom tapped lightly on his crystal goblet, and the clear, melodious ring summoned everyone's attention. He looked at his brother and sister-in-law, then at Crimson. But his eyes, instead of glowing with pride, were shadowed by shame. Why? Crimson wondered. What was going on?

"Ladies and officers of the Seventh," Tom said. "First of all, let me say how glad I am to have General Custer back, and to relinquish command of the Seventh to its rightful commander."

After the respectful applause subsided, Tom cleared his throat and went on.

"My brother has returned with glorious news, which he has allowed me the privilege of passing on to you. Commencing next month, the Seventh Cavalry will return to the field for an all-out campaign to rid the Black Hills once and for all of the dangers posed by hostiles. Ladies and gentlemen, we will take to the field with the greatest army since the Civil War, and the Seventh Cavalry will be the vanguard of that army."

"Hear, hear," Reno said, applauding heartily, and the others quickly joined in.

"I am pleased also to say that my brother has given me the special task of finding Joseph Two Hearts and returning him here to hang. That is one task I am undertaking with the greatest of pleasure."

"Oh," Crimson said, and the others at the table glanced toward her. She looked quickly at her plate, her cheeks flaming in embarrassment.

"I'm sorry, Miss Royal," Tom went on. "I know you and your father feel you owe your life to him. But Sergeant Flynn felt the same way, and it cost him his life. Joseph Two Hearts is a traitor and a murderer. And we will bring him here and hang him."

"Tom, I . . . I can't watch such a thing," Crimson said.

"I know," Tom said. He swallowed and looked down toward his plate for a moment, as if summoning the courage to go on. "That's why special arrangements are being made for you and your father."

"Special arrangements? What are you talking about?" Crimson asked. "What do you mean?"

"Crimson, dear, this is no place to talk about it," Libbie said. "Such things would be better discussed in privacy, don't you think?"

"Tom Custer, I want to know what you are talking about!" Crimson demanded. "What special arrangements have you made which can only be discussed in privacy?"

"Crimson, I . . ." Tom began, then looked at Libbie with a helpless expression.

"Crimson, dear," Libbie said. "The General and I feel, and Tom concurs, that it is selfish of us to keep you here any longer. A remote military post is no place for a young, vivacious, talented girl such as you. And the world is being denied your father's talent. We're sending you back to New York, and oh, how I envy you! I would give anything to return to New York . . . words can't describe how lovely it was this winter."

"But no!" Crimson said. She looked first at Libbie, and then at Tom, in absolute shock.

"Crimson, be reasonable," Tom said. "I will be in the field for the entire summer. I can't expect you to wait here, can I?"

"Of course you can't, Tom," Libbie said, answering for Crimson. "It would be extremely selfish of you to even consider it."

176

Crimson stood up quickly and pushed her chair back, her napkin clutched in her hand. Tears welled in her eyes and she threw the napkin at Tom.

"I *hate* you, Tom Custer!"

## 19

"Be honest with me, darling," Artemus said to his daughter. "Is your heart truly broken . . . or is your pride merely wounded?"

Artemus was comforting his daughter in her quarters shortly after the disagreeable scene that had taken place in the dining room. Crimson, who was patting her eyes lightly with a perfumed handkerchief, looked at her father with a surge of appreciation for his understanding.

"What a fool I must have appeared," she said.

"No, dear, not at all," Artemus assured her. "The fool is Tom Custer. Fool and coward as well."

"Coward? Father, whatever Tom Custer is, he isn't a coward. Why, he's been mentioned in the dispatches even more than the General."

"Coward I said and coward I meant," Artemus said. "He lacks the courage to stand up to his brother for the one thing he wants most in the world."

"Perhaps so," Crimson said with a sigh. She smiled through her tears. "But I am an even bigger coward, for I lacked the courage to tell Tom Custer that I didn't want to marry him. I would have gone through with it."

"Then your heart isn't broken," Artemus said.

"No, Father," Crimson said.

Artemus smiled broadly and rubbed his hands together. "Then perhaps you will take heart at the news I have for you."

"What news?"

"Tomorrow, we are to be escorted into Bismark, where we are supposed to catch the train East."

"I know," Crimson said. "But why should I take heart over such information?"

"Because we aren't going back East," Artemus said.

"We aren't?"

"No. Yesterday I spoke with Mr. Bell of the Bismark Livery Barn. He has agreed to sell us a team of horses, a wagon, and all the supplies we will need to travel through the Indian territories. Now I ask you, do you still want to go?"

"Father, I don't know," Crimson said. "You heard them at dinner tonight. They are planning a major operation against the Indians."

"All the more reason, it seems to me, why we should go while we have the opportunity. Daughter, this may very well be the last year the Indians will follow their old ways. Don't you see? If we don't go now, the chance will be forever lost. Their culture will have disappeared." Artemus looked at Crimson, and his eyes narrowed. "Unless you believe, as does Tom Custer, that Joseph Two Hearts murdered Sergeant Flynn."

"No," Crimson said. "I could never believe that."

"Then our assurance of safe passage by Sitting Bull should still protect us."

"You're right," Crimson said. "You're right. If we don't go now, we will lose the opportunity. And we do have Sitting Bull's promise of safety. All right, Father, we'll go."

Artemus smiled broadly, then kissed his daughter on the forehead. "Then get your things in order, dear," he said. "And get a good night's sleep. For tomorrow, at long last, we shall begin our adventure."

After Artemus left, Crimson packed her pencils, brushes, paints, and some of her drawings in progress. She packaged the finished work to send to Gideon in New York. She started to destroy several drawings of Tom, Libbie, and Autie, which were not intended for public viewing, then decided instead to leave them. It will be my parting gesture to the Custers, she thought as she spread them out on the table.

Crimson had expected Tom to come by to offer some apology, or at least an explanation. But he didn't, and Crimson, rather than being upset, was glad. For in truth, she had no wish to face him again tonight.

Despite the trauma of the evening, Crimson slept well that night and awakened the next morning, fresh and ready for a new adventure. One of the soldiers from the detail came to help her with her belongings.

"Ma'am, this here pitcher, it's one o' Sarn't Flynn, ain't it?" the soldier asked.

"Yes," Crimson said.

The soldier picked up the drawing and looked at it. "You know, Sarn't Flynn always wanted to be in a pitcher. He tole' me about it onct, when we was lookin' at that big paintin' over to the Sutlers' Store."

"Would you like to have that sketch?" Crimson asked.

The soldier broke into a large smile, and his eyes gleamed excitedly. "Yes'm, I truly would," he said.

"Then it's yours."

"Thank you, ma'am." The soldier stuck the drawing under his tunic, then picked up Crimson's trunk and swung it onto his shoulder. "Thanks a lot."

Crimson followed the soldier outside and saw Libbie standing on the boardwalk in front of her own house next door.

"Soldier, you go on and load Miss Royal's trunk," Libbie said. "I wish to speak to her alone."

"Yes, ma'am," the soldier said, and trudged on toward the carriage, which was hitched up and ready to go.

"You didn't stop by for breakfast this morning," Libbie said.

"I wasn't hungry," Crimson replied.

Libbie looked at Crimson, and for just a moment, Crimson saw a hint of sadness in her eyes.

"Crimson, my dear, I hope one day you will find it in your heart to forgive me."

"I'm sure you did what you felt was right," Crimson said.

"Yes," Libbie replied. She walked over and put her hand lightly on Crimson's arm. "One day you will thank me," she said. "For truly, dear, you were not meant for the life of a Custer wife."

"Perhaps not," Crimson said. "But it should have been my decision to make."

"Did you have the courage?" Libbie asked, and the truth of her remark caused Crimson to look down in quick shame. "No," Libbie said. "I didn't think so."

"Goodbye," Crimson said and started toward the carriage.

"Please, Crimson, write to us from New York," Libbie said. "You've been here long enough now to know how lonely it gets, and how we hunger for some news from the East. Promise me when you get to New York you will write."

Crimson wanted to tell her that she wasn't going to New York, but she was afraid that if she did, Libbie would tell her husband, and he would find some way to stop them. Instead she said, "I'll write when I get to New York," enjoying at least the satisfaction of knowing that would not be for some time, yet.

"Daughter, we must be going," Artemus called from inside the coach.

"I must be going," Crimson said.

"Godspeed," Libbie said and spontaneously threw her arms around Crimson.

Crimson felt Libbie against her, and suddenly she realized the woman's terrible vulnerability. Despite her dominating personality, despite her position as the commanding officer's wife, despite her self-appointed role as queen of the Custer Dynasty, she was still a small, frail woman, pitted against the harsh vastness of the West. And despite everything, Crimson felt a sudden surge of pity for the woman who at all costs had to maintain a brave front.

"Libbie, I really will keep in touch," Crimson said, and a lump came to her throat as she saw that Libbie's own eyes were sheened with tears.

Crimson hurried across the quadrangle and climbed in the coach. She heard the detail sergeant order his men to mount, the coach driver whistled at his horses, and the coach started to move.

"Hold it!" someone shouted. "Driver, hold that team!"

Crimson looked out the window to see Tom Custer running toward her.

"Whoa," the driver said, and the coach stopped.

Tom ran to the coach and opened the door.

"Crimson, I can't let you go like this," he said, his face reflecting his anguish. "I don't care what Autie says. I love you, and I want to marry you."

"Tom, dear Tom," Crimson said. She put her

hands in his. "So you've found your courage at last, have you?"

"Yes," Tom said. "Crimson, I don't care if I'm court-martialed, or even kicked out of the service. I won't let you go. I can't let you go. Autie can go hang for all I care. He wants to be president? Let him, if he can. But not if it means I have to give you up."

And now, buoyed by Tom's courage, Crimson found her own, for at last she had the strength to tell him that she didn't want to marry him.

"Tom, you are a dear, dear man, and I shall never forget you," she said.

"Never forget me?" Tom replied, puzzled by her words. "Crimson, that sounds like you are planning on leaving anyway."

"I am leaving, Tom."

"But why? I told you I don't care what Autie or Libbie or anyone has to say. Don't you understand, Crimson? I'm asking you to stay here and marry me, now."

"I know you are, Tom," Crimson said. "But I can't marry you."

Tom started to speak, but Crimson held her hand up gently to his lips.

"It has nothing to do with Autie or Libbie," she said. "Or perhaps it does. But not because she is forcing it, but because she is right. Tom, we simply are not right for each other. I could never lead the life of an army officer's wife."

"I'll resign my commission," Tom said.

"And do what?"

"Anything," Tom said desperately. "I could be an engineer, I'm trained for that. Or I could get a job as an administrator somewhere. I've experience in directing men."

"No," Crimson said.

184

"But why? I love you, Crimson. Don't you believe that?"

"Yes, I do believe that," Crimson said. "But there is something you love even more, Tom Custer. You love honor, and if I married you, you would forever feel your honor stained. We couldn't be happy with that hanging over us."

Tom opened his mouth, but no words came out. Finally he sighed and looked into Crimson's eyes. At that moment a chill ran through her, for in his eyes she saw sadness, not just over the termination of their relationship, but over the hand which fate had dealt him. And, for some inexplicable reason, she saw a suggestion of tragedy. She couldn't understand it, it wasn't even a conscious thought—but subconsciously, she saw a hollow glimpse of doom.

"Goodbye," Tom finally said. He stepped back and looked up at the driver. "You may go," he said.

The driver whistled at the team, and the coach jerked forward again.

"Open the gates!" the driver called, and as the coach rolled through the gates, Crimson leaned out the window to look back at the little fort that had been her home for the last seven months. She felt a small pang of remorse over leaving. She saw Tom standing there, watching the coach pull away, and she also saw several dozen other soldiers busy at their details, a soldier ballet in blue.

And she saw General George Armstrong Custer standing on the front porch of his quarters with his arm around his wife's shoulders, waving goodbye.

Then the gates were closed and the scene was blotted out forever.

To the east of town, the train was beginning to build up speed. A long smear of black smoke stretched up into the crystal clear blue sky, visible for miles across the plains. Even the soldiers in the lookout towers at the fort could see the thin stream of smoke, and most thought of the beautiful young girl and her father who had been so much a part of the fort life through the winter and were now returning to New York.

What they didn't know was that at that very moment, Crimson and her father were not on the train but were closing their deal with Gibson Bell at the Livery Barn.

"Now mind, if the soldiers catch you, you'll not be telling them I know'd where you was a'goin'," Bell was saying. "General Custer'd boil me in oil iffen he know'd what I was doin'."

"Your secret is safe with us," Artemus assured him. "Just be sure we get good animals and a sound wagon."

"You're gettin' the best I got 'n' that's a fact," Bell said. "Why this rig could pull you all the way back to St. Louis if you was of a mind to go."

Bell took them behind the barn and there, as Bell had promised, were two fine-looking horses and a sturdy wagon.

"I got all the provisions you asked for, too," Bell said. "Flour, bacon, coffee, beans, a rifle, and bullets."

"I didn't ask for a gun," Artemus said.

"I know you didn't," Bell said. "But I figured as maybe you'd just forgot, so I throwed it on in."

"I didn't forget," Artemus said. "I just don't want one. I'm going out there to paint the Indians, not to shoot them."

Bell, grumbling, took the rifle out of the wagon. "It's your funeral," he said. "But you'd never catch me out there without a gun, that's for sure."

"It is likely, Mr. Bell, that we'll never catch you out there at all," Artemus said laconically, as he paid the money over to the liveryman for the rig.

"You're mighty right on that, sir," Bell said without embarrassment. "You're right as rain. I ain't in no hurry to get myself kilt, or my scalp lifted, and that's for sure 'n' certain."

"Well," Artemus said. "Climb aboard, Crimson, and we'll get underway."

## 20

The Indian territory was green with spring and running with streams swollen and sparkling with the melted snows. To the west, a ridge of purple mountains thrust into the sky.

Crimson and her father watched as the first pink fingers of dawn spread over their camp. The last morning star made a bright pinpoint of light in the southern sky, and the coals from the campfire of the night before were still glowing. Artemus threw chunks of dried wood onto the fire, and soon tongues of flame were licking against the bottom of the coffee pot. A rustle of feathers caused Artemus and Crimson to look up just in time to see a golden hawk diving on its prey. The hawk soared back into the air carrying a tiny scrub mouse, which was kicking fearfully in the hawk's claws. A prairie dog scurried quickly from one hole to another, alert against the fate that had befallen the mouse.

Artemus poured them both a cup of steaming black coffee and they had to blow on it before they could drink it. They watched the sun turn from gold to white, then stream brightly down onto the plains.

Though Artemus and Crimson didn't realize it, they had been watched since before dawn. An Indian, his face lined with age and experience, sat quietly behind a rock outcropping, studying them. Finally he stood up and walked into the camp. His sudden appearance startled Crimson, and she gasped.

"I am White Ghost," the Indian said.

"I am Artemus Royal, and this is my daughter, Crimson."

"I know," White Ghost said. "I was in the camp when Crazy Wolf brought you to us."

"Then you know that Sitting Bull promised us safe passage," Artemus said.

"That was before the snows came," White Ghost said. "Much has happened since then."

"Yes," Artemus said.

"The soldiers have killed many of my people," White Ghost said.

"I know," Artemus said. "But we are not soldiers."

"Do you have gun?"

"No."

"I will see."

White Ghost began to poke through the wagon. He came across several drawings, and held them out admiringly.

"You have many pictures of soldiers," White Ghost said.

"Yes. We were held at the fort by the soldiers and couldn't come to the Indian territories to paint Indians as we told Sitting Bull. But now we have left the soldiers."

White Ghost, who was looking through the pictures, came across one of Sergeant Flynn and studied it for a moment.

"Flynn was good man," he said.

"Then why was he killed?" Crimson asked. "He was trying to help you."

"Indians have bad men, same like whites," White Ghost said. He put the pictures down and walked over to sit on a rock. He folded his arms across his chest and looked straight at Artemus. "Now you make picture of White Ghost," he said.

Artemus smiled broadly. "White Ghost, we would be delighted to."

"Wait," White Ghost said. He pulled a pistol from his belt and held it in front of him.

"Do you want me to do the preliminary sketch, Father?" Crimson asked, when she saw Artemus wince with pain as he began drawing.

"Yes," Artemus said, rubbing his hand.

"Can woman do this?" White Ghost asked, pointing at Crimson.

"Yes," Artemus said.

White Ghost looked at Crimson with an awed expression.

"I did not know women could do such things," he said.

Crimson's strokes were quick and sure, and within a few moments she had created a picture of White Ghost, a proud, dignified warrior; she had even managed to capture the expression of wonder in his eyes as he watched her work.

"This is good," White Ghost said. "I keep."

"White Ghost, will you tell the other Indians to let us travel in peace?" Artemus asked.

"Yes," White Ghost said.

"Thank you."

"It does not matter," White Ghost said. "The good Indians will let you travel in peace even if I say nothing. The bad Indians will be bad, even if Sitting Bull asks them to be good. So it does not matter what I say."

"Thanks, anyway," Artemus said.

191

* * *

So Joseph thought, Crimson is still here, and now she is in the Black Hills.

Joseph felt a quick surge of heat as he recalled that night in the fort. He had never quite gotten over the strange feelings she had evoked in him, and thinking about it now, he felt guilty, as if he had betrayed his people . . . as if he had betrayed Sasha.

With every nerve in his body, Joseph wanted to ride out into the territories and find her; he wanted to tell her that he had never forgotten that moment, and to ask if she had.

Perhaps she had. He could not expect her to remember him after all this time.

Joseph looked again at the drawing of White Ghost, who told him that the girl had done it. That meant that he was holding the very paper she had only recently held. Joseph lifted it to his nose and sniffed it, as if to recall her scent. But he couldn't.

"Joseph," Fool Dog called, snapping Joseph out of his thoughts. "Sitting Bull is holding a council now, and he asked you to come."

"I will come," Joseph said.

Several Indians were squatting around the campfire when Joseph arrived, many of whom he had never seen before. He was surprised to see so many strangers.

"Is he white?" one of the strange Indians asked of Sitting Bull, pointing to Joseph.

"He was white," Sitting Bull said. "Now he is red."

The simple explanation was enough to satisfy the Indian and the others, and no one expressed any hostility toward Joseph as Sitting Bull began the conference.

"I will tell you a story," Sitting Bull said simply.

"During the geese flying time, Crook's soldiers made war on the camp of Two Moon, the Cheyenne chief, and Low Dog, the Ogalala chief. They came in the night while the people slept, and they killed many and set fire to the tipis and burned food and blankets. They also stole many horses, but Two Moon, who is a very brave chief, stole them back."

Sitting Bull pointed to Two Moon as he spoke, and the others smiled and congratulated him for his cleverness and bravery in recovering the horses.

"Now, Two Moon has something he wishes to speak about."

Two Moon stood up and looked over the assembled faces.

"Soon, I think, there will be many more soldiers and more war," Two Moon said. "I have sent scouts to watch the soldier camp at Fort Lincoln. There Yellow Hair has stored much feed for horses and loaded many wagons. Soon, I think, he will come into the Black Hills to make war against all Indian people."

"But are we not safe here?" one of the Indians asked. "We are beyond the Powder River, and Yellow Hair said the soldiers would not come here."

"That was before," Two Moon said. "But there have been many raids by Indians against the whites who look for gold, and now no place is safe."

"But we have not made such raids," the protesting Indian said. "The soldiers should find those who make the raids, not us."

"Who is making the raids?" another asked.

"It is Crazy Wolf," Sitting Bull said. "He seeks a way to rid himself of shame."

"He is causing us much trouble," Two Moon said. "You should tell him to stop."

"I have told him," Sitting Bull said. "But my words mean nothing to him."

"But you are a chief," Two Moon protested. "Can you not stop him by saying so?"

"Can I stop the rain just because I am a chief?" Sitting Bull asked.

"No."

"Neither can I stop Crazy Wolf. He has plucked the hair from his head and does not know reason now. Evil spirits have stolen his senses."

"Then surely he will anger the soldiers enough so that they will come for us," Two Moon said. "I think we should not wait. I think we should attack the soldier fort now."

"We cannot," another said. "There are too many soldiers there, and they have thick walls and large guns which shoot twice, one time in the gun and again when the great bullet hits the ground."

"Then if we do not attack the soldier fort, what can we do?"

"We can attack all whites who are in the Black Hills," another said. "All miners, travelers, and farmers who are in the Black Hills will feel fear of us."

"No," Joseph said, speaking for the first time.

"Oh, the one who was once white will speak now," one of the strangers said. "And will you ask us not to attack whites?"

"Not all whites," Joseph said. "There are two, a father and daughter, and they are doing no harm."

"Do you speak of the two who draw pictures?" Two Moon asked.

"Yes," Joseph said. "They are no harm to us. We should not harm them."

"I say *all* whites," another said.

"Sitting Bull, did you not tell them they could travel and draw their pictures in peace?" Joseph appealed.

"White Ghost, you spoke with them," Sitting Bull said. "What are your words?"

"I looked for a gun but found none," White Ghost said. "They travel only to draw pictures. They do not bring the road, they do not dig for yellow metal, they do not kill the buffalo, they do not put up fence. They capture only the way things seem to the eye. They will not harm us, and we should not harm them."

"Then we shall not," Sitting Bull said. "For now, I say we shall not harm any whites. Perhaps if we show the soldiers we can live in peace, they will allow us to do so."

"But they are readying for war," Two Moon insisted. "I know this. I say, let them make war. I have fought already. My people have been killed, my horses stolen. I am satisfied to fight."

"Perhaps they will make war only against Crazy Wolf," Sitting Bull said. "I have a plan which will keep them from making war against us."

"What is your plan?" Two Moon asked.

"The Cheyennes, the Oglalas, the Minneconjous, and the Hunkpapas will camp together. Also, the Brules, the Sans Arcs, and the Blackfoot. All nations will come together as one great Nation. We will be as many as the blades of grass, and then the soldiers will dare not attack."

"We will try your plan," Two Moon said. "But I think the soldiers will attack anyway."

"If they do, they will see the strength of many," Sitting Bull said.

The Indians began to discuss how so many Indians would share the water and grass and buffalo and deer, but Joseph didn't listen. He had heard enough to know that Crimson would be safe, and that was all he cared about for the moment.

## 21

It couldn't be going better, Crimson thought. For nearly a month now, she and her father had traveled unmolested through the Indian country. They visited many small Indian settlements, and everywhere it was as if they were expected. The Indians turned out to pose for them and offered them food and shelter. They were so cooperative and friendly that it didn't seem possible to Crimson that there was any danger. She couldn't understand how the army thought the Indians were hostile.

But though she and her father's relationship with the Indians was peaceful, the war between the Indians and the soldiers had already begun. Cavalry and Indian patrols stumbled across each other, and the result was always a clash. After one such clash, in which three Indians were killed, the soldier patrol took something off the body of one of the Indians, and they brought it back to Fort Lincoln to show to General Custer.

"You sent for me, Autie?" Tom asked. He had

been at drill when word came that his brother wanted to see him in his headquarters right away.

Custer was sitting behind his desk with one arm folded across his chest and the other cupping his chin, stroking his golden beard.

"Do you recognize this, Tom?" Custer asked. He slid a paper across the desk, and Tom picked it up.

Tom smiled broadly. "Sure, I recognize it," he said. "It's a drawing by Crimson. Where did you get it?"

"Tell my brother where you got it, Lieutenant Ward."

The young lieutenant cleared his throat nervously. "I took it off the body of a Sioux warrior, sir," the Lieutenant said. "In fact, it is a drawing of that warrior."

"It must have been one she did when she was in the camp," Tom suggested.

"Look at the bottom of the drawing," Autie suggested.

Tom looked where Custer had indicated. There, printed in neat, block letters, was the legend: Royal, Black Hills, 1876.

"Oh, my God!" Tom said. "Crimson is out there! Autie, we have to go get her!"

"Why?"

"Why? Because she could be killed!"

"She and her father knew the risks," Autie said coldly. "I will not risk a patrol on a rescue mission, particularly when the people my soldiers would be risking their lives for don't even want to be rescued."

"You don't have to send anyone," Tom said. "I'll go and take some volunteers with me."

"No," Custer said. "I can't allow that."

"Autie . . ." Tom stopped and looked over at Lieutenant Ward, who was taking it all in with curious eyes and ears. "Uh, Lieutenant Ward, would you excuse us, please? I'd like to talk to the General in privacy."

"Yes, sir," Lieutenant Ward said, snapping a salute, then executed a sharp about-face and left the room.

After the lieutenant was gone, Tom turned back to face his brother. He took a breath, as if composing himself, then spoke, not angrily but sincerely.

"Autie, because of you I did not marry Crimson. It was a supreme sacrifice, you said. You were right, it was a supreme sacrifice, and I have not forgiven myself, or you, for that yet. But that was partly my own fault, for it was my cowardice that allowed you to force such an unhappy decision upon me. But I will be damned, sir, if I will let Crimson wander around in hostile territory, in danger of being killed, because I am too much of a coward to do anything about it. I will go after her whether I have your permission or not."

"You would go despite my orders to the contrary?" Custer asked.

"Yes," Tom said.

"If you do, I shall court-martial you, Captain, and that is a promise," Custer snapped.

Tom smiled, a slow, ironic smile. "General, do you really think you can frighten me with threat of a court-martial? Don't you think I know you wouldn't dare do such a thing and jeopardize your political future? How would it look if you court-martialed your own brother because he went into the Black Hills to try and save America's most famous artist and his daughter?"

Autie sighed. He was defeated and he knew it. He ran his hand roughly through his hair and sighed again.

"All right," he finally said. "You may take two

companies and go after them. But I want you back in this fort within two weeks. Do you understand me, mister?"

"Thank you," Tom said, smiling broadly and reaching out to grab his brother's hand. "But, Autie, I don't want two companies, or even one. I want five good men. That's all. Just five men."

"Five men?" Custer sputtered. "But that's preposterous!"

"Five men," Tom repeated. "And I'll select them. We can travel fast, light, and, most of all, unobserved. There's no way I could conceal two companies."

"All right," Custer finally said, exasperated that Tom had had his way on every issue. "All right. But remember what I said about two weeks, Tom. I want you back then."

"I'll be back," Tom promised. He turned and started out the door, then he stopped and looked back toward Custer. "And when I get back, Autie, I propose to marry Crimson immediately, if she will have me. Nothing you or Libbie can possibly say will dissuade me."

"We won't try to interfere," Custer promised.

Tom left the headquarters sick at heart and frightened at the thought of Crimson and her father alone in the Black Hills, but elated that for the first time in his life he had won a victory over his brother.

Tom told Sergeant Kennedy that he would be going on a rescue expedition to bring Crimson and her father out of the Black Hills, and he asked for five volunteers to meet him at the stables in thirty minutes. Then he went into his quarters to ready his field gear.

Tom looked around the quarters that had been Crimson's while she was at the post, and he could almost feel her presence. How often he had wished that he had not listened to his brother. If he had stood up to him earlier, Crimson wouldn't be in danger now. And, what's more, she would be his wife.

Of course, he had finally gone to her in the carriage and asked her to stay and marry him, she had refused. But what could he expect? After all, he had broken her heart and humiliated her at dinner the evening before. No, he was a fool, and he had let his one chance slip by him. But if he got another chance, he wouldn't let it go by again.

When Tom walked out to the stables a short time later, he was amazed by what he saw. There weren't five volunteers; there were nearly five hundred! He was flabbergasted.

"Sergeant Kennedy, what is this?" he asked. "I said five."

"Everyone in your battalion volunteered, sir," Kennedy said. "If word had gotten around to the regiment, I believe they would have volunteered as well."

Tom looked at the men, all eager and dressed out in full field gear. Never in his life had he felt greater pride in the Seventh Cavalry than at this moment. He stood there, unable to speak; finally he swung up onto his horse.

"I can't pick them, Sergeant Kennedy," he said. "I would be honored if you would select five men for me."

"Four men, sir," Kennedy said. "For I shall be going with you."

"Very well. I'll wait outside the gate," Tom said.

Tom rode through the gate and waited for a few moments, then was joined by Sergeant Kennedy and four other troopers. He nodded at them; then, without a word, they rode off into the hills.

"You know, daughter," Artemus was saying, "a

201

couple more weeks and I think we shall have everything we need."

"I know," Crimson said. "It has been wonderful. The Indians have cooperated so well, and we have drawings of the villages, of the hunt, oh, and I just love this series on the children," she said, holding up a couple of the sketches. The other drawings were propped up against the side of the wagon that served not only as their transportation but as their living quarters and working area as well.

"Here come some more," Artemus said, pointing to a group of horsemen who were approaching the wagon. "They'll be wanting their pictures drawn."

Crimson laughed. "You can't say we haven't been getting cooperation from the Indians, can you? In fact, quite the opposite. They are so anxious to have their pictures drawn that they keep coming to us, so that we have a difficult time depicting them in their villages."

"Well, we can't turn them down," Artemus said. He looked around. "Now, what happened to those charcoal sticks?"

"Oh, I put them in the wagon," Crimson said. "I'll get them."

Crimson climbed up onto the wagon, opened the canvas cover, and went inside. The canvas allowed only a shaded light through so that searching for the charcoal drawing sticks was difficult. She began looking through the blankets, papers, baskets, boxes, and other paraphernalia.

"I said I put them in here," she called out to her father. "But I tell you, I can't find them."

She felt the wagon tip as someone climbed on.

"You don't have to come up here, Father. I'll find them."

The curtain parted and Crimson looked around.

There, grinning obscenely, was the painted face and bald head of Crazy Wolf!

Crimson felt a knife of fear stab into her heart, and she gasped. But she fought the urge to scream and finally managed to regain some measure of composure.

"Crazy Wolf," she said. "Have you come to have your drawing made?"

"Come see," Crazy Wolf said, still grinning hideously. He jumped back down onto the ground, and Crimson, puzzled by his strange behavior, followed him.

"What is it, Crazy Wolf?" Crimson asked. "Why are you acting so strangely?"

Crazy Wolf made a proud, sweeping gesture with his hand. And then Crimson saw the handiwork of which Crazy Wolf was so proud. Her father, with an arrow in his heart, lay sprawled on the ground, his eyes open but unseeing. His face wore a look of surprise and disbelief.

Crimson felt the world spinning, then everything went black.


"Cap'n, these are wagon tracks," Sergeant Kennedy said. "What would wagon tracks be doin' out here?"

"It has to be them," Tom said. "Let's follow."

"It could be miners."

"Not likely," Tom said. "Miners would use pack animals, and I don't think any settlers would be fool enough to come in here alone."

Sergeant Kennedy saw a pile of horse dung between the wheel tracks, and he poked at it with a stick.

"Whoever it is can't be far away," he said. "They was through here no more'n twelve hours ago."

"Let's go," Tom said, urging his horse into a lope.

They covered over ten miles in an hour. Then,

as they crested a ridge, they saw an object in the valley below.

"Cap'n!" Kennedy called.

"I see it!" Tom answered, and he reined in his horse to a stop, then looked down at the wagon. A few Indians were standing around the wagon, but Tom couldn't see what they were doing.

The horses, excited from their long run, stomped and pranced about.

"Dismount," Tom said quietly. "Campbell, you take the reins."

"Yes, sir," the private said, and he took all the horses and walked back below the crest of the hill so they wouldn't show up against the skyline.

"What do you reckon we've got here, Cap'n?" Kennedy asked.

"I don't know," Tom said. "But I don't want our presence known until we find out. Come on, we'll follow the gulley around until we are even with them, then we'll creep up and have a look-see."

"Right," Kennedy said.

"Take off anything that might rattle," Tom whispered.

The soldiers removed their canteens, spurs, and cartridge belts.

"How about money?" Tom asked. "Does anyone have any coins in their pockets? They might jangle."

"Get the money out, men," Sergeant Kennedy said. "Give it to Campbell."

"Hey, what if I don't come back? Does that mean Campbell gets to keep it?" One of the soldiers asked.

"If you don't come back, what the hell will you need with it?" Kennedy asked dryly. "The drinks are free in Fiddler's Green."

"Aye, they are at that," the soldier said, and he emptied his pockets without further discussion.

"All right, men," Tom said when they were ready. "Follow me."

Tom ran in a low crouch, moving quickly and silently through the gulley, following it around the valley until he reached a place he figured was even with the wagon. Then silently he crept up to the top of the ridge and looked down at the wagon.

"Oh, my God!" he said, turning his head aside in quick revulsion. For there before him, the Indians were systematically mutilating Artemus's body.

Suddenly all planning and military discipline went by the wayside. Tom Custer felt only one thing—a blind, killing rage. He gave no orders, formed no plan of attack. He just stood up and ran toward the Indians. "You butchering bastards!" he screamed.

The sudden appearance of Tom and the three soldiers who got up to follow him caught the five Indians around the wagon totally by surprise.

Tom killed the Indian nearest Artemus's body with his first shot. The others started toward their horses.

"Kill the horses!" Tom shouted. "Kill the horses, don't let the butchering bastards get away!"

The three soldiers dropped to one knee and aimed their carbines at the horses as carefully as if they were shooting at fixed targets. Their carbines cracked as one, and three of the horses fell dead. Tom killed the other two with his pistol.

The four remaining Indians realized now that they had nowhere to go, that they were forced into a fight. They turned to face their charging adversaries, holding their lances and war clubs at the ready. The soldiers were unarmed, having expended their lone cartridges on the horses.

"Kill them!" Tom shouted, his rage still out of control. "Kill the murdering bastards! Kill every one of them!"

The Indian nearest Tom threw his lance at Tom, and it stuck in the ground just in front of him. Tom picked it up and charged with it, driving it right through the surprised Indian's neck.

Tom turned then and saw that one of his men was down, a warrior standing over him with a raised warclub. Tom leaped at the Indian, knocking him over, then, wrenching the warclub from him, brought it crashing down on his head, killing him instantly.

Now it was four soldiers to two Indians, and the Indians, finding the odds not to their liking, tried to run away. Tom pulled his pistol, and lying on his stomach with both hands in front of him to steady his aim, he shot both of them.

Now, five Indians lay dead; Tom had killed every one of them.

"Look in the wagon," Tom said from his position on the ground. "I can't."

Sergeant Kennedy hurried over to the wagon and climbed up to look inside. He looked back, relief on his face.

"It's all right, sir," he said. "She ain't in there. They must of took her alive."

"All right?" Tom said. "She'd be better off dead."

## 22

Crazy Wolf stood just inside the tipi and looked at the girl. The tipi was bathed in a flickering gold light produced by two burning torches. In the center of the tipi, Crimson lay nude, staked out on the ground. As Crazy Wolf looked at her, he felt a growing pressure in his pants and a shortening of breath.

Now he would have his revenge upon Joseph Two Hearts. He knew that Joseph felt something for this white woman and that he would be greatly angered when he discovered what Crazy Wolf had done to her.

Revenge was going to be sweet, that was true enough. But even sweeter would be the enjoyment of her. For never had Crazy Wolf felt the heat of his blood nor the fullness of his manhood as he did now.

With the girl's arms stretched over her head, only two smoothly flowing, gently rounded curves topped by straining, erect nipples hinted at the fullness of her body. And there, at the junction of her legs, a patch of red hair glowed in the reflected light like a spade of coals taken from the fire—a thought that made his own loins begin to burn in anticipation of what was to come.

Yes, Crimson would satisfy him in every way. She would provide a just revenge against Joseph Two Hearts, and she would be a sweet prize for his manly hunger. He rubbed himself as he thought of it.

Crazy Wolf had tied her and thrown her across his horse when she had fainted and left the others to the prizes of the wagon. Let them have their fun with the drawings and the blankets and the other booty. This girl was all he needed. Oh, it was going to be so good.

Because of the shadows and her bonds, Crimson couldn't see Crazy Wolf standing in the door. So far nothing had happened to her, but she knew that she would soon fall victim to Crazy Wolf's lust. Then she heard something, and she turned her head toward the sound. She gasped, for there, standing in the edge of the light, she saw Crazy Wolf, completely nude. His face was painted in a grotesque mask; the paint extended onto his bald head. He was grinning demonically.

Crimson had heard the story of Crazy Wolf's humiliation from several of the Indians. She knew that he had plucked himself bald in a rage and was keeping it that way until he had redeemed himself. She was frightened, to be sure, but greater than her fear was her hatred for Crazy Wolf.

"So," she said scathingly. "The coward has returned."

"Woman," Crazy Wolf said. "You will know pain."

It wasn't until that moment that Crimson saw that Crazy Wolf held a whip made of a long thin strip of rawhide. He caressed it, almost lovingly, and the reflected lights in his eyes looked like the fires of hell.

"Do your worst, bastard!" Crimson said angrily, and she spat at him.

Crazy Wolf raised the whip over his head and brought it down sharply across Crimson's breasts. The lash seared her flesh like a hot brand, and she screamed in pain. She looked down and saw a trickle of blood oozing from the wound.

Crazy Wolf struck her again and again, flailing at her breasts, stomach, legs, and thighs with the whip until Crimson's entire body burned with pain.

Despite her screams of pain, Crazy Wolf realized that she would not be seriously injured by the beating, for that would have defeated his purpose.

Finally Crazy Wolf stopped. He dropped to one knee and looked into her face, still grinning demonically. "You will beg me to come to you," he told her.

"Beg you, you bastard?" Crimson said. "Never."

Crazy Wolf's smile changed to a frown and he stood up and raised his whip to beat her again, then smiled and lowered it. He pulled out his knife and looked down at Crimson.

Crimson closed her eyes tightly. She was afraid that she had pushed him too far. But if he were going to kill her, then so be it. At this moment, she would welcome death over the vile degradation to which she was being subjected.

Crimson waited for the cold shock of the knife, and when it didn't come, she opened her eyes.

Crazy Wolf was busy cutting off small pieces of the rawhide from the whip. Then he dropped two of the pieces in a water gourd, then fished them out and held them up, dripping wet.

"What are you going to do?" Crimson asked.

Crazy Wolf didn't answer her. Instead, he reached

down and looped one of the pieces of wet rawhide around the nipple of one of Crimson's breasts.

"What? What are you doing?" Crimson asked, and for the first time, her fear was beginning to win out over her anger.

With the other piece of rawhide, Crazy Wolf tied off the other nipple. The rawhide ties forced blood into the nipples, causing them to protrude like two fingers thrusting upward.

"You will beg me to come to you," Crazy Wolf said, and he sat down beside her to wait.

At first, Crimson couldn't figure out what Crazy Wolf was up to. The rawside thongs weren't excessively tight, they just caused her to feel pressure in her breasts. Uncomfortable, but not painful.

And then, after several moments, Crimson realized what was happening. As the rawhide dried, it grew tighter and tighter, until the sensations passed from pressure to pain and from pain to agony, finally dragging a scream from Crimson's lips.

Crazy Wolf reached down with his knife and cut the strips, but the nipples remained congested with blood, straining upward, rose red, from her bruised breasts.

Crazy Wolf cut two more strips off, dipped them into the water gourd, and started to put them on her nipples. Crimson realized that these rawhide strips would begin where the others left off—as they dried, they would squeeze her even tighter, possibly even rupturing the nipples.

"No," she said. "No, please, for God's sake don't do it."

"Then I come to you?" Crazy Wolf asked.

Crimson closed her eyes as tears flowed down the sides of her head into her hair and ears.

"Yes," she finally said in pain, fear, and shame.

And then, still in pain, she suffered the humiliation of Crazy Wolf over her, penetrating her, driving into her brutally, grunting out his lust. He squeezed her tender nipples so hard that the pain made her pass out.

One word kept running through Tom's mind as he rode back to the fort—betrayal. Betrayal, betrayal, betrayal.

Sergeant Flynn had been betrayed by the Indians when he was leading them to safety.

Crimson and her father had been betrayed by the Indians, and all they had been doing was drawing their pictures.

And he had been betrayed by the Indians because of his eight years of guilt over Washita. He only wished now there were other Washitas. Ten of them perhaps, or maybe a hundred. A thousand, even.

Tom had once heard of a plan, proposed in all seriousness, to infect blankets with smallpox and distribute them to the Indians. The originator of the plan claimed it would kill ten thousand Indians. Tom had turned his back on it in disgust and revulsion. Now he wished it had been put into effect.

As the detail approached Fort Lincoln, the great gates were swung open. Inside, in the quadrangle, the rest of the Seventh stood in parade formation to greet their return.

Custer turned to face Tom and his returning patrol, whipping his hand up in a perfect military salute.

Tom looked at the formation, his face a mask of utter disdain. He didn't dismiss his detail, or return the salute, or even turn the command over to Sergeant Kennedy. Instead he dismounted and headed straight for his quarters.

"Dismiss your battalions!" General Custer called, his voice reflecting his anger at Tom's disrespectful manner.

Tom kicked the door of his quarters open and went right to the shelf where he kept the whiskey. He pulled the bottle off the shelf, uncorked it, then took several deep swallows. He felt the whiskey burning in his throat, through his chest, and down into his gut, and still he drank.

Finally, his head spinning, he looked up to see General Custer standing in the light of the doorway with his hands on his hips, staring angrily at Tom.

The back light cast a halo around Custer's head, and his golden hair and beard glowed as if possessed by some mysterious, inner light.

"They're dead," Tom said, tossing the whiskey bottle toward his brother.

The expression in Custer's face softened.

"I'm sorry, Tom," he said. "If there is anything I can do . . ."

"There is," Tom said dryly.

"What? Just tell me."

"Help me to kill Indians," Tom said.

Custer looked at his brother in surprise. Could this be the same Tom who experienced such agonizing doubt after every military operation? Could this be the same Tom who sympathized with the Indian cause so deeply? Custer smiled and pulled the cork on the whiskey bottle. He took several swallows, then wiped his mouth with the back of his hand.

"You want to kill Indians, do you, Tom, boy?"

"Yes," Tom said.

"That I can promise you. Within the week, we will embark on the campaign that will go down in history as 'Custer's Triumph'."

"I've got a better name for it," Tom said, taking the bottle back from General Custer. He drank from it until the last of the liquid bubbled and slid into his mouth.

"What do you think would be a better name?" Custer asked.

"A name that says exactly what I want to do to all of them," Tom said easily. "I think it should be called 'Custer's Massacre'."

## 23

It was early June, the season the Sioux call the Moon of Making Fat, and the Hunkpapas were holding their annual sun dance. For three days Sitting Bull danced, inflicted cuts upon himself, and sat in the sweat lodge, until he finally fell into a trance. When he emerged from the sweat lodge, he called everyone together to report on the vision that had come to him.

"Hear me," he said. "For voices came to me during my vision, and the words I speak to you are words of truth."

The drums and the music stopped, and warriors and chiefs gathered around to listen. It wasn't only Hunkpapa, but Oglala and Minneconjous, San Arcs, Blackfeet, and even Cheyenne. They all sat quietly to listen to the vision of Sitting Bull.

"A voice came to me and it cried: 'I give you this because they have no ears.' And when I looked into the sky I saw soldiers falling like grasshoppers, with their heads down and their hats falling off. They were falling right into the Indian camp. Because the white men had no ears and would not listen, Wakantanka, the Great Spirit, gave these soldiers to the Indians to be killed. The leader of these soldiers is Yellow Hair."

"Eeeeeeyyaaaaahhhh," a warrior shouted in excitement, and others took up the cry so that the camp roared with their shouts of excitement and challenge. The drums began again, this time more ardently than before, and a hundred warriors took up the dance.

"Joseph," Sitting Bull said as Joseph Two Hearts walked by. He patted the ground beside him. "Come, sit with me and we will talk."

Joseph sat beside Sitting Bull.

"Once I told you that after the battle one of your hearts would be dead and one would live."

"Yes," Joseph said. "My Indian heart chose Sasha."

"But now Sasha is dead," Sitting Bull said. "I was wrong before. I said that only one of your two hearts would win the battle, but now I know both shall win."

"I do not understand," Joseph said.

"When Sasha lived, your Indian heart lived. Sasha is dead, and I think your Indian heart will die."

"No," Joseph said. "I will never betray my people."

"You say you will not betray your people, yet you would betray the heart which yet lives?"

"Sitting Bull, why do you think only my white heart lives?"

"I saw you in the vision," Sitting Bull said. "And I saw a white woman who makes pictures with a stick."

"Crimson Royal," Joseph said. "Yes, she and her father are traveling through the Black Hills making pictures. But I have not gone to see them."

"Evil has struck them," Sitting Bull said. "In my

216

vision I saw the girl's father struck down, and the girl taken prisoner."

"Crimson is a prisoner?" Joseph asked. "Where? Who has her?"

"It is Crazy Wolf."

"Crazy Wolf!" Joseph said, hitting his fist into his hand. "I should have killed him when I defeated him in battle."

"And now your blood runs hot with hate because he has the white woman," Sitting Bull said.

"Yes," Joseph replied.

"Ah, that is good," Sitting Bull said. "I saw your anger in my vision and this is as it should be. You should find her."

"I will," Joseph said. "I'll find her and be back in time for the battle that is to come."

"No," Sitting Bull said.

"What? Why do you say no?"

"You will not fight in this battle," Sitting Bull said.

"Of course I will fight in this battle. I am a war chief. I've earned the right to fight in this battle."

"Hear me, Joseph. If you fight in this battle, against whom will you fight?"

"I will fight against the soldiers, of course."

"And against your heart?"

"Yes. No. I mean, I don't know," Joseph said.

"I would feel great sorrow if you fought on the side of the soldier against your people," Sitting Bull said.

"Sitting Bull, I couldn't do that," Joseph said.

"But I would also feel great sorrow if you fought against your white heart. It would be best if you did not fight in this battle at all."

"But what will I do? Where will I go?"

"You will go find your white woman, and with her, you will go to make a new life. You will become white again."

217

"Sitting Bull, I could never do that, I couldn't just abandon you and the others like that."

"I have spoken," Sitting Bull said.

"But . . ."

"Hear me," Sitting Bull said again, his voice conveying the weight of his authority. "From this day on, you will not be one of us. You may travel in our lands in peace. But you will not live in our villages."

"Sitting Bull, no, you can't do this to me," Joseph said. "You can't turn me out like this."

"I am doing this because you will not," Sitting Bull said. "Now go, find your woman and leave this place."

Joseph stood up and looked down at Sitting Bull. He wanted to argue further, but the chief had closed his eyes and was drifting back into another trance. Joseph knew that any further attempt at communication now would be futile. There was nothing left for him to do but leave the village and look for Crimson.

Crimson had been Crazy Wolf's captive for nearly two weeks. In all that time they had not seen another human being, white or Indian.

Crimson had come to believe that Crazy Wolf was operating outside the limits not only of white man's law, but Indian as well. She harbored hope that she might be rescued, if not by whites, then by Indians. And she looked every day, hoping to see someone, anyone, as she believed her lot could only improve.

Though Crazy Wolf had not tortured her again as he had on the first day of her captivity, he had used her sexually time and time again. It had been a marvel to her that something that could otherwise be so pleasurable could be so painful under such evil circumstances.

Crazy Wolf moved from campsite to campsite, never staying in one place longer than one night. Sometimes he put up a tipi, sometimes he didn't. He rode everywhere he went, while Crimson trailed on foot behind his horse on the end of a tether with her hands tied.

After a long day of traveling, they stopped for camp. Crazy Wolf killed a rabbit and skewered it over a fire. As usual, Crimson sat quietly, waiting for Crazy Wolf to eat his fill so she could eat what was left. Sometimes there was little more than the marrow of the bones to sustain her, but whatever it was, Crimson took it, hanging on to life with a fierce tenacity.

Crimson sat by the fire, dirtier than she had ever been in her life, her hair hanging in matted strands, her dress tattered and torn, her fingernails broken, as wild-looking as any creature who ever wandered the plains. She got a sudden mental image of the reception she attended in New York just before she and her father left. She saw again the elegant gowns, the handsome clothes of the men, and the beautiful carpets and appointments of the art gallery.

For some strange, inexplicable reason, the contrast struck Crimson as amazingly funny, and she began to laugh.

Crazy Wolf looked up in shock. He was holding the rabbit in both hands, and a piece of it was hanging from his lips; his face shown with the rabbit's grease.

Crimson laughed harder.

"Why do you laugh?" Crazy Wolf asked.

Crimson pointed at the rabbit. "I once had to choose between pheasant under glass and leg of lamb," she said, "and was vexed because I couldn't make up my mind. And now I'm sitting here, like some animal, waiting for leftover rabbit!"

Crimson howled in laughter, and tears started

coming down her face. She had no idea why she was laughing, she knew that only she could appreciate the irony of her situation, and its tragedy was greater than any humor. But she couldn't help it. Her laughter was wild, uncontrollable.

"You stop laughing," Crazy Wolf said.

"I can't," Crimson gasped.

Crazy Wolf stood up. "I make you stop laughing," he said, drawing his fist back to hit her.

Even under imminent threat, Crimson still couldn't control her laughter, and Crazy Wolf started toward her, cursing her in his own language.

Suddenly a shot rang out of the night, and Crazy Wolf grabbed his chest. He looked down to see bright red blood spilling through his fingers. Another shot, and Crazy Wolf fell.

Crimson screamed and looked out into the dark. Seconds later, two men stepped out of the dark into the golden circle of light thrown by the campfire. They were both white men, one tall and thin, with a prominent adam's apple and large eyes, the other shorter, stocky, with a head full of bushy hair and a great, black beard.

"Well now, Harley, lookie here, would you?" the short one said, pulling at his beard as he looked at Crimson. "What think ye' o' this, now? This here heathen had him a white woman."

"Cain't be too much of a woman, Luke, 'cause she ain't dead. Any white woman what was decent would'a already kilt herself.

Luke laughed. "Well now, ain't it just our luck that we'uns found us a woman out here who ain't decent?" He rubbed himself gleefully.

With a sinking heart, Crimson realized what the man named Luke meant. She hadn't been saved; she had merely been thrust from one danger to another. The degradations against her would continue.

\* \* \*

It was the next day before Joseph found Crazy Wolf's camp. He spotted the lone tipi from the ridge and dropped back down into the gulley behind the ridge, following it around until he was able to get a closer look at the tipi. He dismounted and crawled up to the top of the ridge on his hands and knees, then crept on his stomach for the last few yards. Finally he reached the summit and peered down toward the tipi.

It was strangely quiet. Crazy Wolf should have been making preparations to move. And there should have been a smell of cooked food in the air, for surely he would have had his breakfast by now. And where was his horse?

Joseph studied the campsite for a few minutes longer, then, looking all around to make certain that no one was watching him, he rolled over the top of the ridgeline, keeping low, and darted quickly and silently down into the camp.

Just as he reached the campsite, he saw the body of Crazy Wolf, shielded by the tipi.

Cautiously he walked the rest of the way into the campsite and opened the flap of the tipi to look inside.

Crimson wasn't there, but Joseph didn't really expect her to be. He sighed, then looked back toward Crazy Wolf's body, wondering who had murdered him.

Joseph dropped to one knee to examine Crazy Wolf's body more closely. He had been shot twice in the chest. And his medicine bag was still hanging around his neck. Who ever did it had no special hatred for Crazy Wolf, or the medicine bag would have been removed to prevent Crazy Wolf from entering the Happy Hunting Ground.

A warrior's medicine bag was a special totem, a magic amulet without which no warrior would feel secure. Its contents were secret, known only to the warrior who carried it, and seen by no other until after his death.

Joseph opened Crazy Wolf's bag and looked inside. There was a tuft of feather, a bear claw, a polished rock, an arrowhead and a small pile of dirt. Each item was symbolic of Crazy Wolf's life. Joseph recognized the bear claw. It had been taken from a rug belonging to Sitting Bear. Sitting Bear had been greatly distressed when it was taken, and he had asked all in the village if they knew anything about it. All had denied knowledge of it, including Crazy Wolf.

Joseph shook his head sadly as he looked at the warrior and the contents of his medicine bag. He had been a liar and a coward even with himself, for the claw of an animal not killed by the warrior himself possessed no special magic.

Joseph replaced the claw and the other items and put the medicine bag back around Crazy Wolf's neck. Then, using the poles and the skins from the tipi, Joseph built a grave for Crazy Wolf. Then he picked up the trail of the two horsemen who had evidently killed Crazy Wolf. They were white men, he knew, because the horses were shod. They had left camp with an unshod pony. The pony wasn't carrying quite as much weight as it had been earlier on the trail, and Joseph figured that Crimson had replaced Crazy Wolf.

For a moment Joseph wondered if he should even go after her. After all, she had been rescued by two white men. Surely she was safe now. They were probably taking her back to civilization and the life she knew before coming out here. If he followed them and saw her, she might not even want to see him.

Joseph also realized that he was a wanted man by the army and that a reward might be out for him. If that were the case, he certainly would not be allowed to talk to her; the moment her rescuers spotted him, they would shoot first and ask questions afterward.

No, Joseph thought. She is safe now, and the chances are that she wouldn't want anything to do with him. It wasn't worth the risk to track her any further.

Joseph sighed, then climbed onto the back of his horse and began to ride slowly away, in the opposite direction of the tracks.

## 24

On June 3rd, 1876, the Seventh Cavalry Regiment set out to join forces with General Terry's expedition against the Sioux. It was the beginning of the grand and glorious campaign that General Custer had been promising Tom and the other officers of the regiment for several months now.

Custer's Seventh was augmented by artillery, infantry, laden ponies, pack mules, scouts, civilian employees, wagons, and reporters. There were seventeen hundred animals and twelve hundred men, and the column stretched for two miles. George Armstrong Custer, Lieutenant Colonel, U. S. Army, Brevet Major General Volunteers, commanded. Beside him rode his wife.

In the mists of early morning, the troops saw a mirage. They saw themselves riding in the sky. The Indian scouts, upon seeing this vision, let out a wailing chant of fear. The soldiers, too, were frightened; many swore that they saw Sergeant Flynn, as well as Howe and Peters, Hamilton and Elliot, and all the other soldiers of the Seventh who had been killed.

It was as if the portals to Fiddler's Green had opened and those cavalrymen who had gone on before were calling to their earth-bound comrades, inviting them up to join them.

"It's just a mirage brought on by the early morning mist," General Custer assured his men.

"Sure, it's a good-luck sign," Colonel Keough said.

Young Autie Reed, General Custer's nephew, rode next to his father, Captain Jim Reed; Boston, Custer's youngest brother, was along as well. Autie and Boston were greatly taken with the mirage, and they asked Mr. Ingersoll, the photographer, if he could get a picture of it, but Ingersoll told them that mirages didn't photograph.

Tom was less enthusiastic than his younger brother and his nephew. Though not superstitious, Tom couldn't help but feel a sense of foreboding over the incident. He suppressed a shudder, and, though he didn't put it into words, he had a feeling that he would never return to Fort Lincoln.

The mirage only lasted for about fifteen minutes, for as the sun rose, it burned away with the mist.

Libbie, Custer's wife, and Maggie, his sister, had ridden along with the column for most of the morning. When the column stopped for lunch, the officers and their ladies picnicked on roast duck and wine. Many photographs were taken, and Mr. Kellog, the special correspondent for the *New York Times*, wrote up his impressions of the grand expedition's first day and presented them to Libbie to send in for him when she returned to the fort with Maggie after lunch. Young Autie Reed and Boston, though both too young for the army, were to stay with the column. General Custer promised his sister to keep the two with him constantly for the duration of the expedition.

"Look at them, Maggie. Isn't that a magnificent sight?" Libbie asked as they watched the column.

"Yes," Maggie agreed. The two women were riding in the paymaster's car, which was to carry them back to the post. "I agree, there is no sight more beautiful or inspiring than this."

The column marched by as if on parade. Flags were snapping in the breeze, officers were holding shining sabers up in a salute, and row upon row of blue-clad soldier stared straight ahead with pride. As they marched by, row on row, the band played stirring marches such as *Garry Owen,* the ubiquitous regimental song.

Several times the paymaster started to call to his horses, but each time Libbie put her hand out to stop him. Finally realizing that she intended to watch the entire procession, he sat quietly until the last of the column had passed. Then they watched the long blue line recede into the distance, listening to the music fade away until only the drum and the high notes of the flutes could be heard.

Finally, only a cloud of dust hanging over the horizon evidenced that the army had passed them by. It was deathly quiet save for the whistling of the wind.

A paper blew across the prairie and plastered itself to the wheel of the carriage. Libbie reached down for it, and looked at it.

"What is it?" Maggie asked.

"It's a poem," Libbie said.

"A poem?" Maggie asked with a little laugh. "What sort of poem? Oh, do let me see."

"It was written by one of the soldiers, I suppose," Libbie said, a strange, faraway look on her face.

"Well, what is it? Is it a love poem?" Maggie asked.

"No," Libbie said. "Here, read it for yourself."
She handed the poem over to her sister-in-law, who
began to read:

> There goes first call blowing,
>     Sergeant Flynn,
> And it sounds like taps blowing,
>     Sergeant Flynn,
> Oh my lad, that's only a fancy
> Take a brace there, Private Clancy,
> You'll feel better when they strike up
>     "Garry Owen."
>
> Ten thousand braves are riding,
>     Sergeant Flynn,
> In the black hills they are hiding,
>     Sergeant Flynn,
> Crazy Horse and Sitting Bull,
> They will get their bellies full
> Of lead and steel from men of
>     Garry Owen.
>
> We'll dismount and fight the heathens,
>     Sergeant Flynn,
> While there's still a trooper breathin',
>     Sergeant Flynn,
> In the face of sure disaster
> Keep those carbines firing faster,
> Let the volleys ring for dear old
>     Garry Owen.
>
> We are Irish, Scotch, and thrifty,
>     Sergeant Flynn,
> We'll sell troopers one for fifty,
>     Sergeant Flynn,
> For each Seventh scalp that's lifted,
> Fifty heathen souls have drifted

228

*To their Happy Hunting Ground for*
*Garry Owen.*

*Here they come like screaming Banshees,*
*Sergeant Flynn,*
*Sioux and Blackfeet and Comanches,*
*Sergeant Flynn,*
*Let your blades run red and gory*
*In their blood we'll write our story,*
*We will die today for dear old*
*Garry Owen.*

Maggie lay the paper in her lap and looked at Libbie. "Oh, my," she said. "Oh, my, Libbie, you don't think . . ."

"What?" Libbie asked.

Maggie looked at the cloud of dust, which was now little more than a small puff on the horizon. "You don't think anything will *happen* to them, do you?"

"No, of course not," Libbie said. "Why, one company of the Seventh could handle the entire Sioux Nation. I've heard Autie say that I don't know how many times."

"I know," Maggie said. "Still . . ."

"Maggie, you saw the army as they left, didn't you? How magnificent they were? Do you really think they are in any danger from savages?"

"No," Maggie said. "No, I suppose not."

"Good. I thought you would see it that way. Now, driver, let us hurry quickly back to Fort Lincoln."

"Yes, ma'am, Mrs. Custer," the driver said, and clucked to the horses.

The column covered thirty-two miles the first day, finally stopping to eat at about ten o'clock that night. Despite that, there was very little grumbling from the men, for most of them were more than willing at last to have left the long winter's garrison.

"There is nothing tastier than trail stew, gentlemen," Custer said, squatting beside the campfire, eating from his mess tin with great gusto. A tin cup of coffee sat on the ground beside him, and he periodically took a drink from it and smacked his lips appreciatively, mostly for the benefit of young Autie Reed, who was enjoying his uncle's antics.

"You'd better not let Aunt Libbie hear you say that, Uncle," Autie teased. "She would grab you by the hair."

Tom laughed. "She wouldn't have much hair to grab. The General shaved most of it off. Did you hope to cheat the Indians of their prize, General?" he asked.

Custer joined in the laughter, and, removing his hat, ran his hand across his newly shorn hair. "I needed a change," he said. "And besides, there's no sense in making it easy for them."

"What does the newspaper think about the General's new look?" Tom asked Kellog.

Kellog, who was reading by the firelight, looked up and chuckled. "I don't think the readers will find him quite as dashing," he said. He ran his hand over his own hair. "But if I thought it would keep the Indians from being interested in me, I'd shave myself bald."

"Don't worry, Mr. Kellog," little Autie Reed said. "If the going gets rough, I'll protect you."

"I'm certain Mr. Kellog will sleep much easier for that, Autie," General Custer said. "Tell me, Mr. Kellog. What do you find so interesting in the paper?"

"Oh," Kellog said. "I just got these before we left the post, and I haven't had a chance to look at them before now. But they have all the latest news of the Republican National Convention."

"Oh?" Custer asked with interest. "And what is the news?"

"Mr. James G. Blaine has announced that he is withdrawing his intention to place a name into nomination in order that his own name may be entered."

"What?" Custer asked in a small voice. "What did you say?"

"Oh, it's all political strategy and hokum anyway," Kellog said. "You see, Blaine's biggest opponent for the nomination is clearly Governor Rutherford Hayes of Ohio. So Blaine spread the rumor that he was going to place another prominent Ohioan into nomination for president, in order to dilute the support for Governor Hayes. Of course nobody knows who the fellow from Ohio was who would be so base as to allow his name to be used for such a purpose. Certainly it could be no one with political ambitions of his own, for such a thing would be the death knell to any future political aspirations."

"I see," Custer said in a small voice. "Did they find out who it was?"

"No," Kellog said, looking through the paper. "No, I don't think so. It may be, though, that the fellow whose name Blaine was going to propose had no idea of the real reason for the nomination, and, when he realized it, he ordered Blaine to withdraw him."

Custer stood and looked down at Kellog and the others for a moment, then turned and walked quickly away into the darkness.

"General," Kellog called. "Are you all right?"

Tom set his plate down and went after his brother.

He found him standing by the front wheel of a wagon, his hands around the spoke, pulling on the wheel.

"Autie, are you all right?" Tom asked.

Custer pulled on the wheel so hard that the hub and axle squeaked.

"Listen to that," he said. "If the teamsters don't keep these wheels lubricated, we shall be having a great deal of trouble before this expedition is over."

"I shall take it upon myself to see that the wheels are all properly lubricated," Tom said.

"And not just the hubs," Custer said. "The tie joints as well."

"Yes," Tom said.

Custer walked around to the other side of the wagon and pulled at the wheel on that side, too.

"I was a fool," he finally said, speaking so quietly that Tom could barely hear him.

"No you weren't, Autie."

Custer laughed, a quiet, self-deprecating laugh. "Oh, yes, I was. I sat there in Blaine's office in Washington, and I let him convince me that he would be submitting my name for nomination for the president because he really believed I would be the best man for the job. Who was I fooling? How could I have been so naive as to think I could be president?"

"You would make a fine president, Autie," Tom assured him. "And you weren't being naive, you were being confident. Your problem is you are too honest a man, Autie. You had no idea that Blaine intended to use you for his own purposes."

"I can tell you that never again will I be such a fool," Autie said.

"Autie, I hope you aren't considering withdrawing from all political considerations," Tom said.

Custer looked at his brother and smiled. "Oh no,

Tom," he said. "Quite the contrary. I shall be even more forceful in my political pursuits. But, I shall do it all myself, and never again will I depend on someone else."

"That's the boy, Autie," Tom said proudly. "And I'll be with you."

"Tom, we start here, now," Autie said. "Have you seen General Terry's orders to me?"

"No," Tom said. "They are secret."

"I authorize you to read them," Autie said. He reached into his pocket and removed the orders and a small reading candle. He lit the candle and handed Tom the dispatch from General Terry:

Lieutenant Col. Custer, 7th U. S. Cavalry
Colonel:

The Brigadier General Commanding directs that, as soon as your regiment can be made ready for the march, you will proceed up the Rosebud in pursuit of the Indians whose trail was discovered by Major Reno a few days before. It is, of course, impossible to give you any definite instructions in regard to this movement, and even if it were, the Department Commander places too much confidence in your zeal, energy, and ability to impose upon you precise orders which might hamper your action. He will, however, indicate to you his own views of what your action should be, and he desires that you should conform to them unless there is sufficient reason for deviating from them. He instructs you to proceed up the Rosebud until you ascertain definitely the direction in which the trail spoken of above leads. Should it be found (as it appears almost certain that it will be) to turn towards the Little Big Horn, you should continue southward, perhaps as far as the headwaters of the Tongue, and then turn towards the Little Big Horn, feeling constantly, to your left, so as to preclude the possibility of the escape of the Indians to the south or southeast by passing around your left flank. The column of Colonel Gibbon is now heading for the mouth of the Big Horn. As soon as it reaches that point it will cross the Yellowstone and move up at least as far as the forks of the Big and Little Big Horns. Of course, its movements will be controlled by circumstances as they arise, but it is hoped that the Indians, if upon the Little Big Horn, will be outflanked by two columns so that their escape will be impossible.

The Department Commander desires that on your way up the Rosebud you should thoroughly examine the upper part of Tulloch's Creek, and that you should send a scout through to Colonel Gibbon's column with the results of your examination. The lower part of this creek will be examined by a detachment from Colonel Gibbon's command. The supply steamer will be pushed up the Big Horn as far as the forks of the river are navigable, and the Department Commander, who will accompany Colonel Gibbon's column, desires that you report to him there not later than the expiration of the time for which your troops are rationed, unless in the meantime you receive further orders.

> Very respectfully,
> Your obedient servant,
> E. W. Smith, Captain 18th Inf.
> Act'ng Asst. Adjutant General

Tom finished reading the orders and returned them to his brother. Custer put them back in his pocket, then blew out the candle.

"As you càn see," Custer said. "General Terry practically gives me the authority to do whatever I wish."

"Not really, Autie," Tom disagreed. "He gives

you his own views, and states that he desires you conform with them."

"Unless I see sufficient reason to depart from them," Custer said. "And I see sufficient reason." Custer smiled. "Tom . . . when we do locate the Indians, we aren't sharing them with anybody."

"What do you mean?" Tom asked.

"I'll tell you what I mean. I mean the Seventh is going to report to General Terry at the Big Horn, with news not that we found the Indians, but that we defeated them. From this moment on, Tom, we aren't on a scouting expedition, we are on a hunting expedition."

"I see," Tom said.

Custer got a faraway look in his eyes. "It will be a clear message to the Republican National Convention and to the American people," Custer said. "I may have missed out on the nomination this time, but I will get it in '80. Not only the nomination, Tom, but the election as well. And it all hinges on this operation."

"Then we must make certain that we find the Indians," Tom said.

"Oh, we'll find them all right," Custer said. "And when we pick up their trail, we won't wait for anyone. We will close with and kill them ourselves. In this battle, Tom, I shall do something which will make my name go down in the history books forever."

# 25

Harley and Luke didn't immediately avail themselves of the opportunity to enjoy Crimson's charms after they captured her. It wasn't that they were being shy; they simply wanted to put as much distance between themselves and the dead Indian as they could, in case any of his companions were lurking nearby.

Though now Crimson rode instead of walked, it was, if anything, more difficult. Crazy Wolf at least had ridden at a slow enough pace to allow her to keep up. But Harley and Luke rode fast and hard, and Crimson, whose hands were tied behind her and her feet tied with a rope that passed under the pony's stomach, was most uncomfortable. She had to hold on with her knees lest she fall and be dragged by the animal, and the constant pressure of her knees turned into agony.

The longer they rode the more her discomfort increased, until she felt as if she would be unable to take it any longer. Finally, as the sky in the east began to lighten, Luke called for a halt.

"We may as well stop here 'n' sleep a spell," Luke said. "Like as not 'ny injun as may have come up on the dead injun, is far away."

"Yeah," Harley said. "Yeah, and besides that, I'm tired. 'N' somethin' else too, if you get my meanin'."

Luke laughed. "I get your meanin', Harley. What about you, girl? You get his meanin'?"

"Please," Crimson said quietly. "Just untie me and let me off this horse."

"Sure, girl, don' mean to discomfort you none," Luke said easily. He walked over and released her bonds, and Crimson, with a grateful sigh, slipped down from the pony.

"Go on over 'n' lie down in the grass under that tree," Luke invited. "You'll be comfortable there."

" 'Ceptin', don't go gettin' yourself too comfortable now," Harley said, giggling and rubbing himself. " 'Cause me 'n' Luke here, we got plans for you. Ain't we, Luke?"

"Damn, Harley, ain't you a mite tired?" Luke asked.

"Yeah, sure I'm tired," Harley said. "But I ain't too tired. Now come on, what do you say?"

Luke sighed. "You go on," he said. He stretched and yawned. "Me, I'm gonna stretch out 'n' take me a nice long nap. Then, when I wake up, why, I'll be fit as a fiddle, 'n' rarin' to go."

"You go ahead 'n' take your nap," Harley said. "Don't let me stop you."

"The onliest thing, Harley," Luke cautioned. "After you get finished, you tie her back up good 'n' proper, you hear? I'd hate to wake up 'n' find she'd done slipped out on me."

"Don't you worry none about that, Luke. I'll tie her so's she ain' goin' nowhere. 'Cause the truth o' the matter is, after I do it now, I aim to catch me a little nap 'n' then do it again."

Luke laughed. "Boy, you sound randy as a rabbit."

"Oh, I am that, Luke. I am that," Harley said. He started toward Crimson, unfastening his breeches.

Crimson's arms and legs were free now, but try as she may, she was unable to run. She tried to stand up, but her legs were cramped from the cruel restrictions, and she was weak from lack of food and rest. She fell back down, and in an instant Harley was on top of her. Crimson fought with what strength she had left, but after her ordeal, first with Crazy Wolf, and now with these two, she had no strength left. She closed her eyes as she felt his calloused hands bunching up her skirt.

"Now, girly, we'll see if you don't think a white man's better'n an injun at this."

Crimson felt Harley's weight press against her bruised, racked body. She wanted to scream out, to protest this final indignity, but she knew instinctively that her protests would do her no good and might even increase the brute's pleasure. So, she suffered his foul penetration in silence.

Fortunately the attack was very brief. In less than one minute, Harley had satisfied himself, and after a few grunts and groans, he pulled himself from her, then collapsed beside her, breathing heavily.

Crimson looked over at him, and saw that his eyes were closed. A sudden thought came to her—perhaps he would fall asleep! Luke was already snoring, stretched out under a tree about thirty feet away.

Crimson lay very still. This was difficult for her to do, for the mark of Harley's lust was running down her thigh, and she convulsed to think of it. But she made no move for fear of disturbing Harley, who lay there with his eyes closed, still breathing heavily.

After several moments, Harley's breathing grew more measured, and then Crimson realized that he was asleep. She sat up, moving very quietly, and looked at him. Yes, she thought, nearly shouting with joy at her unexpected good luck. Yes, he was asleep!

Crimson started tiptoeing toward the horses. Once she heard one of the men snort and roll over, and she stopped, frozen in fear. But she wasn't discovered. She reached the horses and quietly untied the closest one. She led him over one hundred yards away, then climbed onto his back and rode off.

She had escaped!

The steamer *Far West* was playing a very important part in Custer's expedition. It had pushed all the way up the Yellowstone, then up the Big Horn to the confluence of the Big Horn and the Little Big Horn, where it unloaded fresh supplies and mail for the troops in the field. Couriers from Custer's regiment brought mail to the *Far West* and hurried the incoming mail back to the soldiers.

The waiting wives in the fort were eager for word from their husbands, but their husbands in the field were no less desirous for word from home, talk of the daily routine, assurances of a stable domesticity.

Custer received his first letter from Elizabeth in the field and read it aloud to Tom, who had received no mail of his own.

"The servants are doing very well and we are raising chickens," Custer read.

"Oh, what I wouldn't give to have a plate of Libbie's fried chicken right now," Tom said.

"Now, do you want me to read this or not?" Custer asked.

"Yes, yes, go on," Tom said.

Custer cleared his throat and continued.

"We have forty-three chickens. And we have so many cats about the garrison that our rat problem has disappeared. The weather is very hot, but the nights are cool. The lights about the hills and valleys are exquisite. The river now is too high for sandbars to be seen.

"About a hundred men with John Stevenson in command have gone to the Black Hills. Nearly twenty-five teams have passed by.

"Carter has returned and is chief trumpeter. He really sounds the calls beautifully. But his drawn-out notes make me heartsick. I do not wish to be reminded of the cavalry."

After Custer finished the letter he handed it to Tom, who read it to himself. Then the two men sat quietly for a moment, staring into the campfire, which popped and snapped before them. Around them were over a hundred campfires. It was an absolute certainty that every Indian in the territory knew their whereabouts. But a hundred campfires could mean ten thousand men, and they knew that they were perfectly safe from any surprise Indian attack.

Off in the distance someone began singing in a rich, clear voice, and soon he was joined by a few others until the valley rang with song.

Boston and little Autie were hopping around from campfire to campfire. Boston was only a couple of years older than Autie, but he was Autie's uncle and wore that position of authority as surely as if it were military rank. In general, though, the boys got along well together and were much in demand by the soldiers who couldn't read or write, to read messages from their families back home and write letters for them.

Boston finally managed to settle down to write his own letter home to his mother back in Ohio.

My darling Mother,

The mail leaves tomorrow. I have no news to write. I am feeling first rate. Armstrong takes the whole command and starts up the Sweet Briar on an Indian trail with the full hope and belief of overhauling them, which I think he probably will with a little hard riding. They will be much entertained.

I hope to catch one or two Indian ponies with a buffalo robe for Nev, but he must not be disappointed if I don't. Judging by the number of lodges counted by scouts who saw the trail, there are something like eight hundred Indians and probably more. But be the number great or small, I hope I can truthfully say when I get back that one or more were sent to the Happy Hunting Grounds.

Now don't give yourself any trouble, as all will be well. I must write Maggie and Libbie, for if the mail should reach Lincoln without a letter from me there will certainly be trouble in the camp.

Autie Reed is going. He will stand the trip first rate. He has done nicely and is enjoying it. The officers all like him very much. He will sleep with me in my small tent. Tell Ann he is standing the trip nicely and has not been sick a day.

Armstrong, Tom and I pulled down an Indian grave the other day. Autie Reed got the bow with six arrows and a nice pair of moccasins which he intends taking home.

Goodbye, my darling Mother. This will probably be the last letter you will get till we reach Lincoln. We leave in the morning with sixteen days' rations with pack mules.

Love, Boston

Boston finished his letter and dropped it in an envelope, then carried it over to deposit it in the mail sack. He saw Tom standing over by a rock, some distance from everyone else, and he walked over to talk to him.

"Hello, Tom," he said. "Thinking about all the Indians we are going to kill?"

"Bos, I think you and Autie should return with the dispatches tomorrow," Tom said.

"What? Whatever makes you say such a thing?"

"I just don't think what's coming up will be good for civilians, that's all."

"We aren't just civilians, Tom, we're family," Boston said. "Besides, Kellog is going, and he is a civilian."

"Kellog is a newspaper man," Tom said. "This is his job. But it isn't your job, and you don't have to go. Besides, being family has nothing to do with it, except maybe make me more anxious for your safety."

"Tom, are you afraid?" Boston asked, awed by the possibility. "I've never known you to be afraid."

"There are only two kinds of people who are never afraid," Tom said. "Fools and those who want to die."

"Then you *are* afraid," Boston said.

"No," Tom finally replied quietly. "I'm not afraid."

Boston gave a small laugh. "You said only fools and those who want to die aren't afraid. So which are you?" he teased.

"I'm not a fool," Tom said quietly.

243

## 26

Crimson rode as fast and as hard as she could. Though she was so exhausted that she could scarcely stay in the saddle, she pushed on, driven by the fear of what lay behind her. Finally she topped a ridge, then stopped, gasping. For there, spread out in the valley below her, was the magnificent sight of a bivouacked army.

With a small cry of joy, Crimson rode down the hill toward the encamped army, calling out to them. She was saved!

Crimson was spotted by one of the outlying pickets, who notified his sergeant, who notified his lieutenant, so that by the time Crimson reached them, nearly a dozen soldiers had turned out to meet her.

"Oh, thank God," she said, almost falling from the horse when she reached them. "You don't know how happy I am to see you."

"Who are you, ma'am, and what are you doing out here?" the lieutenant asked.

"My name is Crimson Royal."

"Crimson Royal? I'm sorry, ma'am, but that name doesn't mean anything to me, I'm afraid."

"You haven't heard of me?" Crimson questioned. "Well, no matter. Take me to General Custer. He knows me."

"Ma'am, this is Colonel Gibbon's column. Custer is a long way from here. But General Terry is with us, if you'd like to see him."

"General Terry? Yes. Is there a Colonel Gray on his staff?" Crimson asked, remembering the officer she and her father had met on the train nearly a year ago. Was it less than a year? It seemed decades ago.

"Yes," the Lieutenant said. "Come with me."

Crimson followed the young officer, feeling the questioning stares of the soldiers.

"Bet she was an injun squaw," she heard one soldier say.

"She should'a had the decency to shoot herself," another said.

Crimson closed her eyes and ears to the soldiers as she followed the lieutenant. Finally they reached a tent, much larger than the others and with a flag flying out front. The two soldiers posted outside came to attention and brought their weapons up as the lieutenant and Crimson approached.

"Lieutenant Kent to see Colonel Gray," the lieutenant said.

One of the soldiers went inside the tent, and a moment later Colonel Gray appeared in the door flap, a puzzled expression on his face.

"Colonel Gray, do you remember me?" Crimson asked.

"No," Colonel Gray said. "No, I'm sorry, miss, but I don't."

"I'm Crimson Royal. You met my father and me on the train last summer."

"My God, yes, of course," Colonel Gray said. "Miss Royal, what has happened?"

"I . . . my father . . . he was killed, and I was . . ." Suddenly Crimson felt so dizzy that she was afraid she would faint, and she put her hand to her forehead. "Forgive me," she said. "I am so tired and hungry that . . ."

"No, you must forgive *me*, Miss Royal," Colonel Gray said. "I should have offered you food and rest before I began to question you. Lieutenant, see to it that Miss Royal is fed at once. Also, see the quartermaster. I believe there are some dresses in his stock that are to be used as trading material with cooperative Indians. Select one for Miss Royal."

"A new dress?" Crimson said, looking at the tattered rags she was wearing. "As dirty as I am . . ."

"Sergeant, rig up a screen down by the river and post guards to see to the lady's privacy. Miss Royal, if you wish, you may take a bath and change clothes while your meal is being prepared."

"Oh, thank you," Crimson said. "You have no idea how grateful I am to you."

"As soon as you've cleaned up and eaten, we shall have our talk," Colonel Gray offered.

Soon Crimson was bathing in the cool, bracing river. She used soap and even sand to scrub herself pink-clean. And when she emerged from behind the privacy screen a bit later, clean and fresh, dressed in a new if not stylish dress, she felt one hundred times better.

A small camp table and chair had been brought up for her, and she was invited to sit down to eat. The simple fare of beef stew and potatoes was as delicious as any meal she had ever eaten in the finest restaurant in New York.

After the meal, though, everything caught up with

247

her, and she nearly passed out from exhaustion. Colonel Gray tried to question her, but after a few attempts he realized how tired she was and invited her to lie down on his cot to sleep.

"Colonel, as tired as that girl is, she'll sleep right through until after we pull out," Crimson heard one of the officers say.

"No matter," Colonel Gray said. "I can question her back on the post after this is all over. I say let her get all the sleep she can get."

"But what will we do with her if we have to leave before she wakes up?"

"Wright and Hill will be back from their scout by then. We'll leave her with them. They can take her back into the fort. I'll just talk to her when this expedition is over, that's all."

"Yes, sir," the officer said.

Their conversation diminished to a buzz, then grew silent altogether as Crimson fell deeper and deeper into sleep.

Joseph had been watching the encampment for the last two days now. He thought he had it figured out, but he wanted to watch a bit longer, just to be sure. If he was right, this army would sweep up toward the Indians with Sitting Bull, while Custer's army swept down from the north. Sitting Bull and the others would be trapped in the middle.

Sitting Bull had prohibited Joseph from participating in the war that was to come, but he couldn't just stand by while the trap was being closed, either. If the army was successful, a lot of people would die, people who were his friends and very nearly his family. He wouldn't let the trap be sprung.

Joseph watched for the rest of the day. If he was right, the army would leave by nightfall, starting in a generally northern direction. Then he would ride quickly to Sitting Bull and tell him what he had seen.

Joseph knew that he would be riding hard tonight, so he scratched himself a place out of the side of the gulley, crawled in, and went to sleep. It would be dark when he woke up, and if they had left while he was still asleep, it would be easy enough to follow them, for the number of horses the army had was astounding. That many horses would nearly leave a road paved in horse dung. It would be simple to follow, night or day.

It was dark and quiet when Crimson woke up. She lay in bed for a moment but could hear nothing, neither voices nor sounds of men at work. She swung her legs over the side of the cot and looked around the dark tent for a moment. Finally she stood up and walked to the tent flap to look outside. She saw a campfire with a coffee pot suspended over the flames. Two men were squatting by the fire, staring into the flames. Then Crimson remembered hearing Colonel Gray say that Wright and Hill, the two scouts who were out at the time, would be back to take her home.

"Well, you must be Wright and Hill," Crimson said.

"Some folks calls us that," one of the men said. Then he turned toward her and grinned evilly. "Others just call us Luke and Harley."

Crimson gasped. It was the same two white men who had 'saved' her from Crazy Wolf only to subject her to more torture.

"No!" she screamed.

"And now it's my turn," Luke said, standing up and starting toward her.

Crimson was rested and fed, and finding a strength in her legs she had not had before, she ran from Luke.

"Come back here, damn you!" Luke sputtered, starting after her.

Harley laughed at them. "Go get 'er, Luke," he called.

"Well help me, damn you. Don't just stand there," Luke called back.

Harley took a swallow of whiskey, not moving from his spot. "I've had my fun," he called. "Now it's your turn."

Crimson looked back over her shoulder and saw that Luke was gaining on her. From somewhere she summoned an extra burst of energy and started up the hill just behind the campsite.

"Hey, girl," Luke called to her. "You'll get lost in the dark and the injuns will get you. Come on back. Ol' Luke, he's gonna be nice to you."

Crimson ran pell mell through the dark, her breath coming as rasping gasps in her throat. Bushes and low-lying scrub trees formed barriers and the limbs seemed to grab for her. Finally one of them tripped her, and she pitched headfirst into the briars.

"Where'd you go, girl?" Luke called. He had seen her fall, but it was so dark that he couldn't see her in the bushes on the ground. He was walking slowly, moving the bushes aside with his hand, squinting in the moonlight. "Come on, girl," he called again. "You gonna liken what I do to you. I ain't like Harley. I'm good with women, 'n' that's a fact."

Crimson began crawling through the bushes and stepped on a dry twig, which snapped loudly.

"Ahh, trying to sneak away are you?" Luke said. "Well, not to worry, little girl. I'll find you. And when I do, why, I reckon it'll just make our little game all the more sweet."

Crimson crawled away until she felt she had put enough distance between them, then stood up and started to run—right into someone's arms.

"No!" she screamed.

"Crimson . . . it's me, Joseph!"

Crimson, who had closed her eyes tightly the moment she felt the arms grab her, now opened them. She saw Joseph standing there in the moonlight, and she collapsed against his chest, giving herself over to his strong, protecting arms.

"Oh, Joseph," she said. "Joseph, thank God it's you."

"Well, well, well. Now, ain't this just fine?" Luke's voice was right behind Crimson. She gasped and looked around. He was standing no more than ten feet from them, smiling the same evil smile.

"Yes, sir, this is really fine," Luke went on. "First off, I'm gonna kill me a traitor, 'n' collect the reward. Then I'm gonna have me a woman. 'N' it looks like it's your woman . . . that's gonna make it even nicer."

It was only then that Crimson saw Luke's knife. He was holding it out in front of him and tested the point with his finger.

"If you got any heathen gods to pray to, injun lover, you'd best get them said. 'Cause I aim to gut cut you."

Joseph pushed Crimson around behind him, then quickly removed his buckskin shirt and wrapped it around his left forearm. A pelt of black hair stood out against his bare, muscled chest; his skin gleamed silver in the moonlight. He held his arm, padded with his shirt, crooked in front of him, and reached for the knife he carried in his waistband. Then he assumed a crouching stance similar to Luke's, right arm out, knife blade moving back and forth slowly and hypnotically.

It was obvious that the fight would not last long. Both men were going for a quick kill.

Luke danced in, light on his feet for a heavy man, and raised his left hand toward Joseph's face. He feinted with his right, the knife hand, and when

Joseph raised his left arm to block, Luke brought his knife hand back down so fast it was a blur and went in under Joseph's arm.

The knife seared Joseph's flesh like a branding iron along his ribs and opened a long gash in the tight ridges of muscle. Blood began to spill down his side and over the top of his breeches. Joseph brought his left hand down sharply, almost by reflex, and knocked away the knife, which Luke was now holding with an air of careless confidence. He jabbed quickly with his right hand, sending his knife into Luke's diaphragm, just under the ribs.

They stood that way for a few moments, Joseph twisting the blade in the wound and struggling to stay on his feet in spite of the pain burning across his ribs. Finally Luke began to collapse, expelling a long, life-surrendering sigh. Joseph turned the knife, blade edge up, letting Luke's body tear itself off by its own weight. When Luke hit the ground he flopped once or twice, like a mortally wounded buffalo, then lay still.

Joseph staggered back, breathing heavily. The fight had not been physically exhausting; it was over too fast. But it had totally drained him emotionally. He looked into Luke's face. The eyes of the fallen scout were open and unseeing, still registering surprise. He had not had time to know fear or to feel much pain.

Joseph felt along the cut in his side and tried to estimate its severity. He held his fingers up and examined the blood in the moonlight.

"Oh, Joseph, you're hurt!" Crimson said.

"Come on," Joseph answered. "We must get out of here. I don't want to fight the other one, too."

Joseph climbed onto his pony, then helped Crimson up behind him.

"We will go to the village," Joseph said.

## 27

The night passed slowly, almost reluctantly, from the earth. When the darkness lifted, the slanting bars of morning sunlight revealed an army stretched out in a line nearly two miles long. The army was divided into three mobile units and one supply train; as they moved, each mobile unit was smaller and less impressive than had been the sum of all its parts.

All that day Custer continued on the trail of the Indians. Throughout the day many Indian camping places were passed. Every bend of the stream bore traces of a camp, and the Indian ponies had nipped almost every blade of grass. The ground was strewn with broken bones and cuttings from buffalo hides, and the carcasses of recently killed buffalo. One campsite was much larger than the others; still standing was the framework of a large sun-dance lodge.

"Let's hold up the column," Custer said, raising his hand. The command was passed along the line of march and the column halted. Soldiers turned in their saddles and looked over the site. None of them had ever seen a campsite so large.

"General, I don't like the looks of this," Captain Keough said. He took off his hat and wiped the sweat from his forehead.

Custer took a drink of water from his canteen and handed it over to Tom.

"What don't you like about it?" Custer asked, smiling broadly.

"Look at this place," Keough said. He took in the campsite with a wave of his arm. "My God, General, I'll bet there were ten thousand Indians here."

"You worry too much, Keough," Custer said. "This is nothing but a campsite that has been used over and over again, that's all. I don't think there are any more than eight hundred warriors ahead of us."

"There are ten times that many," Keough said. "General, we'd better wait until we link up with Terry's column."

Custer fixed a hard look at Captain Keough. "Keough, if we join Terry's column, then under whose command would the operation take place?"

"Why, as Terry is senior, it would be under his command," Keough said.

"That's right," Custer said. "He would depend on the Seventh Cavalry to haul his ashes out of the fire, but he and his men would get credit for the victory. No, sir, I don't intend to hand him such a prize. We will press on, Captain."

"Then would you at least abandon your plan to separate Reno and Benteen?" Keough asked. "I feel it would be unwise to divide our forces in face of such numbers."

Custer laughed. "Don't worry about it, Keough. When the Indians see three disciplined units attacking from three different directions, they will become so demoralized that we can pick them off like shooting ducks in a barrel. I've enjoyed over a decade of successful campaigns, and I know what I'm talking about."

"Yes, sir," Keough said.

"General," one of the sergeants called from the door of the large sun lodge. "General, maybe you ought to come see this, sir."

Custer swung down from his horse. "Come along, Tom," he said.

Tom followed his brother to the lodge door. Inside, hanging from one of the lodgepoles, were two fresh scalps, obviously taken from white men.

"Who are they, General?" the sergeant asked.

"I'm afraid I don't recognize the gentlemen," Custer said.

"Here's a button on the floor," Tom said. He picked it up. "It's from the Second Cavalry."

"Brisbin's command," Custer said. He made a fist of his hand. "Good Lord, Tom, you don't suppose Brisbin is *ahead* of us, do you?"

"I don't see how he could be, Autie," Tom answered. "We've certainly seen no sign. These men may have been scouts."

"Or deserters," Custer said.

Several others came into the lodge to look around, including Bloody Knife, one of the Indian scouts who was riding with Custer's column.

"The Sioux had a big ceremony here," Bloody Knife said. "Look."

The scout pointed to a drawing in the sand. A line had been drawn with soldiers on one side and Indians on the other. Dead men were drawn with their heads pointed toward the Indians, which Bloody Knife said meant that all the soldiers would be killed.

Custer laughed. "That is what their medicine says, is it?"

"Look at this," Tom called. "What does this mean?" He pointed to a pile of stones, with the skull of a buffalo bull on one side and the skull of a buffalo cow on the other. A pole was leaning toward the cow skull.

"This says that when the Sioux are overtaken, they will fight like a buffalo bull, and the soldiers will run from them like women."

"Well, we shall see about that," Custer said.

Boston and young Autie Reed were among the others standing in the lodge.

"Armstrong, may Autie and I have these skulls as souvenirs?" Boston asked.

"Certainly," Custer said.

"Thank you," Boston replied. "Come Autie, these will make wonderful souvenirs," he said as he gathered them in.

Custer walked back outside.

"Tom, pass the word that we will rest for a couple of hours," Custer said. "Tell the men to make coffee if they want to. Then we'll press on."

"Very well," Tom said.

While Tom was relaying the message to the others, Custer walked to the edge of the campsite and looked out toward the valley that stretched before him. The trail was fresh, and the whole valley was so scratched up by thousands of trailing lodgepoles that it looked like a poorly plowed field. It was apparent that the quarry was not far ahead.

## 28

Crimson heard a sound and sat up quickly. Joseph was smiling at her.

"I'm sorry if I woke you," he said. A trout, tied to a green sapling and suspended across forked poles, was sizzling over a fire. "I'm just cooking breakfast."

"Joseph, the cut on your side," Crimson said. "How is it?"

Joseph looked down at the wound, which he had packed with moss.

"The pain is gone," Joseph said. "The moss will keep it from bleeding more."

Crimson stood up and looked around. It had been dark when they arrived here during the night. Joseph had constructed a rude shelter for them, and Crimson had gone to sleep almost as soon as her head hit the pillow. But now, in the light of day, she saw that there was much to admire about their campsite.

It was located in a glen of flowering trees near a swiftly flowing stream. The valley before them was green with grass and dotted with wild rose bushes. Thousands of bright red roses decorated the plains, filling the air with their sweet perfume. The wind whispering through the trees, the bubbling of the brook, and the delicate song of the birds surrounded them with music.

"This is like the Garden of Eden," Crimson said.

"Garden of Eden?" Joseph asked. "I've heard of that somewhere."

Crimson laughed. "Joseph, you are teasing. Don't you know what the Garden of Eden is?"

"No," Joseph admitted.

"It's from the Bible. It is the place where Adam and Eve lived."

"Oh, yes," Joseph said. "I think the white man's God is very angry with me because I took up the Indian's ways."

"He isn't just the white man's God," Crimson said. "He is the God of all men. And He wouldn't be angry with you for taking up the ways of the Indian, for the Indians are His children just as is everyone else."

"Is the Garden of Eden a pretty place?" Joseph asked.

"It is beautiful," Crimson said. "But in truth, I do not see how it could be more lovely than this place."

"Here," Joseph said, handing a goatskin to Crimson and pointing to the stream. "Get water."

Crimson walked down to the stream to fill the goatskin with water, and by the time she returned, Joseph had taken the trout off the fire and fileted it for them. After breakfast, Crimson asked Joseph to stretch out on the ground and remove the moss.

"Why?"

"I'm going to clean the wound," she said. "Then I'll put fresh moss on."

Joseph did as she instructed, and Crimson gingerly pulled the old moss off. She used the water from the goatskin to loosen the dried blood around the wound.

"It isn't too bad," she said, examining the cleansed wound. "If you don't break it open again."

"Shall we put more moss on it?" Joseph asked.

"Not yet," Crimson said. "I'm sure the air and the sun is good for it. Wait for a bit. We can rest here, can't we?"

"Yes," Joseph said. "We can wait here as long as we need to."

Crimson lay down beside Joseph and put her hands behind her head, then looked up at the sky.

"It is so peaceful here," she said. "I wish we could stay here forever."

"It won't be peaceful for long," Joseph said. "There is going to be a great battle."

"I know," Crimson said. She reached over and took Joseph's hand in hers. "I am glad you are not going to be in it."

"Sitting Bull will not let me fight in the battle," Joseph said. "He has told me that I am white."

Crimson raised up on one elbow and looked down at Joseph. "You are white," she said.

Joseph sighed. "I know. I married Sasha, and I was a good husband to her while she lived. But when she died . . . something changed. It was not good to be an Indian any more. And when Crazy Wolf killed Flynn and the other soldiers who were helping the Indians . . . my heart grew very hard against the Indians."

"Crazy Wolf bragged to me many times how he killed Sergeant Flynn and the others," Crimson said. "And he bragged how he would kill you."

"Crazy Wolf was like his name," Joseph said. "He was crazy. I was sorry for him."

"I wasn't sorry for him," Crimson said, shivering.

"I am sorry," Joseph said. He looked at her with

eyes full of compassion. "I know he killed your father and used you as his squaw. It was an evil thing, and I came to find him, to kill him for it. But when I found him, he was already dead, and I saw a sign which said white men had saved you."

"Saved me," Crimson said. "Joseph, one of the men who 'saved' me was the man you killed. They were beasts. They were worse than Crazy Wolf."

Joseph put his arms around Crimson, and pulled her toward him to hold and comfort her.

They stayed that way for several moments, feeling that same closeness they had known when they had lain together that first time. Crimson knew that she loved him, enough to know that she could find contentment with him, even if it meant living with him as his squaw. She knew she would be giving up everything and would suffer society's ostracism, but she didn't care. She loved him enough to face anything.

They lay full length, body against body, and kissed. As they kissed, Joseph moved his sure and exciting hands over her body, skillfully undressing her, and then he slipped out of his own breeches so that like Adam and Eve, they were naked and without shame.

The heat of their bodies mounted until they were on fire with desire for each other.

Crimson could feel the muscles of his chest and arms and the strength of his legs. She took his hands and guided them over her skin, moving his fingers up the smooth curve of her hips and across her swelling breasts. She rubbed the palm of his hand on her nipples, so small and hard after the soft, firm feel of her breasts; then she guided his fingers over the slope of her shoulders into the softness of her crimson hair, shining copper now in the halo of the morning sun. She could smell the tree blossoms and the wild roses . . . and the softly pungent smell of the earth . . . and her own musk. She was ready for Joseph to make love to her. She lay back in the grass and pulled him down onto her.

First Crazy Wolf and then Harley had brutalized her in the past few days. Now, she was using Joseph to purify her . . . to set right the wrongs they had done to her.

Joseph took her with an amazing tenderness, as different from the brutality to which she had been subjected by Crazy Wolf and Harley as a gentle shower is from a ripping thunderstorm. Yet the passions he released in her flashed through her like charges of lightning.

Crimson had never before felt such intense jolts of pleasure. She cried out in ecstasy as they passed through her, once, twice, three times in rapid succession, then a fourth time that was as great as the first three combined and lasted for several seconds, causing her to arch her body up to him, then feeling him join her as he spent himself in her.

Finally a last shudder of ecstasy convulsed both of them, and they collapsed back on the bed of grass, lying in each other's arms for a long moment before Joseph rolled away from her. Crimson lay with her eyes closed for a long while, listening to the sounds from the valley, the occasional call of a distant bird, the whisper of wind in the trees, the singing of the brook.

Finally she opened her eyes and looked into Joseph's face. He was on one elbow, looking down at her. Somewhat hesitantly, he spoke to her.

"It is not the way of Indian men to speak of love to their women," he said. "And yet, I feel I must tell you that I have a great love for you."

"I'm glad you can tell me," Crimson said. She reached up and trailed her fingers along his shoulder. "For I have a great love for you as well."

Joseph sighed and lay back down. "I don't know what we can do," he said.

"We can get married," Crimson said easily.

"No. For as long as Custer is alive, I will always be a wanted man. Hunted by the whites . . . shunned by the Indians. I am a man without a place in life."

Crimson laughed.

"Why do you think that is funny?" Joseph asked, annoyed.

"Joseph, there is a whole world out there you haven't seen. Do you think Custer would chase you all the way to New York? Or Boston? Or Paris?"

"Perhaps not," Joseph said. "But can I hunt buffalo and deer in New York? Can I fish in Boston? Can I steal ponies in Paris? I know only the things that Indians know. I do not know how to live as a white man."

"I'll teach you," Crimson said.

This time it was Joseph's turn to laugh.

"You think I can't teach you?" Crimson challenged. "You learned to be an Indian, didn't you?"

"Well, yes."

"Then you can learn to be a white man again. And it will be easier for you, because you are white, and things you may have forgotten, will come back to you."

"All right," Joseph said. "I will let you teach me the ways of a white man. And when I have learned, I want to go to Washington."

"Why?"

"I want to work for the president, to help the Indians."

Crimson smiled. "You know, Joseph, you just might do it at that."

## 29

It was a difficult and tiring march, for Custer, after halting only long enough for supper, pushed his troops on through the night. They moved west, alongside Davis Creek, more than twenty miles north of where General Terry expected them to be.

No lights were permitted during the night march, and the only way the troops in the rear had of knowing which direction to take was by the dust cloud raised by those ahead. If they could not smell dust, they knew they were off the trail. Also, the men in the rear of the troop pounded their tin cups on their saddle horns to guide the troop following them.

When the first faint streaks of dawn broke in the east, the scouts told Custer that they could not possibly hope to cross the valley before daybreak, and they couldn't cross after daylight without being discovered by the Sioux.

"I don't want the Sioux to see us yet," Custer said. "I don't want them to get away."

"General, do not fear that the Indians will get

away," Bloody Knife told him. "I think when you find the village, you will find all the Indians you want."

"How many?" Custer asked excitedly.

"Maybe three thousand."

"Three thousand?" Keough asked. He looked at Custer. "General, is he talking about three thousand warriors?"

"Oh, I scarcely think we will be that lucky," Custer said with a chuckle.

"Autie, perhaps we should stop here until dawn," Tom suggested.

"Yes, maybe you are right," Custer said. "Give the orders."

The troops concealed themselves in a wooded ravine situated between two high ridges. Some of the mules were unpacked and some troopers unsaddled, although most simply dropped down with the reins over their arms and went to sleep.

The campsite they chose was a poor one. There was very little grass for the horses, and the water was so alkaline that the horses refused to drink it. Even when the water was boiled and made into coffee, it was unpalatable.

Lieutenant Varnum, who had gone ahead with the scouts, returned at daybreak as Custer was eating his breakfast.

"Sit, Lieutenant, and tell me what you have seen," Custer said.

Varnum wore a shocked expression on his face; he walked over and took a long drink from a whiskey bottle protruding from a nearby knapsack.

"What is it, Varnum?"

"General," Varnum said. "The entire valley on the other side of Crow's Nest is white with tipis. There are so damn many campfires that the smoke covers the entire valley. There are more hostiles

264

ahead than there are bullets in all the belts of all the soldiers."

Custer smiled. "Well, then, I guess we are in for the fight of our life, gentlemen. But I guess we'll get through them in one day."

"Shall we break camp, Autie?" Tom asked.

"Let's go," Custer said, and without finishing his breakfast, he mounted his horse and rode bareback around the camp shouting orders to his officers.

By eight-thirty the command was ready, and they moved out. The men were in high spirits and they laughed and bantered back and forth. The sun was clear and bright, and it was obvious that they were in for an extremely hot day.

Custer had not slept well, despite his exhaustion, because the mosquitoes had kept him awake. In his diary the evening before, he wrote that he would rather face ten thousand Sioux than ten mosquitoes. And now, as he rode in the saddle, he, like his men, hung on the edge of total exhaustion.

Crimson and Joseph, after two days on the trail, rode down from the ridge and saw preparations being made by the Indians in the village below to leave their encampment. He hurried his pony on and arrived on the scene just as the equipment was being loaded onto lodgepole travois.

"White Ghost," he said, spotting the old man. "It is good to see you."

"It is good to see you as well," White Ghost replied. "I see you have found woman who makes pictures. That is good."

"White Ghost, what is happening here?" Joseph asked. "Where is everyone going?"

"Long Hair has been seen," White Ghost said. "He is very near to here, and I think soon there will be a great battle. In the way of the sunset, there is a great village. Some say it is a village as large as the great cities of the white men. We are going there, for no soldiers would have the courage to attack such a large village."

"Custer might," Joseph said. "He is a very brave man."

"Yes, this I know," White Ghost said. "But if he attacks us there, it is he and the soldiers who will be killed. If he attacks us here, it is only Indians who will be killed. You must come with us."

"Sitting Bull has forbidden me to fight," Joseph said.

"All right, you will not fight. But if you stay here the soldiers will find you and they will kill you."

"You are right," Joseph said. "White Ghost, I need another pony for Crimson."

"I will get one for you," White Ghost said, and started out on his task.

"Joseph, do you really think Custer will attack a village as large as the one White Ghost describes?" Crimson asked.

"You know Custer better than I do," Joseph said. "What do you think?"

Crimson sighed. "I think he will do it."

"He is a brave man," Joseph said. "But he is also a very, very foolish man."

"Here is a good pony for you," White Ghost said, returning a few moments later. "Also, a blanket and a buckskin dress. You will be safer dressed in the Indian way."

"He's right," Joseph said.

Crimson looked around and noticed that all the tipis had been taken down. She gave a small laugh. "Where will I change?" she asked.

"Change here," White Ghost said. "I will watch."

Crimson looked at White Ghost with a shocked expression. "What?" she asked.

"It will be good to watch," White Ghost said in perfect innocence, totally oblivious to Crimson's reaction.

"Joseph, is he serious?" she asked.

Joseph laughed. "Yes," he said. "It is common for Indian women to bathe or change clothes in the open. And if she is a pretty woman, it is common for the men and boys to watch."

"I can't do that," Crimson protested.

"You must do it," Joseph said. "Crimson, don't worry. No one will harm you. No one will even touch you. And if you do, you will be accepted as one of them."

Crimson sighed. "Then I suppose I must do it," she said. And, gathering her courage, she began slipping out of her dress.

By the time the dress was off, her face was burning bright red in embarrassment. The nipples of her breasts were drawn up in tight little buds, and they seemed to flame as hot as her face. It was especially embarrassing that, just as Joseph had predicted, men and boys had stopped what they were doing to watch her.

Then she saw in Joseph's face an expression, not of shame, but of great pride. And that pride managed to spread to Crimson, and she lost her self-consciousness. The flame of embarrassment left her cheeks, and the heat she still felt wasn't of embarrassment, but of a forbidden sexual excitation.

Soon Crimson, dressed as the others, was able to lose herself in the crowd of people milling about, so that from a distance, no one would be able to tell that she was a white woman.

The camp moved out, and Joseph and Crimson rode in the front with White Ghost, who was chief of this camp. On the distant horizon, they could see a great dust cloud rising, and they knew that Custer was near.

* * *

Custer's scouts told him of the moving camp, and fearing that the Indians were going to get away, the general ordered Major Reno to report to him.

Reno's command was trailing at the rear of the column, so he had to ride hard to catch up. Finally, with his horse lathered from the exertion, he rode up to Custer.

"Marcus," Custer said. "The Indians are trying to get away. Take your three companies and cross the river to engage them."

"I'm to engage them with only three companies, General?" Reno replied.

"Yes," Custer said. "Engage them, then charge right through. I will support you with the rest of the command."

"Very good, sir," Reno said.

"Tom," Custer called as the major rode off. "Send word to Benteen to attack in the center. We'll go down to the other end of the village and drive the hostiles back this way. Lt. Varnum, take Bloody Knife and join with Major Reno. We've got them cold now. There's no way they can escape."

Reno overheard the exchange between the General and his brother as he rode back to his battalion to execute his orders.

"What did the General want?" asked Captain French, the senior captain in Reno's battalion, when Reno returned.

"He wants us to cross the river here," Reno said. "We are to attack with vigor, and he will provide us with support."

"I don't like the idea of splitting our forces in the face of such superior numbers," Captain French said.

"I don't either," Reno said. "But Custer is the great Indian fighter. I can only hope that he knows what he is about."

"Well, you know the old cavalry axiom, Major: 'Ours is not to question why, ours is but to do or die'."

"Somehow at this point, I don't find that a very comforting thought," Reno said. He pulled a whiskey flask from his saddle bag and drank deeply, offered a swallow to Captain French, who refused, then recorked it and put it back in his bag. "Prepare the troops for the advance," he said.

"Yes, sir," French replied, and passed the word to the others.

The men, excited by the prospect of imminent battle, shouted and cheered as the battalion broke off from the rest of the column and started toward the river.

"Knock off that noise!" Reno ordered. "We are soldiers, not savages!"

"Major, it's good to let the men yell," Captain French said. "It lets them get rid of some of their tension."

"The soldiers of my command will behave as soldiers," Reno said.

The column crossed the river, sending sheets of silver water from the hooves of their horses. On the other side, they formed into a line of skirmishers and started toward the Indian village.

"Forward at a gallop, men!" Reno called, and the battalion swept across the plain to the thunder of hooves.

Reno fully expected the Indians to retreat, but surprisingly they stood their ground. Then, even more surprisingly, those on horseback started charging toward the soldiers.

"My God, they are attacking!" Reno said.

"No, Major, *we* are attacking. They are just coming to meet us," French replied.

"That gulley up there," Reno said, pointing to

a nearby ditch about three feet deep and ten feet wide. "We'll dismount and take cover there!"

"Dismount?" French asked in disbelief. "Major, we can't dismount! If we do, Custer's forces will really be divided!"

"I am in command here, Captain French!" Reno said. "I can't worry about Custer's forces, I have my own men to worry about. Dismount!" he yelled. "Take cover in that ditch!"

As yet, few shots had been fired, but when the Indians saw that Reno had checked his charge, the few who had feinted toward him to fight a rear guard action, suddenly took heart and began firing in earnest.

"Return fire!" Reno shouted, and a ripple of gunfire exploded along the ravine as the soldiers began firing.

"Major, we've got to get the men mounted," French insisted. "We can't fight here."

"This is a good defensive position," Reno insisted. "This is a very good place to fight."

"But we are supposed to be on the offense," French said.

"What do you want from me?" Reno yelled desperately. "Look out there! There are thousands of Indians in front of us! Where is Custer? He was supposed to support us!"

"Major, didn't you say he was going to hit them from the other side? We've got to keep moving or the Indians can crush us one at a time!"

An arrow stuck into the ground just beside Reno and he looked at it with a shocked expression.

"We can't stay here," he said. "They can drop their arrows right down on top of us. We've got to get back into the trees."

By now the soldiers were firing furiously and had nearly checked the Indians' advance.

"Major, look," French said. "The Indians are beginning to pull back. Come on, let's charge them. We can yet link with Custer."

"No. It's a trick. Move back to the woods," he called. "Move back to the woods!"

Reno started back to the woods, and the soldiers, climbed out of the gulley and followed him.

"French, what the hell is going on?" Lieutenant Varnum called. Custer had sent him to Reno as a liaison officer. "Doesn't Reno know the General expects him to attack?"

"He is attacking," French said dryly. "He's attacking the woodline."

With the realization that the soldiers were leaving, the Indians pressed their advantage, and a whole flight of arrows whistled down toward the two officers, who now found themselves virtually alone in the gulley.

"We'd better get out of here!" French said. He and Lieutenant Varnum scrambled up the opposite side of the gulley and ran like deer toward the tree line. Arrows and bullets kicked up the dust around them, but miraculously they weren't hit.

The soldiers, having taken a position in the treeline, opened fire at the Indians and once again had them nearly in check. French and Varnum tried again to convince Reno to rally the men and charge the village.

"You are asking me to lead my men into a slaughter pit," he said. "I simply won't do it!"

"Major, you don't know what you are doing," French insisted. "You are just giving this battle to the Indians! You don't understand the Indian mind."

"I don't, do I?" Reno said. "Bloody Knife! Bloody Knife, come here at once!"

Bloody Knife who had come to Reno with Varnum, hurried toward the commander.

"We'll just see about the Indian mind," Reno said. "Bloody Knife is an Indian. I'll get his opinion."

Bloody Knife joined them and stood before Reno.

"Bloody Knife, these 'gentlemen' are advising me to charge the enemy. They say I don't understand the Indian mind. What do you think?"

Bloody Knife opened his mouth to speak, but at that very moment his head nearly exploded as a bullet crashed into it. Blood and warm, gelatinous brain matter gushed out of the wound and splashed onto Reno's face.

"Oh . . . oh . . . oh my God!" Reno said. He backed away, horror struck, holding his hands out in front of him as if afraid that Bloody Knife's collapsing body would fall on him. "My God . . . oh . . . my God!" Reno said again.

"Major, get hold of yourself," French said.

Reno ran to his horse and leaped on the animal's back, then spurring it, started back toward the river. "Retreat!" he yelled. "Retreat!"

"Major Reno, come back here!" French shouted. Captain French raised his pistol and took a long, careful aim at the retreating major's back.

"French, no," Varnum said softly. "It isn't worth it."

French sighed, and lowered his pistol. "I should have shot the son-of-a-bitch when he dismounted at the gulley."

The soldiers, hearing a second order to retreat, feared the worst. In the space of a few moments they had seen what they thought was going to be a victory turn into a setback, then a defeat, and now a rout. Panic-stricken, they made a mad dash for the river, a mad, scrambling run, with the frightened horses running out of control.

"M Company, form as skirmishers to protect the crossing," French called. But M Company, taking a page from the book of their senior commander, leaped into the river. The pursuing Indians were having a field day, picking off the soldiers as they struggled across the water.

Until the moment Reno's battalion retreated across the river, only four or five had been killed and four wounded. But at the river more than thirty were killed as the Indians came up to the river bank and fired down at the hapless victims.

The soldiers who made the opposite bank started returning fire, and the Indians were driven back slightly. His command decimated by the river crossing, Reno moved into position on the bluffs overlooking the river, where he directed that breastworks be prepared.

The shooting stopped and an unearthly quiet came over the scene. All that could be heard was the heavy breathing and low moans of the wounded who had made it back to the bluffs.

They stayed in position for about fifteen minutes, waiting for what they were sure would be an Indian assault, when Lieutenant Varnum sat up and held up his hand.

"Listen," he said. "Do you hear that?"

From the distance came the low, muffled sound of gunfire.

"It's Custer," he said. "He is engaged."

"Why doesn't he come help us?" Reno asked petulantly.

"Major, I imagine he's got about all he can handle and then some," Varnum said.

"Major . . . Major . . . we are saved!" a trooper yelled. "It's Captain Benteen!"

Reno smiled for the first time since the engagement had begun. He ran down the bluff to meet Benteen, who was approaching from the opposite side.

"Benteen, am I glad to see you!" Reno said. "For

God's sake, stop and help us. We've been badly beaten here, and I've lost half of my command."

"I've just got a message from Custer to come quick," Benteen said.

"Custer? You know Custer, he's in his glory. I'm the one that needs help."

"I don't know," Benteen said. He ran his hand through his thick, white hair and twisted in his saddle to look at the men he had brought with him. "Maybe he meant join up with you. He said bring packs. I'm sure he didn't mean bring them while he was on the attack."

"Yes, yes," Reno said. "I am certain that is what he meant. Now, get your men dismounted and stay here with me. Our situation here is critical."

## 30

Joseph and Crimson had reached the north end of the big village when they heard the sounds of fighting from the south. They were actually hearing the sounds of the rear guard's engagement with Major Reno, though they supposed it was Custer himself.

The village was the largest Joseph had ever seen. In fact, though he had no way of knowing it at the time, it was the largest concentration of Indians ever to gather on the North American continent.

Sitting Bull was standing by his tent in an open area in the center of his village when he saw Joseph.

"Why are you here?" he demanded angrily. "I do not want you to fight against the white man anymore."

"I had to come to the village," Joseph said. "It was not safe for us."

"I will not turn you away," Sitting Bull said.

"I am glad. Now, tell me where I must go to fight."

"No," Sitting Bull said. "I will not let you fight.

You will stay with the women and the children and the old men."

"And the cowards?" Joseph asked sharply.

The expression on Sitting Bull's face softened. "Any who would call you a coward must call me a coward as well," he said. "For it is my wish that you not fight."

"Sitting Bull is right," Crazy Horse said. "It is not right that you should fight in this battle." Crazy Horse, dressed in war paint, reached down and patted his horse on the neck and spoke soothingly to the nervous animal.

"Long Hair comes now," Crazy Horse said.

"So," Sitting Bull said, a faraway expression on his face. "Now the vision will be proven true."

Sitting Bull held up his hands for attention.

"Warriors, Long Hair comes," he said. "We have everything to fight for. If we do not fight, we have nothing to live for. Go, fight well, and be brave."

Crazy Horse let out another whoop and dashed toward the river.

"Brave hearts to the front," Crazy Horse yelled. "Cowards to the rear! This is a good day to fight! This is a good day to die!"

From all over the village, warriors swarmed to join Crazy Horse. Many were mounted but most were on foot, and they crossed the river and quickly disappeared into the ravines and behind rocks and hills. To the person who had not seen the warriors hide, the approach to the river looked deceptively peaceful.

"Oh, Joseph, what is going to happen?" Crimson asked.

"If Custer tries to cross the river, he will be defeated," Joseph said. "In fact, he will be killed, as will all of his men."

"Can't we . . . can't we stop it?" Crimson asked in a small voice.

276

"No," Joseph said quietly. "If we tried now, we would be killed as well . . . and it would do Custer no good."

"But we've got to do something," Crimson said. "Joseph, we can't just sit here and watch Custer's entire army be massacred."

"Crimson, believe me," Joseph said. "We can do nothing."

"What a cruel twist of fate that I should be a witness to this," Crimson said.

As Custer crested the bluffs on the opposite side of the river from the village, he saw that the Indians would not run from him as he expected, but would stand and fight. He also realized for the first time that there were more Indians than he, or anyone else, had expected. At that, he couldn't see all of the village because his view of the section furthest downstream was obscured by the bends in the river and the timber growing along the banks.

"Damn, Autie, look at that," Tom said.

"It looks like New York City, only with tipis, doesn't it?" Custer said. He held his hand up and stopped the column.

"Where is Lieutenant Varnum?"

"You sent him with Reno," Tom informed him.

"Oh, yes, I did, at that. Well, Captain Cooke, select a messenger for me, would you?"

"Yes, sir," his adjutant said, and signalled a nearby trooper, a trumpeter named Martin.

"Trooper," Custer told him. "Get back to Benteen as fast as you can. Tell him we have spotted a big village here. Tell him to come quick and bring packs."

"Yes, sir," Martin said.

Captain Cooke was scribbling a message on a page in his notebook, and he tore the page out and handed it to Martin.

The trooper put the message in his shirt pocket and started off at a gallop. As he reached the bottom of the hill, he saw young Boston Custer coming toward him. Boston had been back with the pack train, but, anxious to be in on the excitement, was hurrying to join his brothers.

"Where is the General?" Boston yelled.

"Go over this hill and you'll find him," Martin replied, the two riders passing each other at a gallop.

Boston spurred his horse on faster, and as he crested the hill, he was rewarded by seeing his two brothers in front of a line of skirmishers.

"Wait!" Boston called. "Wait for me!"

"Dammit, Boston, what are you doing here?" Tom asked angrily. "I thought you were going to stay with the pack train."

"What? And miss all the fun?"

"You call it fun, do you? We'll see how much fun it is about ten minutes from now."

Tom turned back in his saddle and looked down toward the village. If they turned back now and rejoined forces with Reno and Benteen, they might be able to hold off the Indians until General Terry's column arrived. If they attacked, they would probably all be killed.

"Are you ready, Tom?" Custer asked quietly.

Tom looked over at him and nodded. He knew that his brother was aware of their situation. He also knew that they would be attacking.

So it had come down to this, he thought. This would be the end of the Custers. The great dynasty that Libby spoke about would be no more. He had been prevented from marrying Crimson, and now, it was going to end in a lonely valley in Montana. No cheering crowds, no fawning politicians, nothing but Indians.

Tom laughed.

"Well, brother Tom, I am pleased to see that you have maintained a sense of humor through it all," Custer said. "Perhaps you'll share the laugh with me."

"It's a joke," Tom said.

"What is the joke?"

"I don't have time to tell you now," Tom said. "I'll tell you tonight, over drinks."

"Over drinks?"

"In Fiddler's Green."

Custer laughed out loud. "Tom, my boy, you are on," he said.

He stood in his stirrups and looked back over his command. "Shall we, then?" he said.

"Why the hell not?" Tom replied, and nodded at the bugler, who sounded the charge.

The notes of the bugle call drifted down across the stream and into the village. Crimson stood in Joseph's arms, a cold chill traversing her body at the sound. Then she saw the soldiers charging down the hill toward the village. At first, she could hear only the beat of the hooves, then the jangle of gear and the rattle of sabers. Finally she heard the soldiers themselves, shouting and screaming at the top of their lungs as they approached.

Closer and closer they came, until the great blue mass became distinguishable as horses and riders, then closer yet until even the individual faces were visible. Crimson saw General Custer riding in front, but she didn't see Tom.

The Indians who were waiting in ambush held their fire until the soldiers hit the stream, then opened up. Several soldiers were hit, and the column was divided. Custer and several more crossed the stream and made it to the edge of the village, but the soldiers on the opposite side of the bank were caught in a murderous crossfire and were driven back.

"General, our line has been cut!" Captain Keough called.

"Damn, they must come across!" Custer called. He turned his horse and with his hat began to wave his troops over. But the soldiers wouldn't abandon their positions.

"Tom, start killing the women and children!" Custer called.

"What?" Tom replied. "What are you saying?"

"Do it, Tom, do it!" Custer shouted. "It's the only way to get the warriors over here!"

"Autie, I can't," Tom said.

"Do it, Captain! That's an order damn you!" Custer shouted.

Tom rode up from the bank of the stream, and pointed his pistol toward a group of children. A pained expression on his face, he cocked the hammer.

"Tom, no!" Crimson screamed, darting out from behind one of the tipis. Joseph ran out with her.

Tom couldn't have been more shocked if his own mother had suddenly appeared before him. He lowered the gun and stared at Crimson, then at Joseph, and his face grew deathly white.

"Crimson . . . you . . . what are you doing here?" he asked.

"Please, Tom, don't kill any of the children," Crimson begged.

"If you do, I'll kill you," Joseph promised.

Tom laughed. "Joseph, don't you know I'm going to be killed anyway? What difference does a few minutes make?"

Joseph put his arms around Crimson and pulled her to him, and they gazed at Tom. Finally the bitter smile left Tom's face, and Crimson saw in it the most incredible sadness she had ever beheld. Not fear . . . sadness. Finally he saluted with his pistol, then slipped it back into his holster.

"Kill the kids by yourself, General," Tom called, turning his horse back toward the river. "I'm going back to help our men."

Tom and the troopers started back across the river and Custer had no recourse but to follow them. On the other side of the river, the Indians were swirling around the soldiers like a swiftly flowing stream around pebbles. The soldiers rallied when Custer reached their side of the stream, and he led them in an organized withdrawal. Gradually they worked their way to the north end of the ridge, where they dug in to make a defensive stand.

Custer may have been able to mount a spirited enough defense here had it not been for the influx of hundreds of Indians from the south end of the valley. With Major Reno retreating, Gall and his warriors were able to join with the ones who were fighting Custer.

Gradually the volume of shooting diminished, and then the women and children of the village rushed across the stream and up onto the battlefield to witness the final stages of the battle.

Crimson was swept along with the others, and she had no choice but to go along with the swirling mob or be trampled. She found herself in the front rank of the spectators crowding around the battlefield to watch the final scenes as if they were the audience of a macabre play.

The horror and shock of what she had been subjected to so benumbed Crimson that she was able to watch almost with a sense of detachment. Her mind suspended reality, sparing her from further anguish as the grisly scene unfolded.

All around her, Crimson saw dead soldiers. Among the dead, she noticed with the same surrealistic sense, was Tom. One by one the remaining soldiers were gunned or clubbed down, until finally only General Custer himself remained alive. He had been shot through the side, and he was on his knees, holding his pistol in front of him. He pulled the trigger and the hammer fell on an empty chamber.

Custer looked at the pistol with bewilderment, as if unable to understand why it didn't fire. Then he looked at the Indians who surrounded him and laughed.

Even in Crimson's numbed state, she was shocked by his laughter, a strange, high-pitched eerie sound, as if it were echoing from the halls of hell.

One of the Indians nearest Custer raised his rifle and pointed it at Custer's head. Custer began to laugh even harder, and he shook his head.

"Yes," he gasped. "Yes, yes, yes!"

One dull, cracking sound, and Custer pitched onto his back, his laughter silenced forever. The sound of the rifle shot rolled back from the hills; for several seconds after the echo of the shot died away, there was absolute and total silence.

The Indians stood around for several moments, too shocked by what had happened to do anything. There was no celebration of victory, nor wailing for the dead. No one spoke a word.

Quietly Joseph took the reins of two unwounded horses that were standing by their dead cavalrymen, and he walked over to Crimson, leading the animals. He helped Crimson mount her horse, then climbed onto his, and slowly, without looking back, they rode away.

## 31

It was late afternoon. Major Reno, Captain Benteen and the other soldiers in the hills at the south end of the valley saw the Sioux pulling out of the village. In an orderly fashion the Indians headed south down the valley of Greasy Grass toward the Big Horn Mountains. The column of Indians was from two to three miles long, and consisted of from eight to ten thousand people, including about 4,000 warriors and countless ponies.

"Major," Benteen said, watching the exodus. "It's been several hours since we've heard the last gunshot. I think we had better go north now and link up with Custer."

"No," Reno said. "We will stay here. Suppose they have Custer surrounded, just as they do us. If we tried to link with him, we would walk right into a trap."

"A trap? Major, who is left to close the trap? My God, half the Indians in North America were in that column we just saw."

"That may be, Captain," Reno said. "But the

other half may be up there, just waiting for us." He pointed north, and from the agitation in his voice, it was obvious that he wasn't going to be persuaded to leave his position of safety on the hill.

"Then if you have no intention of attempting to link with Custer, you should at least consider moving to a better position," Benteen said. "The hills just to the north of us would be easier to defend. Also, the stench from the dead men and horses is unhealthy."

"Yes," Reno said. "Yes, perhaps you are right about that. All right, we'll move upstream and take up a new defensive position."

"And, don't you think we should send out messengers to try and make contact with Custer?"

"No," Reno said. "Custer is the senior commander in the field. It is his responsibility to make contact with me. My only responsibility is to the safety of my men."

Benteen made a few more suggestions to Reno, but Reno was unresponsive. Finally, Benteen took upon himself the responsibility for the soldiers, becoming commanding officer in fact if not in name. He saw to it that the cooks prepared as good a supper as was possible under the circumstances, and the troopers relaxed for the first time in almost two days.

At dusk Benteen had the horses and mules led down to the river, where they were watered and put out to graze. The animals had suffered severely. Many had been killed, and many more were so badly wounded that the soldiers had to kill them as well.

During the night a few stragglers returned, men who had been separated from the troops during the fighting. The men slept half on and half off during the night, and they kept their weapons at the ready for any contingency.

Joseph and Crimson slept the sleep of the exhausted that night. Crimson's fatigue spared her any nightmares she may have had as a result of having witnessed the horrible battle the day before. Joseph, who normally slept so lightly that the landing of a butterfly could awaken him, was also totally exhausted, which may have accounted for the fact that the four men dressed in soldier blue were able to sneak up on the two sleeping figures.

"Wake up Injun lover, or I'll kill you where you lay," said the man wearing sergeant's stripes on his arm. He was in a semi-crouch position with his pistol in front of him, steadied by both hands and aimed right at Joseph's head.

Joseph sat up quickly and just as quickly appraised the situation. He froze, not wanting to startle the four men who were pointing pistols at him.

Crimson woke up and she let out a little gasp and sat up. Joseph put his arms around her to comfort her.

"What is it?" she asked. "What is going on?"

"Hey, she speaks English, Sarge," one of the soldiers said in surprise.

"Of course she speaks English," the sergeant said. "She's a white woman. You ever see an injun with hair that color?"

"You mean she's a *squaw?*"

"You might say that," the sergeant said. "Then again, you might not. You see, we got us a good bit o' fortune here."

"Who are you?" Crimson asked. "What do you want?"

"Who am I?" the sergeant asked. "Well, I'll just tell you, missy. I'm Sergeant Tucker of the Second Cavalry, and these here men is my patrol. We was supposed to be lookin' for injuns, but we ain't found any." He smiled broadly. "What I found though, was a lot better. 'Cause what I found has just earned me a furlough, and enough reward money to have a fine time while I'm furloughin'."

"What are you talkin' about, Sarge?" one of his men asked.

"You mean you don't know?" Sergeant Tucker answered. "Why, unless I miss my guess, this white man here, who is all dressed up like an injun, is Joseph Two Hearts. He's a traitor. The question is, who are you, missy?"

"I am Crimson Royal," Crimson said. "And this gentleman has saved my life."

Sergeant Tucker squirted a stream of tobacco from between his teeth, then wiped his mouth with the back of his hand and smiled.

"Well, now, you don't say. Saved your life, did he? That's a mighty fine thing, ain't it?"

"I think so," Crimson said.

Sergeant Tucker laughed. "Well, now. From the looks of things, I mean, the way you two was all cozied up in bed when me 'n' my men come sneakin' up here, why, I'd'a thought there was a little more to it than that. 'Course it could be that you was just bein' grateful to 'im. Was that it, missy? Was you bein' grateful?"

"Sarge, let's get them back to the column," one of the other soldiers said. "I'm gettin' spooked bein' this far away from the others."

"Yeah, me, too," one of the other soldiers said.

"All right," Sergeant Tucker replied. "But I think we ought to tie this feller up good 'n' proper. I don't want to take no chances on loosin' him."

"Yeah, Sarge, I'm with you. From the looks of this guy he might be pretty sneaky. I don't want him around me iffen he gets loose."

Joseph's hands were tied roughly, and he was shoved toward his horse.

"Hey, Sarge . . . look at these two horses. Did you see the saddle blankets and the brands?"

Sergeant Tucker walked over to the horses. The

286

blankets were blue with a gold stripe and crossed sabers in the corner. On the flank of the horse was the brand **3/7** and another crossed saber.

"These here animals belong to the third of the Seventh Cavalry," Sergeant Tucker said. "Where'd you come by them?"

Joseph, who hadn't spoken a word yet, was silent.

"Maybe he don't savvy white man's lingo, for all him bein' white," one of the soldiers said.

"He savvy's all right," Sergeant Tucker replied. "Maybe he just don't want to talk for no mere sergeant. Maybe he wants to talk to General Terry."

"General Terry?" Crimson asked. "Are you with General Terry's command?"

"Yeah," Sergeant Tucker said. "What of it?"

"Is Colonel Gray with your column?"

"Yeah, I think he is," Sergeant Tucker said, his face reflecting surprise over her comment. "How come you to know him?"

"Never mind, Sergeant," Crimson said. "I just know him, that's all. Joseph, don't worry. Everything will be all right now."

"Yeah?" Tucker said. "Well, we'll just see about that. Now mount up, girl. We're gonna just go see General Terry and your friend Colonel Gray."

With Joseph and Crimson mounted, the soldiers surrounded them and they rode down the side of the hill and out into the broad valley below.

This valley looked exceptionally peaceful when contrasted with the valley of death by the Little Big Horn. Under the morning sun the valley was especially green, and the river, which snaked through the valley like a large letter *S,* was shining gold.

They rode at a jog for about an hour before they reached the approaching column. The officer at the head of the column called for a halt.

"What do you have here, Sergeant?"

"General Terry, this is that white traitor that General Custer put out paper on. His name is Joseph Two Hearts."

"Is that right?" General Terry asked Joseph.

Joseph didn't answer.

"Lookit the horses they's ridin'," the sergeant said. He squirted another stream of tobacco between his teeth.

"Third of the Seventh," General Terry said, looking at the brand. "Those animals belong to Custer's regiment."

"That's right, General," the sergeant said.

"Who are you?" General Terry asked Crimson.

"I can answer that," another officer said, riding abreast of the two prisoners.

"Hello, Colonel Gray," Crimson said.

"You know this woman?" General Terry asked.

"This is the lady I told you about," Colonel Gray said. "This is Crimson Royal."

"The daughter of the artist?"

"Yes, sir."

"I see," General Terry said. He looked back at Crimson. "Well, madam, I imagine there are those who will be glad to discover that you are safe. Just as there are those of us who will be interested in your explanations."

"It's as I told these men," Crimson said. "This gentleman saved my life."

"What are you doing here in the first place?" Colonel Gray asked. "I left you under the protection of two of my scouts."

"Some protection," Crimson said. "If it hadn't been for Joseph, I'd be dead by now. Your scouts were . . . despicable men, and they attempted to assault me. Joseph saved me from them."

"Joseph. So you are Joseph Two Hearts?" General Terry said. "You admit it?"

288

"That is what the Indians call me," Joseph said, speaking for the first time since his capture.

"Well, I'll be damned, he does know our lingo," one of the soldiers who had been with Sergeant Tucker said.

"General, you'll keep it in mind who it was what brung him in, won't you?" Sergeant Tucker reminded him. "When it comes time for the reward, I don't want to miss out none."

"I don't have anything to do with a reward," General Terry said.

"They's paper out on this fella, I know they is," Sergeant Tucker said. "General Custer put it out."

"Then we shall let Custer handle the matter. I imagine he will be pleased enough to see him. I guess he'll be glad to see you too, Miss Royal. After all, I understand you were his guest at Fort Lincoln for the winter."

"General Custer?" Crimson said weakly.

"Yes. We are going to link up with him shortly."

"General Terry . . . Colonel Gray . . . you mean you don't know?"

"Know what?"

"Custer," Crimson said. "He . . . he . . ."

"He what? Come on, girl. Speak up."

"Custer is dead," Joseph said.

"Dead? How, when?"

"He was killed in battle yesterday afternoon," Joseph said.

"No," General Terry said. "No, I am certain you are mistaken. If he had been, a messenger would have reached me with the news by now. It is standard procedure. His next in command would have kept me informed."

"There is no next in command," Joseph said. "And there is no one to send as a messenger. They are all dead. Custer's enitre command was killed."

289

General Terry laughed. "What are you trying to say? Are you trying to convince me that a handful of half-naked savages not only defeated Custer, but killed every man jack in his command as well?"

"Yes," Joseph said.

"General, you don't think that could be true, do you?" an officer asked.

"No, no, of course not," Terry said. "You two, ride up here in front with me so I can keep an eye on you. Colonel Gibbon, order the column forward. We'll have a look-see."

"Very well, General," Colonel Gibbon said, and the order was passed down through the troops.

"Miss Royal," Colonel Gray said, riding beside her. "What is this preposterous tale you and Joseph Two Hearts are trying to tell us?"

"It's true, Colonel Gray. Every word of it, I swear. Though, God in heaven, I wish it weren't."

Colonel Gray, a strained expression on his face, hurried his horse up to catch up with General Terry, who was now riding about twenty yards in front of the column. Colonel Gray said a few words to General Terry, speaking too quietly for Crimson to hear, then hurried back and gave some instructions to Colonel Gibbons.

"Lieutenant Bradley," Colonel Gibbons called.

A young officer pulled his horse out of the formation and rode quickly up to Colonel Gibbons.

"Take a scouting detail out and survey the area. Be especially watchful."

"Yes, sir," the lieutenant said. He stood in his stirrups and yelled for the first platoon of D company to follow him. They broke away from the main column at a gallop, and shortly disappeared over the hills ahead.

Several more minutes after the scouts left, the column ascended a line of low sandstone bluffs. From the top of the bluffs they looked down into the Little

Big Horn valley for the first time since the battle. General Terry halted his men, and they stared down at the valley that the day before had rung with the sounds of battle.

Today the valley was very quiet. From this vantage point they could see some abandoned tipis and a few horses grazing in the timber near the stream. Nearly all the river was black and smoking, and Crimson dimly remembered the smoke rising behind them as they left yesterday.

Where the great Indian camp had stood yesterday, there was now only the funeral tipis and a great pile of garbage abandoned by the Indians.

"It looks quiet enough, General," Colonel Gray said.

"There is no danger," Joseph said. "The Indians have gone. They left last night."

"Mr. Two Hearts, I wouldn't trust you any further than I can throw you," General Terry said.

"He's telling you the truth, General," Crimson said. "Why don't you believe him?"

"Miss Royal, you are scarcely in the position to vouch for him. I'm not convinced of your credibility either."

"Shall we send scouts down first, General?" Colonel Gibbon asked.

"No," General Terry said. "Inform the men to be on extra alert, and we'll go on down together."

"Yes, sir," Colonel Gibbon replied, and the command started down into what was left of the village.

As the soldiers rode into camp they were greeted with a smell which let them know in no uncertain terms that here was a place of death. Dogs running in packs darted around, barking and snarling at the invading army and nipping at the heels of the horses. But the dogs were the only resistance they encountered.

Terry halted his men just inside the perimeter of

where the village had been and pointed at one of the lodges which was still standing. "Check that out," he ordered.

A lieutenant and a sergeant dismounted and stepped inside, then came back out after a few seconds.

"There are eight warriors in here," the Lieutenant said. "All dead. "They're dressed up in their finest costumes and laid out on scaffolds."

"General, look at that," one of the soldiers said. He slid off his horse and ran over to pick up an object lying on the ground. He examined it, then brought it back to the General.

"What is it?"

"It's a pair of underdrawers, sir," the soldier said. "There's blood on them, and the words, 'Sturgis— Seventh Cavalry'."

"General, look at this . . . there's an officer's tunic with a bullet hole in it," Dr. Paulding said.

"Oh, my God!" someone called, his voice tinged with horror. He came running from one of the other lodges. "Oh, my God, do you know what is in there?"

"What? What is it?" one of the men called.

"Heads," the trooper screamed. "Dozens of heads. Heads of white men."

Crimson felt dizzy and nauseous, and she leaned forward in the saddle, grabbing onto the saddlehorn.

"Are you all right, Miss Royal?" Colonel Gray asked.

"Yes," Crimson said quietly.

Lieutenant Bradley, who had ridden out on the scouting party, returned then, and, in a voice trembling with emotion, reported to General Terry and Colonel Gibbon.

"I have a very sad report to make. I have counted one hundred and ninety-seven bodies lying in the hills."

"White men?"

"Yes, sir. I've never seen General Custer in person, but from pictures I've seen, I believe one of the bodies to be his."

A ripple of shock passed through the men.

"Where did these two get Seventh horses?" one of the soldiers shouted.

"Yeah, that's what I'd like to know."

"How'd they know Custer was dead?"

"He's a traitor, you heard him say he was Two Hearts."

"Let's kill this son-of-a-bitch!"

"Hold it!" General Terry ordered, riding back quickly to position his horse between Joseph and the angry soldiers of his command.

"General, what are you protecting him for? Custer and all his men are dead because of him."

"You're a general," one of the others shouted. "You got the right to execute the bastard right here. Give us the word 'n' we'll do it for you!"

"No," General Terry said, holding up his hand. "Men, listen to me. If we killed him here, it would be no more than a lynching, no matter what power I have. We've got to take him back to Fort Lincoln where the full story can come out. If he is guilty, he'll hang there, I promise you. And the woman . . ." General Terry looked at Crimson, and his lips curled into a snarl. "By God, she'll hang, too."

## 32

The slanting bars of a late afternoon sun shone through the barred windows and made squares of light on the floor. Crimson lay on the bed and watched the floating dust motes, wondering about her fate. It had been almost two weeks since she and Joseph were returned to Fort Lincoln. Two weeks, and in all that time she had talked to no one, except the private who brought her her meals.

Her "jail" wasn't all that uncomfortable. In fact, it had been the quarters of one of the officers who had been killed with Custer. She was thankful she hadn't been given Tom's quarters. They had not been offered to her, but she wouldn't have wanted them if they had.

Crimson had been certain that Libbie would come to speak to her, and hoped that she would. But in the two weeks since she returned, Libbie hadn't come, nor had she even sent word.

Crimson was desperate to know about Joseph, but no matter how often she begged for information, the private who brought her her meal told her nothing.

The one encouraging sign she did have was the fact that a scaffold hadn't been built. There could be no hanging without a scaffold. And from that, at least, she was able to take scant comfort.

But why hadn't anyone come to see her, or to tell her anything? That was what bothered her the most—the waiting and the uncertainty.

And then one afternoon there was a change in the routine. She heard the door being opened, and by the position of the sun, she knew that it was much too early for her supper to be brought to her. She had a visitor!

Crimson sat up and self-consciously put her hand to her hair as if to adjust it. Despite herself, she nearly laughed at this bit of vanity.

"She's right in there, sir," the private said, pointing to the bed where Crimson sat. "If you need me, I'll be right outside."

"Why should I need you, for heaven's sake? Do you suppose she is going to try and attack me?"

"Paul!" Crimson shouted happily. "Paul Gideon! My God, you have no idea how happy I am to see you! What are you doing out here?"

Her father's art agent smiled broadly and held his arms out to her. She ran to them with a short cry of joy, and feeling the comforting embrace of another human being for the first time in over two weeks, began crying.

"There, darling, you just go ahead and cry all you want," Paul said comfortingly. He patted her on the back and rocked her back and forth soothingly. "Paul's here now. Everything is going to be all right."

Finally, after a few moments, Crimson regained some of her composure. She walked back over to her bed and offered him a seat.

"I'm sorry, they don't allow me to have a chair," she said. "I hope the bed is all right."

"It's fine," Paul said. "Really it is."

"Paul, have you heard about Joseph? How is he?"

"He's fine," Paul said. "In fact, that is one of the reasons I am here."

"Why? What do you mean?"

"Well, it seems that Fort Lincoln has a most interesting visitor right now . . . and Joseph's services are needed."

"Paul, don't be so mysterious," Crimson said. "What are you talking about?"

"I'm talking about Sitting Bull," Paul said. "He's here, in the fort."

"Sitting Bull? You mean the army captured Sitting Bull?"

"No, not exactly," Paul said. "He came under a flag of truce to hold a peace conference with a personal representative of President Grant. But he insisted that Joseph be used as his interpreter. And Joseph refused to interpret unless you are allowed to attend the sessions. He said he wanted to see you."

"Oh, I want to see him, too," Crimson said. "Yes, yes, I'll go. Besides, I'll be glad to get out of here for a while." She looked around the room. "I know Joseph is being kept in the guardhouse, and I know it is much worse than this. But believe me, Paul, when you are a prisoner, anywhere is bad."

Paul smiled. "Well, then, perhaps I can tell you the second reason why I am here."

"Oh? What is the second reason you are here?"

"To tell you that you are free," Paul said. "The army is dropping all charges against you. It seems that people are already beginning to ask a few questions about the battle. Questions like, Was Custer a gallant leader who died a brave death with his men, or was he a glory-hunting fool who, in self-serving violation of orders, led his men into a senseless slaughter? That's why they are so anxious to talk to Sitting Bull. He is the first spokesman from the other side."

"Joseph or I could have given an account of the battle," Crimson shivered. "Though I don't believe I would want to."

"No, nor would the army want you to. Especially now that they are dropping their charges."

"What about the charges against Joseph?"

"No, they still stand," Paul said. "In truth, the army never really had much of a case against you, anyway. You and your father clearly had permission to paint the Indians, and they were clearly unable to protect you. But the case against your Mr. Two Hearts is quite another matter."

"Oh, Paul, please, you must do everything you can to save him. Promise me that you will," Crimson said.

Paul looked at Crimson, then sighed. "You must really love that savage."

"He's *not* a savage!" Crimson said hotly. And then, when she realized how loudly she had made that declaration, she gave a little laugh. "I'm sorry," she said. "But he isn't a savage. He is a gentle, honest, and honorable man. And, yes. I do love him. I love him more than I ever thought I could love anyone. Now, Paul, you must promise me you will help him."

"I'll do what I can," Paul said. "Now, come on. You do want to see him, don't you?"

"Yes," Crimson said. "Yes, very much."

"Then you shall." He walked over to the door and rapped on it. The private opened it and looked inside.

"We are both ready to come out," Paul said. He pulled a paper from his pocket. "Here is an order signed by the general, authorizing her release."

"What?" Crimson said. "You mean you had that

all along, and you made me stay here while we talked?"

"Believe me, Crimson, this was the best place to talk," Paul said. "Wait until you see the Sutlers' store where the hearing is."

Paul was right. Crimson had never seen so many people at the store, even during the dances. Soldiers were crowded around outside as Paul and Crimson approached.

Crimson heard a buzz of excitement from the soldiers, but she could not make out what they were saying. But for the moment, she was so happy to be free from confinement that it wouldn't have made any difference, anyway. Let them say whatever they wanted. She was free, and in just a moment, she would be seeing Joseph.

"Make way, men, make way and let her through!" Colonel Gray called from the porch of the store. "Miss Royal, come right on up this way."

The crowd of soldiers parted further, and Crimson walked up onto the porch, where Colonel Gray saluted her.

"Thank you for coming," he said. "Your friend is being most difficult for us. He knows how desperately we wish to talk to Sitting Bull, and he won't interpret for us unless you are present."

"I'm not doing this for the army, Colonel Gray," Crimson said resolutely. "I'm doing this for one reason and one reason only—so I can see Joseph."

"Very well, madam," Colonel Gray said. "But whatever the reason, you have the army's gratitude."

Colonel Gray opened the door to the store and Crimson stepped inside. A few lucky enlisted men had managed to find room along the walls to stand, and one or two of them even had a barrel to use for a seat. But the chairs were all taken by officers and civilians, both commissioners and journalists. A photographer set off a flashpan of magnesium powder the moment Crimson stepped inside.

A swell of sound greeted her arrival, and a civilian seated behind a table in front of the room pounded a gavel until the sound quieted.

"Please, ladies and gentlemen," the man said. "This is not a court of law, but an official inquiry into facts surrounding the incidents that occurred in the field two weeks ago. I am representing the president of the United States, and as such, have the authority to conduct this hearing behind closed doors if necessary. If you are to witness it, you must be quiet."

The man's words had their effect, and the crowd quieted.

Crimson looked toward the front of the room, where she saw Libbie. She smiled at her, and her heart went out to her for her sorrow, but Libbie looked away. Crimson looked at the floor in sadness.

"Now, would you bring in our witness and the interpreter, please?"

Crimson looked toward the back door, and then her heart leaped for joy, for there was her Joseph. How wonderful it was to see him! And yet, sad too, for Joseph was in handcuffs. Instead of the buckskin breeches she had become used to seeing him wear, he was dressed in denim trousers and a red flannel shirt. It was the first time she had ever seen him in white man's clothing.

He looked over at her and smiled broadly. Crimson returned his smile, and started toward him, but Colonel Gray restrained her.

"I'm sorry, Miss Royal," he said. "But they won't let you get near him."

"But I must," Crimson said. "Don't you understand? I must!"

"I'm sorry."

Crimson looked back at Joseph and smiled again, only now there were tears in her eyes, her joy at seeing him again made bittersweet by the distance between them still.

Sitting Bull came in then, and Crimson looked over at him. It was the first time she had seen him since that terrible afternoon in the village during the battle. Sitting Bull was wearing a black and white calico shirt, black cloth leggings, and moccasins magnificently embroidered with beads and porcupine quills.

Sitting Bull began to speak in his own language. It was sometimes guttural and barking, sometimes musical and lilting, but always spoken with the force of a man who knew his words would be listened to. He spoke quietly so that Joseph's simultaneous translation could be clearly heard.

"This land belongs to us. It is a gift to us from the Great Spirit. The Great Spirit gave us the game in the country. It is our privilege to hunt the game in our country. The white man came here to take the country from us by force. He has brought misery and wretchedness into our country. We were here killing game and eating, and all of a sudden we were attacked by white men. Now we are tired of fighting and we want the soldiers to stop fighting us. The Great Spirit sees the bloody deeds going on in this country. Though he gave us the country, he did not give us the right to dispose of it. It is our duty to defend our country. We did not want to fight the white man, but now if they wish to withdraw, they may. We do not wish to fight them, but if the whites wish to keep up the war, we can fight for three years. We have plenty of game and everything else."

"Yes," said the commissioner, a man named Morris. Morris was a small man with wire-rimmed glasses and a tiny moustache, which he rubbed with his finger as he talked. "Yes, well, that may be so. But you will never be able to withstand the forces of the entire United States. So, we won't speak of wars yet to come. Though I do wish to speak to you of the war which was. Now, I know you are a great chief, but—"

"I am no chief."

"You aren't a chief?" Norris asked in surprise.

"No."

"Then, what are you?"

"I am," Sitting Bull said, crossing both hands upon his chest and smiling slightly, "a man."

"What does he mean by that, Mr. Two Hearts?" Morris asked.

"It is difficult to explain," Joseph said. "But white men tend to use the word 'chief' far too much. Sitting Bull has influence over his people. He speaks and they listen. But he does not demand."

"You mean he is only a medicine man?"

Joseph smiled. "Don't use the term 'only' in that way when you are talking about Sitting Bull as a medicine man. In fact, he is a medicine man, but a far more influential one than any I have ever known."

"I see," Morris said. "And it is my understanding Mr. Two Hearts, that you have known a few."

"I have," Joseph said. "I am a member of the Soldier Lodge. It is impossible to be a member without knowing a few medicine men."

"What is the Soldier Lodge?" Morris asked.

"Mr. Morris, may I answer that?" General Crook suddenly said, standing quickly.

"You, General? Yes, of course you may."

"Mr. Morris, I, too, am a member of the Soldier Lodge," General Crook said.

There was a gasp from many of the onlookers and General Crook went on.

"It is a privilege reserved for very few people

of any race. Besides Mr. Two Hearts, whose real name is Baker, I know of only one more white person besides myself who is a member. It is a unique honor in Sioux society, akin to the highest order in Masonry. I have nothing but respect for any who would hold such a position."

"But General, I don't understand," Morris said. "How did you come by such an honor? You have been the enemy to the Sioux."

Sitting Bull spoke then, with Joseph interpreting.

"For the Indian there is as much honor in being a good enemy as in being a good ally. General Crook is a man who is much feared and hated by the Indians. And for that he is much honored and respected. Hate is a prized emotion among Indians and is given away no less easily than love."

"I see," Morris said, then looked up in surprise. "How did Sitting Bull know what we were saying?"

"He speaks English," Joseph said. "But he understands easier than he speaks, so he wishes to speak with my tongue."

"Very well," Morris said. "So Sitting Bull is not a chief, he is a medicine man. How did he become a medicine man?"

"I see. I know," Sitting Bull said. "I began to see when I was not yet born; when I was not in my mother's arms, but inside of my mother's belly. It was there that I began to study about my people."

"I don't understand—" Morris began, but Joseph interrupted him.

"Let him speak," Joseph said. "He is explaining his medicine. This is a rare thing."

"I was," Sitting Bull went on, "still in my mother's insides when I began to study all about my people. The Great Spirit gave me the power to see out of the womb. I studied there, in the womb, about many things. I studied about the smallpox that was killing my people. I was so interested that

I turned over on my side. The Great Spirit must have told me at that time that I would be the man to be the judge of all the other Indians. A big man to decide for them in all their ways."

"And you have since decided for them?"

"I speak. It is enough."

"Well, we must move on, Sitting Bull. I want to speak to you about the battle in which General Custer was killed. Here is a map of the valley where the battle took place. Can you understand the map?"

Sitting Bull looked at a large map, showing a long village stretching up and down on the east side of the map, a river running down the middle, and a ridge of hills running down the west side.

"Now, where was the Indian camp first attacked?"

"Here," Sitting Bull said, pointing to the south end of the village where Reno made his first assault.

"About what time was that?"

"It was two hours past the time when the sun is in the center of the sky."

"What white chief attacked you here?"

"I believe it was Long Hair," Sitting Bull said.

There was a buzz in the store, and Mr. Morris looked up warningly.

"It was actually Major Reno," Morris said. "But of course, you had no way of knowing that. Was there a good fight there?"

"No," Sitting Bull said. "That was a trick. The soldiers did not fight hard there, because they thought to fool us. The real fight was here." He pointed to the north of the village at the place where Custer made his attack.

"But what of the fight here?" Morris asked, pointing again to Reno's position.

"Not much fighting there," Sitting Bull said. "The soldiers come, and the soldiers run away. Some stay on the hill, I think, and the others come to attack the village up here. So all the warriors came up here."

"But what about the warriors down here? Major Reno was pinned down on that hill for twenty-four hours. How many warriors were there?"

"No warriors," Sitting Bull said. "Only some old women and young papooses."

One or two enlisted men laughed derisively. But the officers who had been at the hill saw no humor in the situation.

"I see," Morris said. "Now, tell me about the fight here." He pointed to the point on the map where Custer made his attack.

"Our young men rained lead across the river and drove the white braves back," he said.

"And then?"

"And then they rushed across themselves, from the sides. The soldiers were exhausted, and their horses got in the way, and they could not take good aim. Some of the horses broke away and left the soldiers to die. Long Hair had the bugle blow and the soldiers fell back, still fighting, but they could not fire fast enough because there were too many Indians."

"Did the command fight until the last?" Morris asked.

"There were no cowards," Sitting Bull said.

"What about Long Hair," General Crook asked from the floor. "How did Long Hair equip himself?"

"Long Hair stood like a sheaf of corn with all the ears fallen around him."

"Not wounded?"

"No."

"How many stood by him?"

"A few."

"When did he fall?"

"He was the last to fall," Sitting Bull said. "He

tried to shoot his pistol, but it would not fire. And then he laughed, and then he was killed."

"You mean he cried out?"

"No, he laughed," Sitting Bull said. "He laughed at death. He was a very brave man."

A chair scraped across the floor, and everyone looked over to see Libbie standing. At first, they thought it was because the testimony was too painful for her, and General Crook opened his mouth as if to apologize. But then they saw that Libbie was smiling proudly.

"Thank you, Sitting Bull. Thank you very much," she said. "You have made me very happy to confirm my belief in my husband's bravery."

The audience gasped as she left the Sutlers' store in haughty pride.

## 33

Crimson was in her quarters, the same ones she had occupied during her confinement. But now the door wasn't locked and the cabin wasn't guarded. But with no word as to the fate of Joseph, she felt just as miserable as she had when she was a prisoner.

Then, one week after the hearing, Paul came into her quarters, a large smile on his face.

"Paul, you have something?" Crimson asked excitedly. "You have some news for me?"

"Sort of," Paul said.

"Well, tell me. Don't keep me in suspense."

"You shall be happy to hear that I have negotiated a painting for you."

"You have what?" Crimson asked, crestfallen. She had hoped for news about Joseph, and he brought her word of the sale of a painting.

"After all," Paul said. "You are a painter, and you must continue your work. And now that your father is gone, you must carry on."

"I don't know," Crimson said.

"Crimson, what do you mean you don't know? This is Paul Gideon speaking. Remember me? I'm your agent. You have me to look out for too, you know."

"But Paul, I can't work now. Not until I know what is going to happen to Joseph."

"Wait until you find out what the painting is before you say you can't do it," Paul said.

"All right, what is the painting?"

"It's Custer's battle."

"Custer's . . . oh, Paul, no," Crimson said. "No, I couldn't . . . I wouldn't do that. It's too . . . it's just too horrible. I don't even want to think about it. And I especially don't want to paint it."

"Crimson, it might be good for you," Paul said gently. "If you paint it, you might be able to get it out of your mind, once and for all."

"No," Crimson said. "Even if you were right, even if it would help me forget . . . I couldn't do it to Libbie. I couldn't put her through it."

Paul laughed.

"What's funny, Paul? I mean it. I don't want to hurt Libbie anymore than she has already been hurt."

"I'm sorry, Crimson," Paul said. "I shouldn't have laughed. It's just that . . . this painting is for Libbie, didn't you know that? She is the one who wants it done."

"Paul, surely you are mistaken," Crimson said with a horrified gasp. "Why would she want anything so . . . so terrible?"

"Oh, no, my dear. You misunderstand. She doesn't want it terrible . . . she wants it heroic."

"Heroic?"

"Oh, absolutely," Paul said. "She is a fascinating lady, that woman. Do you know what she intends to do?"

"What?"

"She intends to make Custer into the greatest hero in American history. In fact, she told me she intends to spend the rest of her life doing just that."

"Yes," Crimson said with a sigh. "Yes, I can understand that. She couldn't make him a president while he lived, so now that he is dead, she'll promote him to an even higher honor. Well, she's going to have to do it with someone else, because I won't help her. It's just too bizarre."

"Crimson, wait until you hear the price she is willing to pay," Paul said.

"The price? Paul, I won't do it at any price," Crimson said.

"At least listen to it, will you?" Paul pleaded. "I'm telling you, this is a good price. I'm a good agent, aren't I? Do you think I would even let you consider such a thing if I didn't think you were getting a fair price for it?"

"I don't care what it is," Crimson said. "She could offer me five thousand, ten thousand, even twenty thousand dollars, and I wouldn't do it."

"She's offered two hundred and fifty dollars," Paul said. "That's all she can afford."

"Paul, it isn't the money, and you know that," Crimson said.

Paul smiled. "Yes, I know it," he said. "That's why I got another concession. The army is dropping the charges against one Joseph Baker."

There was a moment of stunned silence, as Crimson looked at Paul with an incredulous look on her face. "Paul, you aren't just telling me this, are you?" she asked in a small voice. "Because if you are . . ." she let the word hang.

"No, darling, I'm not just telling you this," Paul said. "I've made a bargain with her. If you will paint the heroic picture she wants, she will use her influence with General Terry to have the charges against Joseph Baker dropped."

Suddenly Crimson screamed and flew through the door of the small cabin.

"Joseph!" she yelled. "Joseph, you are free, you are free!"

Crimson ran across the quadrangle so fast that she scarcely felt her feet touch the ground; she didn't even see the formation of soldiers under the flagpole.

When she reached the guardhouse, one of the guards stepped in front of her.

"Get out of my way, you fool!" Crimson shouted. "Don't you know he's free?"

The confused guard looked toward the officer who was drilling the soldiers in the quadrangle, and the officer looked toward the commandant's house. There, on the front porch, Libbie nodded her head ever so slightly, and the officer signalled for the guard to step aside. Crimson threw the latch and a second later Joseph was outside, holding her in his arms, smothering her lips with kisses.

On the porch Libbie watched the scene, and for just a moment it wasn't Crimson and Joseph, but Libbie and Autie . . . Sunshine and Bo . . . and the guidon snapping sharply red and white in the afternoon breeze wasn't held by an orderly but her own sweet Armstrong. Her eyes dimmed with tears, but her heart surged with joy. Custer would live in the pages of history forever.

On the parade ground the band suddenly struck up a song. It was *Garry Owen.*

# Paula Fairman

## Romantic intrigue at its finest—
## over 2,000,000 copies in print!

# The Windhaven Saga
## by Marie de Jourlet

### Over 4,000,000 copies in print!

# Patricia Matthews

**...an unmatched sensuality, tenderness and passion.**
**No wonder there are over 14,000,000 copies in print!**

☐ **40-644-4 LOVE, FOREVER MORE** $2.50
The tumultuous story of spirited Serena Foster and her determination to survive the raw, untamed West.

☐ **40-646-0 LOVE'S AVENGING HEART** $2.50
Life with her brutal stepfather in colonial Williamsburg was cruel, but Hannah McCambridge would survive—and learn to love with a consuming passion.

☐ **40-645-2 LOVE'S DARING DREAM** $2.50
The turbulent story of indomitable Maggie Donnevan, who fled the poverty of Ireland to begin a new life in the American Northwest.

☐ **40-658-4 LOVE'S GOLDEN DESTINY** $2.50
It was a lust for gold that brought Belinda Lee together with three men in the Klondike gold rush, only to be trapped by the wildest of passions.

☐ **40-395-X LOVE'S MAGIC MOMENT** $2.50
Evil and ecstasy are entwined in the steaming jungles of Mexico, where Meredith Longley searches for a lost city but finds greed, lust, and seduction.

☐ **40-394-1 LOVE'S PAGAN HEART** $2.50
An exquisite Hawaiian princess is torn between love for her homeland and the only man who can tame her pagan heart.

☐ **40-659-2 LOVE'S RAGING TIDE** $2.50
Melissa Huntoon seethed with humiliation as her ancestral plantation home was auctioned away, suddenly vulnerable to the greed and lust of a man's world.

☐ **40-660-6 LOVE'S SWEET AGONY** $2.75
Amid the colorful world of thoroughbred farms that gave birth to the first Kentucky Derby, Rebecca Hawkins learns that horses are more easily handled than men.

☐ **40-647-9 LOVE'S WILDEST PROMISE** $2.50
Abducted aboard a ship bound for the Colonies, innocent Sarah Moody faces a dark voyage of violence and unbridled lust.

☐ **40-721-1 LOVE'S MANY FACES (Poems)** $1.95
Poems of passion, humor and understanding that exquisitely capture that special moment, that wonderful feeling called love.

**Buy them at your local bookstore or use this handy coupon:**
Clip and mail this page with your order

---